Beyond
the
Shadows

The Land of Riandus

Linda Boulanger

Beyond the Shadows
By Linda Boulanger

Cover Design/Interior Design:
Tell~Tale Book Covers

Published by TreasureLine Publishing

ISBN: 978-1-61752-196-6

Also available in eBook publication

PRINTED IN THE UNITED STATES OF AMERICA

To my mom, who listened patiently to my detailed
retelling of every little thing I did in life.

And to my Dragon Guardians.
You have my heart… and my back. Love you!

Chapter 1

Standing in the shadows, his back against the cool, stone wall of Dorengar's Great Hall, Redahn Sharanis turned his head from left to right in a slow, deliberate motion. He looked past the group of women gathered around him. It wasn't hard, given his height.

A smile tugged at the corners of his mouth when he finally found what he was looking for. The lady, with her blonde-brown hair falling down her back and her body clad in fitted gold, was busy, discreetly assessing those around her and giving him the opportunity to watch her in action. He chuckled under his breath, finding himself every bit as amused by her antics as he had the past few nights. Only tonight, she had no idea what she was in for.

It was hard to believe they were already into the fourth night of the yearly Dremis celebration. The women who had been marked years ago, their bodies injected with a chemistry changing serum that would match them to one of the first born elite warriors, had been claimed the first night, leaving all others vying for the affections of the rest of the King's noble guard. Most hoped to secure a match that would guarantee a life of luxury and status, though the majority would end up moving into still coveted positions as Ladies of the Court. Their reason for being, as far as Redahn was concerned, was to provide pleasurable companionship to the men of royal lineage whenever they desired. He supposed there were those from the Ladies

Chambers who still got the chance to marry one of the elite, which seemed to be what all women wanted.

Not *all*, he thought. Even dressed in her alluring gown, it was obvious the maiden who had snared his attention had no desire to leave with any of the men who had approached her those first few days of the Dremis. Her demeanor certainly wasn't that of one who had chosen to be among the clamoring maidens. She appeared to want nothing to do with any of the would-be suitors she was working so hard to keep at bay. He could have told her she needn't have worried. Not those first three nights, anyway. Redahn chuckled again. Her life and her luck were about to change.

Dragging long fingers through his thick, dark hair, he brushed away an errant thread from his sleeve and pushed off the wall. Strolling away from the current conversation, he was surprised by the discontented murmurs that followed him. He shrugged it off, their comments seeming unfounded since they'd surely known they'd been boring him for the past half turn of the hour. His silence and lack of attention should have alerted them that their drivel and the way they fawned and pawed were turning his stomach.

Or it would have if he'd cared. Surly these women knew he had no intent of falling into the clutches of any woman's arms longer than it took to satisfy his lusty appetite. Still, it was the same every year, and even more so as time went by. They'd try anything to find their way into his bed in hopes of snaring his heart. Even his family, the people he would have expected to know him best of all, had begun to profess that he needed to find a wife.

When the lady dressed in gold looked away from one of the warriors she had just succeeded in putting off and saw Redahn staring at her, she quickly averted her gaze. Redahn just smiled, anxious to see the tactics she'd use to dissuade him when he confirmed her fear that she was his intended target. There'd be no getting away for her tonight.

"Ladies." He bowed when he reached the group. They curtsied in near unison.

"Lord Redahn! How nice of you to join us." One of the ladies giggled behind a gloved fist. Redahn had to stifle another laugh when his intended rolled her eyes. She'd thought no one had noticed, but he had, even with the unwelcomed distractions around him.

Another maiden fanned herself in an attempt to bring his attention to her kohl-rimmed eyes, leaving no doubt she believed them her finest feature. They all tried their own tactics to get him to notice them… except the one he wanted to see trying.

The true object of his interest turned toward him. "My lord, if you'll excuse me…" She nodded and tried to step beyond the little circle only to find Redahn's arm blocking her way, the contact sending a surge of excitement through him. The hunter had most definitely found his prey.

"You would leave so soon after my arrival and deprive me the pleasure of your company?" His voice was low, his face close enough to her cheek that he could feel her body heat. "I've a feeling you'll add much to the liveliness of this conversation, my lady. I'd like you to stay."

His dark brown eyes locked with carefully masked, blue orbs, and even though her disdain was obvious, she didn't break the stare. He hitched a brow after several seconds when he felt her slight shiver.

Her mouth pressed tight, forehead creased in a sharp V, she took in a deep breath that she expelled quietly before moistening her lips and setting them in a well-rehearsed smile. "Very well, my lord," she told him while stepping back, her words dripping with unfelt sincerity that matched the placating smile.

He suppressed a burst of laughter brought on by the rush of meeting up with a worthy opponent, though he expected her games would be no real match for his. They both knew he held the final card. Like all the women in the Great Hall, her sole purpose in life was to indulge men like him. He smiled as he watched her move back toward the wall and turn around, her mask slipping for a mere second before she bristled at his blatant stare. *You should have stayed beside me,* he thought, *out of my direct line of vision.* Not that her standing beside him would have made him stop. His eyes seemed drawn to her of their own accord.

"I feel at a disadvantage," he told the group, looking at each of the others before settling back on the maiden that whetted his appetite more with each passing moment in her presence. He enjoyed a leisurely perusal of the gold dress that shimmered in all the right places, accentuating what lay beneath. "It's quite obvious you know who I am..." His sentence trailed off, leaving an opening for their tittering, which they filled for the next few minutes with each trying to imprint herself into his mind.

With an inward chuckle, Redahn watched as the gilded maiden tried to dispel her unease by shifting from foot to foot, feigning interest in what each of her companions had to say. When a couple of the ladies moved in, tightening the circle, her breathing sped up. The way her eyes darted about had Redahn fighting the urge to bite his lower lip. Did he make her that nervous? Maybe he'd miscalculated this woman, though he couldn't accept that his instincts had been that wrong. He surely hadn't grown so soft in his time away from the battlefield that he could no longer read his opponent. He watched, expecting her to redeem his sense of judgment by regaining control of herself and the situation just as she'd done time and time again over the past few nights. Instead, she shook her head and began to move toward him.

"I... I'm sorry. I need some air." She stumbled in his direction and pushed hard against him, knocking him out of her way before she rushed from the group, startling them all, even Redahn.

He moved after her with the stealth of the warrior he'd once been, ignoring the pleas from the other maidens for him to remain. He could hear their comments about the fleeing maiden, was surprised by the anger their words kindled inside him, though he chose to continue after her instead of turning back to blast them. The unspoken thoughts he had of what he'd like to say to them were as far from kind as their own words had been about the only woman whose company he currently desired.

Chapter 2

Redahn had to pull up short only three steps out the door to keep from knocking the maiden into the arms of another man. She stood rod-stiff, her hands clenched at her sides, breaths coming in ragged, shallow gulps. In a semicircle around her, a small group of tipsy warriors showered her with *compliments* on her feminine virtues. Their chatter stopped immediately when Redahn's hands closed over her shoulders and he pulled her against his broad chest.

"Gentlemen." His dry greeting had the men standing taller. Several of them stepped back and offered bows.

"Lord Redahn." The youngest of the warriors rose from his bow, apology etching lines on his young face. "We didn't realize the maiden was with you."

Others nodded in agreement, though more than one set of hungry eyes flicked from him to the maiden. Redahn pulled her to his side noticing her trembling when she slipped her arms around his waist.

"Now you do." He moved forward, forcing them to step back to let him and the maiden through.

"Good evening, my lord," they called in a manner befitting the great grandson of the King. He could feel them watching as he escorted the lady down the path and away from them.

Redahn noticed her shoulders relaxing a little with the fading of their voices, though she still shook. "Are you cold?" he asked, reaching across her body to rub her arm with his free hand.

"No." The shaking of her head was louder than her whispered response. She glanced back in the direction of the Great Hall, a sigh accompanying the widening of her blue eyes before she looked up at him.

Redahn stopped and took her face in his hand. "You wish for me to return you to them?" He laughed at her attempted head shake. "Then why be concerned with my taking you away? Surely you realized where your path would lead when you left the comforts of an overcrowded gathering of male dogs sniffing after willing bitches."

She sucked in sharply at Redahn's calculated words. "Do you truly believe that, my lord? That we're all willing?" She spoke through lips that were barely moving. "Some of us have our positions chosen for us."

He thought about her words for several seconds before nodding, his eyes remaining on her lips. "Fair enough." His own lips lifting at the corners, he chuckled before dipping his head to brush a light kiss across the thin line of her mouth. She tried to pull back, but he held her tight and continued, his voice a husky whisper, "Tonight, *I* shall be the one to choose for you. And my position of choice is you flat on your back beneath me." He laughed, enjoying the shocked look that turned quickly to insolence as her hand raised, fingers swiping across her lips. "There's always a price to be paid when a man rescues a lady from the greedy clutches of would-be, unwanted lovers, is there not? And we will start with a quick lesson. Do not wipe away my kisses." He didn't give her time to respond before he closed his mouth tightly over hers, his one hand moving to cup the back of her head, the other pressing firmly against her lower back to keep her against him.

Redahn was frowning when he finally pulled away from the most unpleasant kiss he'd ever experienced. Frustrated when she didn't look up to see his displeasure, he turned her harshly to continue their journey away from the gathering hall. She didn't resist, though she remained every bit as rigid at his side as she had during the kiss. What was wrong with this maiden? Redahn was used to women turning to thick gelatin in his arms. And what of him? Why should he care?

"What's your name, Maiden?" The irritation that edged his voice made her jump. A slight squeeze to her arm made her answer.

"Mahryn," she told him with yet another look back at the nearly out of site hall.

"Relax," he commanded. "I'm not going to hurt you. At least not much." He snickered, amused at his own comment, though his mirth quickly faded. His scowl returned when her blue eyes finally made contact with his and she blasted him with a scathing glare. Slowing their pace, he considered turning back. He certainly didn't have to put up with a maiden with an attitude. But something kept him from turning around. As bad as the kiss had been, as unresponsive as she seemed, and regardless of her obvious disdain for him, there was something about this woman that entranced him. He'd been unable to shake his thoughts of her ever since he'd spotted her among the maidens that first evening, and each night thereafter.

He hadn't planned to take advantage of his growing interest at first. She was intriguing and pleasant enough to look upon, though she wasn't the type of woman he usually found himself attracted to. She was smaller and fairer than most, her pale skin a testament that the outdoors was not a place she spent a lot of time. That paleness, a testament of how different their lives were, contrasted with the bronze tones of the broken warrior who felt most at home in the open, with the sky his roof and the earth his flooring.

With the ends of her hair tickling his arm, he was reminded as well that her thick mane, as unique as the woman herself with its equal parts of dark blond and light brown, had been left down every night. He much preferred to see a woman's hair pulled up, allowing him to kiss her bare neck before loosening the pins. He relished the feel of silky tresses as they cascaded down over his hands and arms in those first moments of exploration.

She also dressed differently than most, not that the gold silk was rare. More so, the cut of the dress—the straight, slip-like lines that draped strategically around her small body exuded fine tailoring and skill that accentuating her soft curves well beyond what might be needed for a hungry warrior's notice.

He wasn't sure any of it mattered, even though somehow it seemed it should. No, he argued with himself. Using a woman for one's pleasure required nothing this one didn't possess. He didn't need her hair to be up, or her to be of a certain height or shape. She didn't need the delicate buttons running up the back of a dress that he so loved to undo one at a time. The one she wore would come off easily. The thought of his hands entwined in her hair, silky material pooled at her feet, flitted through his mind and he quickened their pace again. He may be a warrior too damaged to regain the battlefields, but he certainly would not allow a woman, especially this one, to make him question what he was doing.

Running a hand through his hair, he turned them off the main path and onto the road leading to Zanak, his family's home.

Chapter 3

"Are you taking me to Zanak?" Mahryn knew her voice sounded higher than it should, felt certain the man at her side could feel her hand trembling where he'd tucked it into the crook of his arm and covered it with his own.

He chuckled, a deep rumble low in his throat. "Unlike my brother who thwarted propriety and filled his family bed whenever and with whomever he wanted until his Chosen came of age, I must say I never thought it right for a man of my position to return home with a Lady of the Courts."

She was on the verge of asking why it was a man of his position came to these gatherings in the first place. He could have any woman, anywhere, and yet…

"I enjoy the allure of fresh maidens," he told her, raising a single dark eyebrow when she looked at him, her own brows rising first. He chuckled again, which he seemed to do quite often. "You were wondering why I bother with the Dremis Gathering when I have no intent to find a wife, were you not?"

Mahryn thought about denying the claim, though she'd never been very good at lying. She didn't see the point. Instead, she nodded. "Partly, though I was also wondering… Can you not find better maidens elsewhere?"

The ever-present chuckle erupted into a roar of laughter that caused Mahryn to cringe. It seemed a legitimate question to her.

"*Better* maidens," he repeated her words, patting her

hand and leaning his head closer to hers as they walked. "Dremis Maidens are magic," he whispered.

"Magic!" Her unladylike snort caused yet another chuckle. "I suppose one might try to make claim that the marked ones are. Perhaps. Though you're a younger son from an elite family, so one might also believe you've the smarts to have had no experience there since your head does appear to still be attached to your neck." Her eyes flitted to the neckline of his cream colored shirt. She shook her head. "Whatever would possess you to think any woman magical?"

"I've never slept with a marked woman," he whispered, stopping her and pulling her hair aside slightly before leaning down to press a kiss to the side of her neck, "but I've had my share of Dremis Maidens and I can tell you it's a week of blissful magic." He stood beside her, his mouth exploring the curve of her shoulder.

Mahryn wasn't sure about magical maidens, but his touch seemed to be putting her under some spell. "Magic," she mumbled after several seconds.

Low laughter rumbled from Redahn while his hand slid down her arm. A quick squeeze and he was grabbing her wrist and tugging her onto a barely visible path, his motions pulling her from her trance.

"Where…" He was moving faster now, the terrain more difficult to maneuver.

"You're quite the inquisitive one." He clucked his tongue. "I hope you don't plan to question my every move this night."

Her father's voice filled her head as she thought back. "You've always been too inquisitive for your own good, Mahryn. It's what got you into trouble in the first place." The glare her father had leveled at her would have made the boldest warrior cow down and back away. But not Mahryn. Not the second child of the King's closest confidant. She'd stood her ground as he'd narrowed his blue eyes and pointed a menacing finger in her direction. "Some questions are better left unasked for the good of all involved. See that you remember that."

He'd told her all that when she'd questioned him again about her sister's death, demanding answers to some of the parts of the equation that simply didn't add up. Three days later she'd been informed via messenger that there'd been a change of plans—that her arranged marriage proposal, the one she'd sincerely doubted from the beginning, had been rescinded and she would be required to participate in the Gathering of the Dremis Maidens.

Mahryn had squeezed her eyes shut in an attempt to still the spinning room.

"Have you a return message for your father, my lady?" The courier who'd boldly read the decree from her father asked when she opened her eyes. His mocking tone and lascivious stare had her fighting the urge to offer him the slap she'd like to present to her father.

She'd been on the verge of telling the man he could tell her father to go to hell, a most unladylike response, she knew. Though that's when another thought flashed through her mind. She clasped her mouth closed in a tight line and held up a single finger indicating the courier should wait, before she turned away, giving herself a moment to fully contemplate her next move.

She'd been surprised her father hadn't told her where she could take her petty requests. Instead, he'd agreed and she'd felt hope for the first time in a long time, though she realized now he'd known a week's worth of putting off the advances of every man looking for an available maiden was an impossibility. Her eyes bore into the back of the man leading her to her doom, her disdain for her father momentarily transferring itself to this nearer target.

"*Where* are you taking me?" she demanded, yanking her hand free of his. The sudden motion caused her to stumble. A hand beneath one elbow, the other around her waist was the only thing that kept her from going down. She'd never seen anyone move that quickly. That was her last rational thought before she found herself pulled against the hard planes of his broad chest, his dark eyes first assessing, then penetrating.

Kiss me again.

Maybe *that* was actually her last thought, irrational as it was, before his lips pressed to hers, moving until she began to understand the phrase 'kissed senseless'.

Mahryn wondered at what point her limbs began to liquefy, then realized that wasn't entirely true either. Her arms were wrapped around his neck, her hands entwined in the thick strands of his dark hair—hair considered too long, even for the standards of the day. She didn't care. She liked the way it looked, loved the silky feel of it threaded through her fingers. *Soft, yet manly*, she thought. Just like his scent. He didn't wear the sandalwood worn by most men, though she couldn't quite put her finger on what her nose registered as simply strong and masculine without being overbearing.

When his mouth left hers and her head lolled back, she somehow knew he'd take advantage of the moment. That knowledge did little to keep at bay the shudder that streaked through her when his warm lips began to caress the tenderness of unexplored flesh.

"You have a sweet spot, my lady," he mumbled against her neck at that spot just above her collarbone.

Mahryn wasn't sure what he meant, only that her knees

buckled when his tongue dipped into the hollow at that exact spot. She grabbed fistfuls of his shirt, her breath hissing out with the tightening of his arm around her waist. It was another low rumble of internal laughter that pulled her from the moment, causing her body to stiffen. Her arms trembled as she pushed against him.

"Be still, Mahryn. I'm not finished."

She started to object only to be swept away on another wave of awakened feelings. His mouth moved upward while a finger trailed down her chest toward the hollow between her breasts. She caught his hand in her own, somehow aware that if he didn't stop, at some point he'd be unable to, that he'd take her right there on the forest floor.

Just like Hahna.

The words came out of nowhere, slamming into her heart. A wave of panic further hindering her ability to breathe, she struggled against this man who was by far stronger than…

Stronger than who?

Flashes of another forest, other men clouded her vision. Redahn's hands were no longer the ones pawing at her. It wasn't his lips that seared her skin. She felt herself being sucked into an old nightmare, one where she relived those moments, not even her own—they'd been Hahna's last.

"Please, don't do this. Don't hurt me." She fought against the one who held her, her voice sounding pathetic and small. Self-loathing pumped bile into her throat and she was afraid if she didn't get away, what little she had in her stomach was going to wind up all over them.

Him.

Redahn's voice and gentle shaking of her body brought her back to the moment.

"My lady? Mahryn?" His dark eyes bore into hers as she regained focus. The depth of concern emanating back surprised her. He was stroking her hair which had become damp at the temples. "What happened? Where'd you go?" he questioned further when she didn't answer. No doubt the confusion that clouded her thoughts showed in her eyes. "It's okay," he told her when words still eluded her. "You're safe now."

"It wasn't me," she whispered as his hand slid across her shoulder and he pulled her close to his side. She couldn't help wrapping her arms around his waist as they continued their journey, feeling a certain sense of security she hadn't felt in a long time... if ever.

Chapter 4

Redahn felt Mahryn stiffen the moment she caught sight of the cottage in the clearing ahead of them. They'd come up to it from the back, though it was still a lovely little place, even from that view, with the whitewashed fence playing backdrop to carefully arranged trees and shrubs interspersed with a vast array of colorful flowers. Even in the moonlight, he felt that unexpected warmth that never failed to fill him whenever he went there—a warmth that had nothing to do with the reason he usually visited the place.

Mahryn had been so perfectly fitted against him that he felt a sense of loss when she lifted her head from his shoulder and moved away a step or two. He grabbed her hand then turned to watch her take it all in, enjoying the appreciation in her blue eyes. They were eyes he was anxious to get a good look at once they were in brighter light.

"Whose house is this?" She turned to look at him.

"How do you know it's not mine?"

Shaking her head, she laughed. "I do know who you are, my lord. You've already said you do not take maidens to your family home. And you certainly don't live in a cottage, though someone does." She tilted her head and looked up at the smoke drifting out the chimney top.

A smile crinkled the corners of Redahn's eyes and played across his full lips.

"Is there humor in my statement?"

Redahn shook his head, wondering if he should admit he admired her thought processes and sense of deduction. He liked the way she studied him too, the way she'd been sizing him up from the moment he'd walked across the floor of the Gathering Hall, much as he might have an opponent on the battlefield. They were tactics he knew well and he felt certain she would have made a good warrior had she not been born one of the fairer sex.

"I was thinking you're as perceptive as you are inquisitive, my lady. No need to get your hackles up." The last was thrown out when her lips pressed tightly together and her eyes narrowed. His words were accompanied by a thumb smoothing out the line created in her forehead.

She jerked her head away from his hand. "I am *not* taking offense."

Redahn had to admit he was a bit puzzled. They weren't words that should have annoyed her, though her stance told him they had. *That* would have been her undoing on the battlefield—her inability to keep minor offenses, real or imaginary, from burrowing beneath skin that was not nearly thick enough.

Speaking of skin, he remembered how silky smooth the flesh of Mahryn's neck and arms had been. He loved the softness found only in those just old enough, before the world could harden them or mar their beauty.

And not just their outsides. His favorites of those maidens sent to the Dremis Gathering were the ones who were innocent and without guile—or as much as any woman could be. He'd yet to meet one who didn't have her sights set on snaring some man, whether even she realized it or not. Most of them had been drilled with the idea that a good match would bring honor and happiness. And he, being the King's great grandson—even the second son in the family and a warrior who could no longer fight—qualified him as *good match* material. He shook his head, his chuckle sounding sour even to him.

Mahryn's frown had deepened. Her eyes searched his face.

"It doesn't matter," he told her, tucking her hand back into the crook of his arm where he could steer her toward the other side of the cottage. "Let's go meet the owners of this home willing to let us enjoy the magic of the Dremis without interruption."

"Are you serious?" Mahryn's bottom jaw had dropped with his words, only to be clamped shut again.

"Oh, you'll enjoy it, all right. As will I…"

"Please! Don't insult me with your witty speech. You know that's not what I'm talking about. Whose house is this?"

"Insult yo… How dare you!"

Mahryn clapped a hand over his mouth, only to have it yanked away and pushed behind her back where he grabbed both her hands and held them with one of his. She tried to wrench her face free from the vice like grip he had on her jaw. Both pairs of eyes—the dark browns and the unusual blues—burned as they glared at one another.

"I will do with you as I please, *my lady*. And you will address me with the respect I deserve." Looking down at her, he realized he was much too aware of the rise and fall of her chest against his. When she moistened her lips, he found his eyes riveted to them, his body registering even before his brain did, just how much her boldness had excited him.

"Yes, *my lord*." She answered, using the same belittling tone he had. Ignoring the warning in his frown, she attempted to drop into a mock curtsy.

He tightened his hold on her wrists and her face and she stopped. His eyes boring into hers, he shook his head. "Is this really a battle you wish to pursue?" His whispered words hissed out between tight lips.

She held his stare for several more seconds before looking away, the silence stretching between them. "No, my lord," she answered just as he'd begun to tighten his hold on her jaw, her voice so quiet he couldn't make out her tone. Regardless, he'd take it as an apology. It was probably the best he'd receive from her.

After a moment more, he release her, his hand wrapped around her upper arm as he steered her in the direction of the front door.

"The couple who tends the gardens of Zanak," he said after he'd rapped three times on the wooden door. When Mahryn just stared at him, he continued. "The cottage belongs to the couple who tends the gardens of Zanak." He spoke with deliberate slowness that had her narrowing her eyes at him.

"And you have no qualms about barging into their home whenever you wish in order to indulge your lust?"

Now it was Redahn's turn to close a slack jaw. "You simply do not know when to stop speaking, do you?"

The sound of movement beyond the cottage door stilled her response and Redahn chuckled quietly. Yes, he came to their house whenever he wanted. He'd had the house built and paid them well to let him do so, which should have been evident by the size of their cottage compared to most craftsman servants. He believed in taking good care of those who took care of him. And this set up served him well and had for many years now. He frowned. The *rightness* of it had never crossed his mind... until Mahryn had questioned it.

Chapter 5

Three quick knuckle taps to the smooth wood, a short pause, and then two more raps brought the sound of the bolt sliding free on the other side of the door.

"Master Redahn. You've returned home."

Mahryn frowned, the pleasant, song-like voice that greeted them filling her with an unsettling sense of familiarity. She stared at the bent head, though she couldn't tell much about her. The woman kept her face down, her eyes cast low as was proper for those of a lower station when the house master brought home a Lady who was not his own. A Lady of the Court may not have much say in where she spent her nights or with whom, but her position was still considered one of privilege, and propriety was demanded.

"No need for pretenses tonight, Dara, this one has already figured out my ruse. She seems to be brighter than most." He ushered Mahryn through the door then turned to the woman and pressed a kiss to her cheek. The affectionate pat it earned him made Mahryn smile though his next words wiped it away and had her lips curving down. "That being so, I can't understand how she has found herself amidst the *Ladies,* and certainly you might think she could have kept herself out of my clutches."

"Psht!" The woman known as Dara dismissed her master's comment with a wave of her plump hand before turning around. "I'd say wisdom is her kin and fortune has shined down on her. At least if she is with you, she has a far better chance of her first... encounter being a pleasant one. Begging my forwardness, but if I were a young maiden again, I would do my best to catch your fancy, my lord."

The woman's boldness caused Mahryn to break through their laughter with a sincere melody of her own. Redahn turned to her, his smile an indication he was pleased at the sound. Dara, however, sucked in a hard breath, her face sobering, her eyes growing in dimension as she looked fully at Mahryn for the first time. The older woman covered her mouth with her hands, slowly turning her head from side to side.

"It can't be," she whispered, taking a step toward Mahryn.

Arms immediately crossing over her front, Mahryn began to back away. She darted a quick glance at Redahn, though her rounded eyes and shaking head seemed to give Dara all the signal she needed. The older woman stopped just as Redahn reached out and took hold of her elbow.

"Hahna? Is that really you?" Dara asked, her focus remaining steadfast on Mahryn's face.

A mixture of horror and confusion contorted the young maiden's features. She eyed the woman with guarded curiosity and, after several moments of silence, she shook her head. "No. Hahna was my sister."

"Your... sister?" Dara's hand returned to her mouth. "What on earth have you been told?" she whispered.

Mahryn shivered, feeling an unexplained tenseness and her ire rose along with her chin. "Yes. My sister. Though I cannot fathom how that would be any of your concern."

Redahn gaped at Mahryn's cold tone.

Dara looked as though she'd been slapped. "Forgive me, my lady. I once had the pleasure of knowing the Lady

Hahna. I didn't realize she had relations other than her father, and I thought perhaps…"

"You knew her?" Mahryn's voice softened, her hand covered her heart. Could this woman have known the sister she had no recollection of, though desperately wanted to remember? Her sister. The one who had been killed that night… Her father's favorite. Mahryn had always felt it should have been her that died instead of Hahna…

"Y… yes. When she was young." Dara proceeded with a cautious tone. "May I inquire as to your name, my lady, since I do not recall a younger sister?"

Mahryn looked from Dara to Redahn then shifted her gaze back again. Her eyes squinted in contemplation for an extended moment before she spoke. "I am the Lady Mahryn."

Dara moaned loudly right before her knees buckled. She would have gone down had Redahn not been by her side, his hand already beneath her elbow.

"Hell's fury!" Redahn growled when Dara fought against him, trying to steady herself. She pushed him away, smoothing the front of her skirt, her hands visibly shaking.

"Forgive me, my lord." She didn't look at him, instead casting a quick look at Mahryn, though her eyes didn't remain there long. She looked away, blinking furiously and wiping at a tear that had broken free of the well of moisture in her eyes. "My lady," she said, clearing her throat and nodding in Mahryn's direction before turning and running from the room.

Redahn stared at the door that closed behind Dara, his jaw slack and arms dangling loosely at his sides. As a seasoned warrior, he was used to processing tenuous situations, turning them into logic problems to be solved quickly, but what had transpired within the walls of the cottage had him completely baffled. He took a step forward, prepared to follow Dara, believing she held the answers he needed, only the thud that sounded behind him stopped him and had him changing directions. He turned to see Mahryn pressed against the cottage door, and watched as she slid down to the floor and covered her face in her hands. Running his fingers through his dark hair, he began to count silently and breathe slowly as he walked toward her—it was something he'd done from an early age, even before he'd needed it to keep his wits on the battlefield.

Silently, he lowered himself to the floor next to her. She didn't move, didn't speak, though he could hear her breathing in through her nose and out through her mouth. He stared down at the gold silk pooled in crumpled waves around her, then reached over and ran the material through his fingers and pulled on it slightly to see if he might gain her attention.

"I'm sorry, my lord." With a shaky voice, her words broke the silence just before she lifted her head and looked at him. She attempted a weak smile then shook her head. "I'm afraid I let my surprise get the better of me."

Redahn chuckled. "So it seems." He laughed again when she rolled her eyes. Without preamble, he stood and offered her his hand. "Come and sit by the fire and tell me what this is all about."

A trembling hand slipped into his, though she shook her head as he pulled her up to face him. "No, my lord. This night isn't about the past, nor is it about me…"

Redahn snorted. He might put on airs that refuted such in front of the majority of the people he knew or met, but he prided himself on making these nights of firsts as much about the lady as they were about his own satisfaction. They might call him a cad everywhere else, but he'd certainly not allow it to be said about his ways in the bedroom. He especially enjoyed leaving a good impression of his abilities with the maidens of the Dremis Celebration. And for some reason, it seemed even more important with this one.

He frowned and she stepped back, prompting him to settle a smile on his handsome features. "Well then, let's not talk, about that anyway. I would still like to sit by the fire and enjoy a glass of wine. So, go. Sit." A sweeping gesture with the hand in which he held hers had her headed in the direction of an elegant sofa, perfectly positioned in front of a low, glowing fire. Dara and her husband always made sure everything was just right...

Redahn's forehead creased. He moved toward the cabinet that held the glasses and the bottles of his favorite wine and wondered why the two women had reacted so dramatically. So, Dara had known Mahryn's sister. Since he believed his speculation of her identity to be correct, he knew it wasn't like she hailed from a Drille so far away from Zanak to where her path and Dara's might never have crossed. He might have understood it otherwise, since depending on where the Dremis maiden's came from, they might never see a familiar face again. But he knew that wasn't the case for Mahryn, even with her unusual situation. He planned to ask her about it the first chance he had to weave it into the conversation.

He thought about her eyes. They'd been the telltale giveaway. He'd been unsure she was who he suspected until her eyes met his while they sat with their backs against the door. The brighter light of the cottage, along with their close proximity told the truth—at least part of it. The rest would all come out, though none of it would change his plans for the evening. Even now, as he poured the wine and took in the curve of her nearly bare shoulder beneath silky tresses, his mouth twitched. He wished he was close enough to press his lips to the very spot, his body stirring, reminding him that he really was the self-serving man everyone believed he was. He wondered if she was aware of his eyes on her. Did she have any idea that he was once again devouring her in his thoughts?

He watched her head move slowly as she took in the finery of the room and he thought of Dara—it may have been his money that paid for the materials, but the wife of Zanak's master gardener had managed to find craftsmen that had turned certain parts of this little cottage into areas fit for a king. Well, the great grandson of a king, anyway. He'd never really thought of it before, but Dara certainly had the touch of someone well above her station.

Redahn stood motionless, his hands resting on the base of the two wine glasses while he stared at a nonexistent spot on a far wall. The night had turned into a puzzle with many more pieces than he'd originally anticipated. A surge of renewed excitement shot through him. He had a mystery on his hands. It had been a while since he'd allowed himself to enjoy anything beyond those too brief moments spent with a woman in his arms. While enjoyable, they never lasted. One simply could not spend all of one's time in bed. Especially with his mother as mistress of the house he had to go to when the night ended. He shuddered at the thought of her overly cheerful voice coming in to rouse him after he'd returned to the comforts of his own bed too soon before her entrance.

He knew the reason. The woman was terrified her second son, the broken warrior who wished daily he'd been allowed to die honorably on the battlefield, was going to take to his bed and never get up. He'd tried that after the doctors had *fixed* him and he'd realized his fighting days were over. He shook his head, remembering how angry he'd been, how he was just getting used to his uselessness when his brother's chosen had arrived.

Elenya—beyond beautiful, smarter than any woman he'd ever met, except perhaps his mother's sister who lived with them. He remembered how his brother's young bride had been abandoned too soon after her arrival when the warriors of Dorengar had been called into battle and how his great grandfather, the King, had asked that he watch over her and the potential heir of Dorengar. She'd challenged him daily during that time, both mentally and physically, annoying him with the things she would say or do, pushing him to the point where she could finally show him he still had strength enough when it counted most, though his true skills now resided in his mind. He hadn't understood that at first, and was still trying to come to terms with using brain instead of brawn to make himself useful on the battlefield.

He shook his head. All those were thoughts for another time, he thought, when Mahryn turned to look at him and succeeded in pulling him back from his ruminations. He made a show of picking up the wine bottle in one hand and both glasses in the other before heading toward her. He liked how her eyes roamed over him as he walked, making him feel appreciated, not that he wasn't acutely aware of his looks. Very few women back at the Great Hall wouldn't have gladly traded places with this maiden.

She jumped at the brief meeting of their fingers when he handed her one of the wine glasses and he chuckled. How ironic that he'd chosen the one woman who was not so eager for his attention. He wouldn't hold it against her. It was obvious Mahryn was not eager to share a bed with any man, not just him. He sat down beside her, the thought running through his mind that she lived under shadows of her own past that were every bit as real as his, though perhaps even more nefarious in nature.

What secrets do you hold, Mahryn? What shadows must she dance beyond in order to live her life in the blissful state he suddenly desired for her?

Chapter 6

Mahryn wondered if she should be afraid of the momentary ferocity that flashed across the face of the man at her side. With her emotions such a jumbled mess, she contemplated the fact that she may have imagined it. She took a rather large gulp from the wine glass, closing her eyes as the liquid hit her stomach, and waited for the spread of tiny fingers of heat to radiate through her body. The desired relaxation didn't come, tempting her to tip the glass to her lips once more. Her eyes popped open when Redahn chuckled and removed the glass from her hand.

"Please tell me you at least ate dinner before the Ball, lest I refuse you any more of Zanak's fine wine. I'll not allow drink to rob me of the pleasures of your company as it did my brother with his Chosen on her Dremis night."

She knew the story of how Elenya had fallen asleep on his brother due to the strong wines of Zanak. Everyone did. Mahryn scowled. It wasn't like she was anyone's Chosen and she was hardly afraid of a little wine. She told him as much and he laughed while slipping an arm around the back of the sofa. She marveled at how free he seemed in spite of all that he'd been through and wished she could be more like that—knowing what she wanted and simply taking it.

When she looked down, he tightened his arm, pulling her closer. He definitely knew how to get whatever he set his mind to.

Mahryn had a sudden desire to stay as they were

forever. She'd started out wishing to get as far away from him as possible when she'd noticed him and realized his attention was directed at her back at the Great Hall. Truth be told, she'd known of Redahn much longer than this gathering of the maidens. She'd seen him in passing many times when she'd been called to her father's side and this great grandson had been leaving the King's hall. Her head always down, she was sure he hadn't noticed her, but he was not the kind of person to go unobserved. Not this man—the epitome of an elite warrior.

She'd heard he could no longer fight due to injuries that had healed improperly. It was also said part of his animosities arose because that particular battle called Dorengar's warriors to defend the borders of Aleone, an exiled Drille—the one that just happened to be home to his brother's Chosen and a lifelong enemy of Zanak. She realized those who said he was no longer a warrior were wrong. It was obvious he had a warrior's heart. No wonder bitterness had crept in with the loss of the one thing he wanted most and couldn't have. It seemed in contrast to the quick laugh that warmed her and revived her many daydreams of him.

She let her mind return to those memories, envisioning the thick biceps that warred against the fabric of his finely tailored shirts. Her fingers tingled at the thought of running them through his dark hair that always lay just a bit unruly and hung to the perfect length to guide the hands from its ends to his training-thickened neck and down to a chest that was both broad and firm.

Mahryn swallowed hard and closed her eyes, the face she knew so well filling her mind with every detail, from the chiseled jaw line, to the penetrating deep brown eyes, perfectly sloping nose, and full lips that easily spewed venom yet, she felt certain, would also offer great pleasure. She moistened her own lips with the tip of her tongue, her mouth suddenly dry and her breathing more shallow. It seemed unbelievable that she now sat here next to the man who'd so often been the center of her fantasies, or that she was willing to admit even to herself that he was, in fact, the same man.

The warmth of his hand on her shoulder radiated intensity beyond any daydream. His fingers traced the delicate vine-like pattern of her dress strap. He must have noticed she was having trouble swallowing past the knot in her throat because he leaned forward to retrieve her wine glass, bringing his body in closer contact to hers. Mahryn accepted the glass with great thanks and downed the liquid inside making Redahn chuckle.

"You're a greedy one where drink is concerned, my lady," he said, just a breath from her ear. The warmth made her shudder and he nuzzled her ear just before his lips grazed the tender spot where her jaw and neck met. A sigh escaped her even as her head lolled to the side, offering him a better vantage before she realized what she was doing and tensed, straightening herself, her eyes opening wide. Had she ventured a look in Redahn's direction, she would have seen those full lips set in a satisfied smirk.

"My..." She had to clear her throat, her voice unsteady, sounding foreign to her own ears. "My Drille is responsible for the grapes used in the King's fine stock, my lord, which also feeds Zanak's supply." She turned her head to catch him masking a moment of confusion. "The grapes are grown in the land of Bander."

Redahn sat back, the loss of his body heat sending an involuntary shiver through Mahryn. He rubbed a hand down her arm. "You say you're from Bander Drille and yet your father sits at the right hand of the King, advising him as no other." Her sharp gasp made him laugh. Grasping her chin, he turned her face toward his. "Your eyes give you away, my lady." She stared at him, silent seconds ticking by before one of his brows inched up.

Mahryn nodded. "You are correct, my lord, though we have not always lived in the King's castle."

"Tedran has been here for some time," he countered.

"Yes, the King realized my father's ability to ferret out information and use that in well thought out strategies that brought success in a short time. His *gift* had him quickly rising through the ranks to his current position after he married my mother." Mahryn's chin drifted toward her chest. "She had no desire to live within the castle walls."

Redahn was quiet, thoughtful. "So your father made his home here, traveling to your mother whenever time permitted."

Mahryn nodded, a sad smile tugging the corners of her lips. Conventional love seemed out of reach for the women of her family.

"Loving a warrior is never a conventional relationship," he said, almost as if reading her mind. "There's never a guarantee they'll be around, or even if they'll come home once duty calls. I suppose it's the same for a man married to the King's service."

"Is that why you've never married?" Mahryn asked.

The volume of Redahn's laugh made her jump. "Some men are not meant to marry." He leaned toward her, his mouth so close to hers she could feel his breath on her lips. "If I did, I might be expected to give up certain... pleasure." He snorted softly. "I'm certainly not of a mind to deprive myself." His statement seemed to push away the man filled with concern and caring, bringing back the lust-filled warrior who ran his tongue along the crease of her lips. Mahryn sucked in, slightly opening her mouth, allowing him to gain entrance to plunder the uncharted territory inside before pulling away abruptly.

"The real question here," he whispered, his breath tickling her moistened lips, "is why the daughter of a man in Tedran's position would find herself thrown into the midst of lusty dogs." He paused, shaking his head. "That, I cannot fathom."

Mahryn remained completely still, almost limp, during his impromptu speech. Slowly, she expelled the breath she'd been holding. "If your intent is to confuse my senses with these abrupt bursts of passion and wayward questions, my lord, you are succeeding quite well in your mission."

Redahn laughed, his grin rather lopsided, as he asked, "Passion? Dear lady, you have been treated to mere morsels of what you might expect this evening." His smile grew more seductive at Mahryn's struggle to swallow down a tiny groan.

He kissed her again, his mouth barely touching hers, brushing back and forth over the softness of her full lips, though enough to have her temperature rising and her hand moving of its own accord to feel the hard planes of his chest. "And you are an expert at avoidance." He whispered, tapping her nose with his before moving back a bit, leaving her frustrated once again. "I still wish to know. Why has your father allowed this?"

She stared at him, willing her body to calm, and shook her head, a curt laugh laced with barely contained bitterness ringing from her. "Power and control," she said, looking away. "And great disdain because others died and I did not," she added in a whisper.

Redahn sat back, his mind resting on the words she'd uttered, trying to decide if he'd actually heard her say what she'd said... as well as what she hadn't. So, his great grandfather's right hand man had forced his daughter into the Dremis mating ritual to punish her? He wondered if his contempt toward Tedran could be any more hypocritical.

For years, Redahn had freely partaken of the maidens' wares offered up at the Dremis Ball, knew there were many families who thought the ritual an honor and truly believed it would bring their daughters a more favorable marriage by matching her up with one of the King's warriors. But he didn't believe in it. Not really. If he was being honest, he thought it a bit disgusting, degrading to women—no doubt a thought heightened by the constant bombardment of his brother's wife telling him so.

At eighteen, he'd been eager to attend his first Dremis Gathering, though what he'd seen had rather sickened him—the elite warriors whose *Chosen* had arrived darting through the crowd of maidens, each blinded by the madness of the scent of the one woman among many who had been injected with that particular warrior's blood, her chemistry altered over time to make her irresistible to her warrior. Once they were gone, the other men, warriors deprived, kept away from a woman's touch far too long on the practice fields, were left to descend on the remaining starry-eyed maidens, each willing to trade her innocence for a chance at an elite marriage.

He hadn't really realized until now, or maybe he'd just never stopped to care, that along with hope, the women were also filled with fear. Most of them hid it well, but it was there. It had been unmistakable, undeniable in Mahryn's eyes. How could it not be frightening—these rituals that were supposed to assure the strength of future generations, the pairing of the elite warriors with the daughters of the finest, to make certain the King's military forces would not only thrive but surpass all others. It was an intensely insane and truly antiquated custom, though he hadn't fully understood that until he saw his brother and his Chosen go through it, and now as he looked into Mahryn's eyes.

He laughed to himself, feeling the sting of hypocrisy, knowing he would have received nothing short of a scathing scowl from the lovely Elenya at his nearness to the daughter of the King's top advisor. He was angry at Tedran for submitting her to a ritual that sickened him, and yet he knew his intent to take pleasure in her had not waned, just as he'd continued to enjoy the Dremis maidens every year since his eighteenth birthday. Life wasn't fair and it didn't always make sense. *That* was the only thing he was certain about.

He contemplated delving further into Tedran's reasoning but found the more he thought, the more his need to have this deed completed increased. Regardless of the reasons, Tedran had, in fact, resigned his daughter to the fate of the King's warriors. Even though he was on uncertain leave from that group, unable to fight alongside those men, Redahn was still considered part of the elite forces. His position was furthered by his kinship to the King, affording him his pick of the unmarked women.

He'd known from the moment he first saw Mahryn dressed in the enticing finery of the Dremis Maidens that she was his, though it had taken him four nights to respond. Three other maidens' hopes had been taken, along with their innocence—young women who had done little to quench the fires his thoughts of Mahryn had set to burning within him. Tonight, that fourth night, he had decided to make his move. Or more so, life had prompted him to make his move when he'd noticed others becoming braver in their consideration of her. He supposed they thought he'd lost interest when he'd quit asking about her and chosen others the previous nights.

He stood abruptly, scooping the round-eyed maiden into his arms and turning toward a short hallway in the opposite direction from the door Dara had taken. He may not agree with the rules that allowed him to do as he pleased with this woman, but damn it, if not him, it would be one of those other men. He'd tried not to care. But he did. He wanted her for himself, before anyone else. And now, he would claim his right, and her.

Chapter 7

Mahryn's heartbeat notched up a level when Redahn scooped her from the sofa's soft cushions. She'd thought she had more time, had planned to consume more wine before this moment of inevitability. Now, as he held her, carried her to a part of the house unknown to her, the urgent desire in the depths of his deep brown eyes told her time was up.

She pulled in a shaky breath, knowing it wasn't so much the act itself that she was afraid of. More... Her gut clenched when she thought of that moment when he would realize—when her secret would be discovered. A lesser man might have been fooled. Intuition told her this one would not. She needed to tell him, needed to explain. Instead, she remained silent as he dropped her to her feet in the middle of a nearby bedroom. Closing her eyes for a brief moment, she willed divine intervention to help get her through this.

Attempting to quell her fears, Mahryn studied the details of the room. She tried, without success, to control the visible trembling of her body by focusing on the elegant attributes. Surprisingly much smaller than she'd expected, the room still held all the regal elegance fitting the chamber of one within the direct line of the King. Complete with the standard deep burgundies and golds, their severity had been broken up with the addition of creams and a soft buttery yellow.

A small smile tugged at her trembling lips when she

realized it was the same yellow that adorned her room back in the castle, though she'd paired it with a deep lavender and a dusty rose so pale the color was near nonexistent. That room had been the only thing she'd truly loved within the castle walls, she thought with a scowl that she quickly worked to hide. This was not the time to be thinking of her father or the sour hand life had dealt her. Instead, she turned to take in more of the room, hoping she might keep Redahn at bay just a little longer while she tried to figure out what to do.

The fire blazing in the oversized fireplace at the far end of the room complete with the clichéd plush rug in front of it had Mahryn rolling her eyes. An armchair, sitting on one side, cuddled a couple of soft pillows and a blanket. Opposite, a two person sofa with a table just the right size to hold two wine glasses and a chilling bottle completed the romantic ambiance of the area.

Moving from where Redahn had put her down, Mahryn pulled back the layers of heavy gold and burgundy brocade. Pushing aside the cream sheer, her breath caught as she looked out at the moon-bathed garden shimmering with subdued color that she knew would burst with the morning light. She heard Redahn chuckle and turned to look at him.

"It's a beautiful sight to wake up to," he said quietly.

"I can only imagine," she answered, realizing she may not have to *only* imagine it much longer, unless he... Her eyes went to the bed that stood stately against the wall behind him and she wondered why he'd bothered to let her down in the middle of the room instead of depositing her directly on its soft center. With the heat in his eyes as he'd carried her down the hall, she'd expected swiftness. Instead, he watched her, waiting... for what? For her to confess?

Her heart beat faster as she stared at the place that

might well be her undoing. Fighting to swallow, Mahryn moved to the bed and ran a hand down the narrow width of the silk draped post adorning one corner. The beauty of the setting contrasted sharply with the ugliness inside her. She bowed her head as Redahn moved closer to her.

"It won't be so bad," he whispered, his lips grazing her neck from his position behind her.

Mahryn's attempted smile faltered and she ended up biting her lower lip in an attempt to keep her tears at bay. She shook her head, wishing she could believe him.

Redahn had grown weary of watching her take in the beauty of the room while he'd pondered a course that might help the lady warm up to the idea of sharing his bed. After a few minutes he'd decided showing her was the only way.

"More wine?" she asked, twisting in his arms as she gestured toward the table holding the bottle and glasses.

Redahn shook his head then pulled her more firmly against him. "Wine is not the drink I thirst for now, my lady," he whispered near her ear, his tongue teasing the sensitive lobe before his lips brushed her neck on his way to where his teeth gently grazed the tender flesh at the top of her shoulder. He smiled when she shivered, an involuntary sigh urging his added kisses. "Ah, Mahryn," he breathed into her hair, inhaling the light rose scent while he ran his hands down and then back up her arms. The softness of her skin against his rough palms heightened his need to feel more of her and he slipped a finger beneath the thin, vine-like straps of her gown only to have her cover his hand with her own.

"My lord... the lights..." She turned and looked up at him, her eyes wide, pleading.

"My preference is to enjoy what lies beneath this gown

in every way, with all my senses. How am I to do that without the lamps?" When she tried to look down he caught her chin in his fingers and forced her to look back up at him. "Modesty is something you'll be unable to maintain as a Lady of the Courts, you know."

A sad smile raised the corners of her lips followed by a silent laugh that accompanied the shaking of her head. "It's not that, my lord. It's…" She shook her head again. "It doesn't matter anyway." With a deeply drawn breath and downcast eyes, she removed her hand and waited, looking up again when he didn't respond. She winced when she took in the tight downturn of his mouth. "Forgive me. Please. Continue."

Redahn wasn't quite sure what was happening to him. Something akin to protectiveness welled up in him. He fought it, knowing it was crazy since he was about to take from her what she didn't really want to give, to force her to do more than she desired, and yet he felt the need to shelter her. From what? From him? He wasn't sure which was more crazy—him or the situation. It made him laugh, which caused her brows to draw down, her lower lip jutting out just a bit.

A hint of anger flared in the depths of her blue eyes, making him smile. He much preferred the feisty maiden to the demure one and realized she probably felt the same about him—that he wavered between a solicitous soul and a lusty barbarian. No doubt which one she preferred, though he had every intent of changing her mind and showing her lust did not have to go hand in hand with barbarian.

"I'm not laughing at you, Mahryn," he told her, his voice low, soothing. "My laughter is directed only at myself, though I do hope I can make that sweet sound ring from you, and even laugh with you, long before this night is through. You're a beautiful woman, Mahryn, made even more so when you smile, which you don't do near enough." He paused. "What took away your smile?"

So many emotions crossed her face—incredulousness, uncertainty, fear... and a desire to believe. He was sure he saw that. "Our lives are not always what we thought they would be. They're not carved from our dreams. And I am not the person you believe me to be. I am..."

"You're the woman I have chosen to be with tonight," he interrupted her, pulling her firmly against him with a fierceness that had her sucking in and bracing her palms against his chest. "*I* chose *you!*" Redahn waited for his words to sink in. "That should count for something," he told her before his mouth crushed down on hers, coaxing, demanding, urging her to give in and forget anything beyond the two of them. Even if just for a little while.

Releasing her, Redahn took her hand and led her to the side of the bed where he kissed her again before pulling back to stroke a hand down the side of her face. He turned to extinguish the bedside lamp, another light still burning across the room, along with the fire in the massive fireplace. Still, Mahryn smiled at him, her tight, quivering lips turning upward in her show of gratitude.

Moving closer to her, he noted only a slight stiffening when he placed his hands over the straps of her gown. He ran a finger under each of them, enjoying the way she squirmed as he came closer to the tops of her breasts. She was going to be an amazing lover, he felt certain just from the way her body responded to his simple touch.

...And his body to her. It was time. He pulled his fingers free and stepped back to remove the wide leather belt and fawn colored tunic before pulling the soft creamy shirt over his head. He watched Mahryn, her eyes traveling from his own to quickly shoot downward.

"Oh, my lord," she whispered, surprising him by stepping forward to place her hand on his chest. He knew the places she touched, knew them by heart, by feel, knew exactly where and how he had received each one. She kissed his arm where the largest scar by far still held the pinkness that would eventually fade with age. Redahn groaned. That scar exemplified his undoing as a warrior.

He didn't want to think of that, though Mahryn's tenderness, the feel of her lips on his skin was nearly his undoing as a man, especially as she proceeded to kiss each scar. Unable to bear it, he lifted her face back up to his.

"Those scars are a reminder of what I gave up so that I and others might continue to live. I earned them and wear them with pride, all except one."

Mahryn nodded. He felt her fingers gently tracing the scar on his upper arm, the one made when they tried to *fix* him. The physician was certain he could restore Redahn's ability to wield a sword by sewing the torn up pieces of his muscles and tendons back together. It hadn't worked in spite of his efforts to let himself slowly mend and then gradually retrain. Oh, he could brandish his sword for short periods of time, had regained his ability and strength in fleeting bursts. But he would never be a true warrior—the one who had been in line behind his brother as best of the elite.

"You didn't deserve this one." Mahryn's voice cut through his thoughts. "A… any more than I did."

She stepped back, leaving Redahn dazed at the loss of her touch and at her words. "I don't understa…" His words froze as she reached for the vine-like straps and inched them from her shoulders. He watched her push them down until she uncrossed her arms and the gold material that had

encased her body slid to the floor. His breath whooshed
from his body at the beauty on display before him, his eyes
sliding over her as easily as the fabric had. Once, twice,
three times, he feasted, devouring her perfection with his
eyes.

That's when he noticed... just above the gold lace that
covered her breast, there on the right... the fine line of faded
white, barely noticeable against the paleness of her skin.
And another, a larger one on her left side closer to where
the silk and lace of her garter belt began. He recognized it,
the size and shape. There was no mistaking a healed knife
wound. "Oh dear God," he whispered, stepping toward her.

She turned around, sliding her hands beneath her hair
and lifting. He understood now why she left it down.
Another scar streaked across the plane of her perfect back.

"Who did this to you?" His voice was so soft her ears
barely picked up the words. She closed her eyes, her arms
coming down to cover his as he pulled her to him, encircled
her in a tight embrace. "How, Mahryn? Why?"

His hands felt hot where they covered the scar on her
breast and the one on her side. "Mahryn?"

She shook her head. "I... I don't know." She turned in
his arms, her eyes remaining at chest level a minute before
she dared to look up at him. "It was so very long ago... I
have never been able to remember." She bit at her lower lip
as tears welled in her eyes, tears she refused to let flow.
"If... if you'll release me, I'll prepare so you may take me
back now." She tried to push away, looking at him in
surprise when he tightened his hold. He moved his hands to
her upper arms, not realizing how hard he was squeezing
until she cried out. "I'm sorry, my lord. I should have told
you."

Redahn bristled at the self-depreciating tone of her

- - 42 - -

voice, hated that she thought her own scars from some repressed battle would have him pushing her away, that he would find her less than perfect. He stared down at her, noting the fear and uncertainty in her eyes and knew he should say something. Instead, he crushed his mouth to hers, worked his hand up into the back of her hair, winding the strands between his fingers. His other hand sought the silk and lace covering her backside and pressed her firmly against him, leaving no doubt that his desire for her remained.

Still kissing her, he turned and tumbled them onto the bed, his body covering hers. She surprised him, meeting his ardor with the arching of her back and the scorching of her tongue where she tasted him. He could scarcely believe how perfectly she fit against him, his body responding of its own accord to the feel of her.

"Mahryn," he groaned, his eyes feasting on her beauty when he'd pushed away from her just enough to relieve them both of their remaining garments. His hand skimmed down her arm, across the soft curve of her hip and down her leg, stopping right behind her knee. He lifted, bringing her leg up to cover his and smiled at the deep intake of her breath when his fingers danced up the back of her thigh, stopping just short of the apex of her legs. He wanted badly to touch her, to feel the heat, the moist pool that would tell him she desired him every bit as much as he did her. But the trepidation in her eyes, orbs that had burned moments before, had his teasing touch moving upward. He chuckled when she squirmed as his fingers crossed her waist, and he bent to kiss the spot he'd just tickled. Her breath whooshed out when his lips touched the scar just below her ribcage, her trembling increasing as he kissed a trail upward, replacing his lips with his tongue when he reached the crevice between her breasts. He looked at the scar not far from her heart and ran his mouth across it. How could anyone have hurt this gentle creature, especially when she was just a little girl?

Glancing up, he was surprised to see her watching him and his desire fired to a new level, especially at the hunger he saw in the depths of her unusually colored eyes. She may have concerns, as any unseasoned maiden should, but she still wanted him, wanted this to happen between them, every bit as much as he did. When she moved against him, he was certain everywhere they touched must have ignited the same sparks in her it did in him. He could feel her flinching, pressing closer, and savoring the contact. His instincts were right. She was quickly proving herself as a fantastic lover, and he couldn't wait a minute more to find out just how high her desire would take him.

Pushing himself up, he covered her mouth with his and moved over her, his hands continuing to assault her senses as his fingers slid across her soft flesh, memorizing her curves and everywhere his touch made her flinch. Her tongue warred with his in a lover's dance that had her panting and arching her back, her legs willingly falling wider apart as he pressed himself between them. More than once, Redahn had to remind himself to slow down, only to forget himself in the feel of her, and have having to rein himself in time and time again. It was a battle he was quickly losing.

She sucked in sharply when he began to push himself inside her and he tightened his hold. Her body stiffened and he pulled back slightly, having met her maiden barrier. He took a moment before driving hard to penetrate to her inner depths deep inside and could have sworn he heard her whisper *I'm sorry* as he sheathed himself with her, piercing her moist softness to join them as one, fully, for the first time. That thought evaporated with a roar when she bit into his shoulder at the precise moment he'd claimed her innocence.

"I'm sorry. I'm sorry!" she cried out.

There was no missing the apology that time. Eyes filled with pooled tears looked up at him when he pulled back to stare down at her.

Her tiny hand rubbed against the tender spot on his shoulder. "I hadn't expected…"

"Do they teach you *nothing* during your time before the Dremis Gathering? You surely do not expect me to believe you to be so naïve as to not know…"

Mahryn shook her head. "No, my lord," she whispered. "I knew. I know." Eyes pleading, he sensed she was willing him to understand something he seemed unable to grasp. After a moment she sighed, her arms falling to her sides against the soft matting beneath her. The tension in her body was replaced by defeat and she lifted her arms again, her palms pressing against his chest in an attempt to move him. Redahn remained immobile, pinning her beneath him. She bit at her lower lip drawing his attention to her mouth. "Please…" He watched her lips as she spoke, feeling his hunger to taste them again. "I know I've made a shambles of this evening. Let me up so that I may prepare to leave. The night is still young enough that you may find another maiden to enjoy."

Redahn's instant scowl was eased by a chuckle. "Would that be a *better* maiden?" His use of her words from earlier caused Mahryn's cheeks to redden and he trailed a finger over the fiery surface, shaking his head. "Be still, Mahryn. You're not going anywhere, so enough talk of you leaving. Tonight, you're my chosen maiden. I intend to enjoy you and to make good on my word."

"Your... word?"

He pressed himself more firmly into her, smiling at the sharp intake of her breath. "You will enjoy this night as much as I will."

Chapter 8

Fighting her way through the haze of sound slumber, Mahryn breathed deeply, the delightful scent of fresh flowers tickling her senses. She smiled, remembering the garden in her dreams, knowing the real scent came from the bouquet she'd picked earlier that afternoon to bring color to her drab surroundings. She pushed away the dark thoughts that tried to creep in, thinking instead about her dream of the god-like warrior. It had been so vivid, more real than ever before. No doubt her idealistic views of the King's great grandson had moved to a new level, leaving her to wonder how such a caustic man could be so gentle and attentive in her mind. She'd never heard of him being either of those. Granted, she only knew him from afar, having observed him from the shadows of darkened hallways, or corners of the King's chamber when he was unaware she was even there. Yet, in her mind, his fierceness had dissolved into tenderness as he'd taken her, taught her... seeming to enjoy driving her to heights she never knew existed, though her body must have known for it to have seemed so real.

Sighing, she turned, wincing when her muscles protested. Goodness, she was sore, almost as if... The thought was stilled when her bent knee contacted the solid warmth of another leg that didn't belong to her. Extending an arm, her palm stopped against the muscled planes of a distinctly male chest and her eyes opened in a hurry to find herself staring into the soul of the man in her dreams. Startled, she pulled back then scrambled to move away from him.

"No you don't." Redahn's hands clamped around her waist to pull her back and rolled her to where he could settle her beneath him. "Was all that we shared washed away with a few hours of sleep?" He inched his hand down between them and quirked a brow then chuckled before whispering, "Your body betrays you, my lady. Already I feel your response."

Just the thought of his touch had Mahryn trembling and mortified by the wantonness of her reaction. She pressed into the mattress in an attempt to distance herself from him. He laughed, continuing with an intensity that had her sucking in air. Assured by a tiny moan she couldn't conceal, he leaned down to nuzzle the side of her neck, the shadow of stubble on his chin tickling the tender flesh there. Of their own accord, Mahryn's hips lifted toward him and she uttered an oath that had him pulling back to look down at her.

"You have spent too much of your time lurking in the corners of chambers where men alone should be present to conduct dealings necessary for our preservation." Her mouth dropped open as he continued, "What goes on within the King's chambers may not always be pretty, but we do and say what we must. And you should use those lovely lips for something much more pleasing." His eyes dropped to her mouth, which she had clamped shut, and Mahryn inched her tongue out to moisten her suddenly dry lips, then cursed herself, silently this time, for her actions. It was too late. She felt the increase in Redahn's desire seconds before he claimed her mouth with his own and moved his hand away to press himself inside her. She moaned, loudly this time, unable to restrain the noise. How could something so simple instantly have her soaring away from her world and all her cares?

It was over an hour before Redahn rolled away from her to sit on the edge of the bed. "I'd best get you back before the Court sends someone to fetch you."

Mahryn sat up, clutching the coverlet to her, and pushed her hair away from her face. "My father won't care."

Redahn twisted to look at her, wrapping a strand of her hair around his finger. "You're no longer under your father's rule alone," he reminded her, giving a gentle tug before running the silky strands between his fingers. "I confess I fear the head mistress of the Ladies of the Courts far more than Lord Tedran." He laughed. "I can guarantee she's made inquiries and knows where you are and who you've been with. She's already allowed you to remain longer than I expected, though she won't let you stay indefinitely, even for me."

Mahryn felt an impish surge, and wondered if she had the ability to entice this man to keep her longer. He stood before her unschooled mind could devise a plan of action, though her eyes were quick to watch him walk away. Mesmerized, she didn't turn away to rise herself until he looked back at her and smiled. With heat creeping into her cheeks, she bit her lower lip to suppress her smile, and pulled the sheet over her shoulders. She heard him chuckle and she rolled her eyes at the silliness of her remaining modesty. Had he been closer, he would have heard her echo his quiet laughter.

"May we leave through the garden?" she asked him just after she'd clamped a gold bracelet around her ankle. Redahn watched her fingers play along the thin metal, stroking it with affection. She'd been near frantic when she'd realized it was no longer on her leg, her eyes shining with gratitude when he'd handed it to her with an explanation that he'd removed it to keep it from getting broken during their… entanglement. She'd blushed, then told him the bracelet had belonged to her sister, Hahna, that it was the only thing she had left tying them together. She'd put it on and quickly turned her attention to the garden.

"There's no exit from the garden," he told her, his eyes snapping to lock with hers when her skirt slid down to cover her legs and she rose to stand before him. He smiled, hit anew with her size, thinking of the way they'd fit so well together.

She looked puzzled and turned toward the door that he'd opened before she'd awakened to allow the sweet fragrance to fill the room. "All gardens have a way out," she told him, unsure of how she knew that or why it should matter.

Redahn watched her after she'd walked out into the morning light. He enjoyed the inquisitive tilt of her head as she studied the flower-crested walls that enclosed his sanctuary. *A beauty among many*, he thought. She was as splendid as the blooms around her… and smelled just as lovely. That thought made him chuckle.

"Come, my lady. There is no way out through these walls." He walked out and took her hand.

"Ah." She nodded. "Much like my life."

Mahryn tried to pass her statement off with a chuckle, but knew she wasn't quick enough to hide the sadness in her eyes when he frowned. Averting her gaze, she looked around one last time. With a soft sigh, she slipped her hand into the crook of his offered arm, refusing to feel the loss as she headed back to begin her new life as an official member of the Ladies of the Court.

Chapter 9

The walk back to town seemed to take a lot less time than it had the night before. She supposed that could have been in part to the multiple stops under the moon. She wondered how much farther it was to the Zanak compound. Since the direct descendants of the King were always allotted prime land around the castle, she assumed it wasn't all that far. She'd never been there, though she'd heard it was a beautiful home nestled against one of the few hillsides within the land, with the rest of the terrain gently sloping down to the sea. Their riches, it seemed, were derived from their ownership of the harbor and the men's abilities to serve among the King's elite forces. They were rumored to have been very good at all they did, and must have been to have gained all that they had.

Mahryn wondered who she was kidding. She *knew* they were good. Redahn had been right about one thing—she did often lurk in the corners of the King's chambers, listening to discussions most ladies were never privy to. She knew a great deal more than she probably should have about a great many people—information that might have been dangerous in the hands of anyone else.

The stares and questioning eyes that met them when they reached the town square had Mahryn tugging at her skirt, her chin remaining lowered. Redahn's shirt, left untucked and untied at the neck, lent an air of daytime casualness over the tan pants he'd worn. Mahryn had disguised her dress, as best she could, using Redahn's tunic to cover her nearly bare shoulders. His wide belt, laced as tight as she could possibly get it, settled more at hip level, allowing the tunic to gap open exposing a good deal of creamy flesh above the neckline of her gown. Her cheeks burned, knowing they all knew where she'd been, what she'd done, and who she'd done it with. She was feeling the sting from the brand of her reality.

She felt the back of Redahn's hand brush her own just before he laced his fingers with hers. He squeezed and she returned it, turning her head to look up into his smiling eyes. She couldn't help but smile.

"Perhaps you might break your fast with me, my lady?" When she hesitated, he nudged her upper arm with his. "Unless you prefer the company of your mistress and those chattering featherheads to mine?" He made a face and she laughed, leaning her head against his shoulder. A loud grumble from behind his belt had her covering her stomach with her free hand and him turning them down an alleyway darkened by the close proximity of the buildings to one another. He led her past the backs of the shops there, over a well-worn path, and to a back gate into the castle grounds.

"Lord Redahn," one of the guards greeted them, motioning the other guards stationed at intervals along the path from the gate to the castle itself to let the couple pass.

"The castle's kitchens?" She looked at him like he'd lost his mind.

Redahn nodded. "No finer food in the land than what is prepared for the King."

Mahryn laughed and shook her head, not that she wouldn't agree about the food. She'd just thought he'd meant to save her from a too soon encounter with those who now ran her life, not deliver her into the beast's belly.

"Lord Redahn!" A man in less than formal attire greeted them with a flourished bow. "It's been some time since you've graced us with your presence." He straightened and nodded to Mahryn. "And never have you showed up with such a radiant companion. Do tell, my lord. To what do we owe the honor?" The graying man in chef's attire lifted Mahryn's hand to his lips.

Mahryn might have taken offense had his bright eyes not been filled with such kindness and fun. Instead, she laughed and allowed him to tuck her hand into the crook of his arm before turning to lead her away from Redahn's side.

Glancing over her shoulder, she raised her brows at her new lover. He just shrugged and followed them, laughing and exchanging greetings with the workers scurrying about to prepare dishes for the castle's masses.

"It's the Dremis, Waylan, or has the preparation of all these extra meals escaped your notice?" Redahn finally answered the man's question, his voice floating to them from close behind.

"I feel sorry for you, having to endure the company of that one," her escort said, turning his head to make sure Redahn heard. Mahryn sucked in hard, surprised at his impertinence. She held her tongue though, noting Redahn's ease and willingness to play along with the man.

"She seems to have *endured* quite well, not that I would expect the Lady Mahryn to wish to share the details of her Dremis Night with you."

Mahryn dropped her head, the lightness of the atmosphere gone from her, replaced by a deep blush in her cheeks.

"Cheer up, dear Lady," Waylan whispered to her. "You could have done far worse, believe me. There are many within the castle walls who would be quite pleased to learn of you and his lordship…"

Waylan's comment was cut short by a loudly cleared throat behind them. When Mahryn looked back at Redahn, she noticed the deep crease of his forehead, a frown tugging at the corners of his lips, though it was all washed away, replaced by a broad smile when a comely woman bustled in to demand the couple be seated.

"Corrina! How are you?" Redahn asked the woman who was maybe a handful of years older than himself. He pulled her into a bear hug before nuzzling her neck, and she pushed him away, unable to keep the smile from her eyes even as she chastised him.

"Mind yourself, my lord. I'm sure your lady doesn't wish to see you pawing some other woman!"

Redahn laughed, his lopsided smile lifting his mouth on the same side as a raised brow. "You'd best be careful how you apply titles, Corrina. We all know how this works. She is no more mine than you are."

"Pftt!" She waved a hand at him before turning to Mahryn and leaning close. "That's why you're still with him well after sun up." Her voice was low, her face kindly when she patted Mahryn's reddening cheek.

"Don't give her false hope, Corrina. You know full well that I plan to go to my grave unshackled by any woman."

He squinted at Mahryn's slackening jaw when she wheeled to look at him. Unanswered challenges passed between them before Mahryn clamped her mouth into a tight line and turned to follow Corrina to a table set for two nestled in a nearby corner.

"As if any woman would choose to be your shackle," she mumbled.

"I heard that," he whispered, catching up to her in a

few long strides.

Mahryn shrugged off the hand he placed on her shoulder, then sat. Once he was also seated, they stared at one another from their chairs on either side of the small table.

"You have no right to be offended, my lady," he told her once Corrina and the others had moved away from them.

"Who says I have taken offense?" She shrugged. "Did you not inform me of my place last night, as well as who would choose it for me?"

He scoffed, taken aback by her tone. "I took nothing from you that I had no right to. Had it not been me, it would have been one of the others."

Mahryn shook her head, the tips of her golden brown hair brushing against his tunic covering her shoulders. "You foiled my intent of evading all advances when you joined our little group. Had everything gone according to my plan, I would have been absolved of the ludicrous *rules* of the Dremis at the end of the week. *I* would have been free to make my own decisions should some man ever deem me fit to take any one of the positions you chose for me last night."

Looking through her, he squinted then stared at her so intently she had to look away. "Had it not been me…" He spoke slowly, leaning forward to emphasize his words. "It would have been one of the others. I guarantee." Reaching across the table, he forced her to look up with a finger beneath her chin. When their eyes locked, he continued. "Every man in there knew of my interest. Their hesitation to make a move had *nothing* to do with your well executed *plan*." Mahryn pulled her chin free with a jerk, though she maintained the eye contact, her lips pressed tightly closed.

"I have no idea what your talk of absolution from the rules means, but I can assure you, my lady, you have been cheated of nothing as far as I'm concerned." His jaw muscle clenching and unclenching, he shook his head. "As Waylan said, you could have done far worse."

Mahryn sat back, hiding her moment of surprise, wondering if she had imagined the flash of hurt she was sure she'd seen in Redahn's eyes. Their stare down was interrupted by Corrina returning with a handful of waiters, each carrying a tray loaded with delectable enticements.

Shrugging off what had just been said between them, Mahryn put on her best façade and shook her head. "There's no way we can eat all this." She laughed when the fifth platter was sat before them and looked up to see Redahn smiling at her.

"Speak for yourself, my lady." Her eyes lingered on the upturned corners of his lips as he spoke, though his next words had her looking back into his dark eyes. "The pleasantries of a night more magical than most I have experienced have left me hungry." She swallowed with effort, her breath suddenly shallow and she found herself pulling each side of his tunic closer together to cover the flesh caressed by his gaze. "Eat," he told her, his voice becoming thick. "It's well past time to go."

Chapter 10

Sated by the exquisite food, her senses still reeling a bit from Redahn's words, Mahryn accepted hugs and an open invitation to return to the castle's kitchens from Corrina and Waylan. She liked the couple, especially when she'd learned they were a *real* couple, happily married, thanks to Redahn's meddling. Those were Corrina's word, not hers.

Following Redahn, she walked along the path and stepped beyond the same gate they'd entered to break their fast, though Redahn led her down a different road, next to the castle's outer wall and well away from the merchants' alleyways. She sighed as they neared the main entrance.

"Chin up," Redahn commanded, moving closer to her side. "Not every Court Lady returns with the King's blood kinsman." They both laughed when she rolled her eyes, though she readily accepted his hand as they crossed under the heavily guarded archway, no one questioning their right to enter.

Mahryn's feet felt heavy, her body tensing with each trudging step toward the lowered drawbridge that would allow them to easily cross the moat and move through the inner wall and then into the castle itself. "I left here a girl and I return a woman," she whispered, full well expecting him to make fun of her the moment the words tumbled from her mouth.

Instead, Redahn changed their direction, steering her a short distance off the path to one of the few trees growing between the inner wall and the castle. "You weren't certain, were you?" He waited, continuing only when she didn't answer. "That's why you said you were sorry... whatever happened... the same incident that caused your scars... you believed they had taken more from you..."

"Please," she interrupted, shifting from one foot to the other and looking around to make sure no one was within earshot. "It doesn't matter. Besides, I only know what I was led to believe, that there was a likely chance I had been compromised."

Redahn started to speak then shook his head. She had been compromised, but not in the way she'd always thought. It was obvious damage had been done, but this was not the time or the place to delve further. "Perhaps you're correct. You know the truth now." *At least that part of it,* he thought as he pushed away from the tree. "Come on," he told her, extending his hand. "It's time I let you go."

Mahryn's shoulders dropped in unison with a soft huff of relief before she placed her hand in his for the short stroll to the castle entrance. She bit at her lower lip as they walked, almost certain she could hear the wheels in Redahn's head squeaking as they turned in thought. She hated the pang of disappointment that had come with him speaking of letting her go. She was going to have to work to make herself believe what she'd told him back in the kitchen. If only she could accept her fate and move fearlessly forward into this life chosen for her by others.

The head mistress' back was to them when they entered the main hall of the wing that housed the Ladies of the Court. Mahryn stifled a nervous giggle that threatened to bubble up with every step they took toward the overbearing, portly woman. She wondered if Redahn felt the same titter of angst she did, thinking back to his comment about fearing the head mistress more than he did her father. He'd surely been jesting, though Mahryn knew she was not alone in dreading this encounter. She'd heard too many stories from the other maidens who happened to know ladies living under the mistress' charge. The older woman didn't care for her well-ordered sanctum becoming disorganized, and Mahryn had done just that by disappearing until close to the noon hour the day after her first night as one of the Ladies.

Taking her time to look over some sort of paper, the head mistress finally handed the parchment to the waiting assistant, who bobbed a curtsy and darted away from the mistress' impatient hand sweep. With a deep, then loudly expelled breath, she turned her ample body toward the couple, now standing a mere two feet from her in the middle of the hall.

Looking first at Mahryn, the dark, penetrating eyes shifted upward to Redahn's face before clicking back down to settle on Mahryn again. "I see you have *finally* returned my girl, Lord Redahn," the house mistress huffed. Mahryn had to work to keep herself from squirming under the woman's scrutiny, her discomfort mounting as the woman continued to speak to Redahn while staring at her. "I trust the *rules* of an overnight *visit* merely slipped your mind. Once again," she added.

Schooling her features, Mahryn refused to let on that her mistress had hit the mark in letting her know she was nothing special simply because the man beside her had broken the rules and kept her so long. No doubt, it wasn't the first time, nor would it be his last... with others, though probably not with her.

Working her hand free of his, Mahryn wiped her palm along the side of his tunic that still covered her evening dress. The mistress glanced down, a satisfied smirk toying just under the surface on her full face. *That's not what Corrina said.* Mahryn heard the words whispered in her mind. The woman down in the kitchen had made out that him keeping her as long as he did was special. But what did Corrina know? She couldn't possibly be aware of all Redahn's... activities.

Her mind swirling, head becoming fuzzy—no doubt in part thanks to a lack of sleep, Mahryn missed most of the conversation between her mistress and Redahn, tuning in just in time to hear him thank the woman for *a lovely evening of entertainment provided by a truly mesmerizing companion.* He assured the woman a *gift* would be forthcoming for his indiscretions in keeping one of her *girls* beyond the bounds set by propriety.

With a nod and a barely bobbed curtsy, the woman stepped back and motioned for Mahryn to take her leave, sweeping her arm in the direction of the hallway that led to the girls' tiny rooms within this section of the castle.

Mahryn took a step away from Redahn, then turned back begging her mind to light on the right words. His face, showing no emotion, did little to help her. Dark brows rising over eyes that shuttered feelings, he smiled at her— that lopsided grin of his tugging up the corner on one side of his mouth.

"My lady." The formal tone of his words lined up with the flourishing bow he offered her had Mahryn dropping into a respectable curtsy fitting the man's station. When she heard him turn, the sound of his boots retreating on the polished tile, she rose, not bothering to lift her downturned eyes as she walked away from her mistress and down the hall toward her room.

"Let Ceeda know when you're ready for your bath and she'll have it drawn," her mistress called.

"Yes, my lady," she called back, her voice a weary whisper.

"Mahryn."

Mahryn stopped, waiting for the lady to continue. "Guard your heart and your emotions," the older woman walked up beside her and whispered. Surprised, Mahryn's eyes snapped to the pudgy face to see compassion there for the first time. "Emotions have no place within our halls unless you wish your heart to get broken many times."

Mahryn stared at her, then nodded. "Yes, my lady," she answered again as she turned toward her door. "Thank you."

As the door closed behind her, Mahryn heard the other woman clear her throat and call out to someone, no doubt one of her assistants lurking in the hallway. "Go and inform Lord Tedran that his daughter has returned. And be quick about it. He wanted to know immediately," she commanded, her voice again hard and uncompromising. Mahryn leaned against the door imagining the satisfied smirk on her father's face.

"You have won again," she whispered before pushing away from the cold wood and walking the few steps across the room to stand beside her bedside table. She sniffed the bouquet, pulling the flowers' fragrance deep into her lungs while softly running her fingers across the metal cross that lay on the table beside the glass vase. He had won—his victory beginning many years ago when she'd been fed a lie that had changed her whole life, distorted how she'd felt and what she'd thought of herself for all these years.

Removing Redahn's tunic, Mahryn reached for the bell pull to let Ceeda know she could have her bath drawn, only to let her hand drop to her side. Later, she thought, moving to the tiny bed nestled against the wall. She lay down, drawing her knees up and flipping the coverlet over her silk covered body. The tunic still clutched in her hand, she rubbed the softness of the material against her cheek and inhaled deeply. The scent was a mixture of her own and his—a heady mix, she thought, as she drifted into the welcomed abyss of sleep. At least for a while, she wouldn't have to think, wouldn't have to feel, and didn't have to come to terms with the fact that the one person who should have loved her the most had betrayed her so fully, simply because she had not been the one to die.

Chapter 11

The sound of a fist against her door had Mahryn bolting upright in her bed, the coverlet and tunic both clutched against her pounding heart. Unlike the first few nights she'd been there, Mahryn seemed to wake knowing exactly where she was. What baffled her foggy brain was why she was still in her clothes and clutching a man's garment as if her very life depended on it.

"My lady," a quiet voice floated in to her through the now barely cracked door and Larina's features began to take form within the opening. Mahryn smiled, pleased to see a friendly face. She wasn't sure she was ready to endure Ceeda's brashness, which would no doubt border on the crude side now that she was no longer one of the innocent maidens.

Thankfully, Larina seemed to like her as well and understood what she was going through. A Lady of the Courts herself, Larina had been there for several years—far longer than she ought to have been, in Mahryn's opinion. The woman's mild temperament and sweet countenance, coupled with looks that were slightly above average, should have captured the attention of one of the lesser warriors looking for the perfect wife. Yes, Larina would have made an excellent wife. Perhaps that was why she was often overlooked as a nightly companion. *These men want lovers, not wives.* She'd heard one of the Ladies say that before the Dremis. *They stumble upon those quite by accident, though their faulty steps are few and far between.* She wondered where she would find herself in the end. Would she wind up serving the younger Ladies as her age inched upward, or the accidental wife of a man who merely needed someone to tend his children and his household? Neither idea much thrilled her, though she really couldn't expect to find love, now could she?

Larina's cleared throat brought her back to focus on the unwanted *pleasantries* of preparation for yet another night with an unknown end. Her body, sore from the night before, tingled with memories she'd just as soon forget. Men seldom asked the same Lady to accompany them from the Ball, and it was especially unlikely for one whose reputation flaunted his appetite for the *magic* of the Dremis Maidens. No, Lord Redahn would not ask for her again. Of all the unknowns in her life, that was one thing of which Mahryn was certain.

Climbing from the security offered by the less than comfortable bed, Mahryn motioned Larina inside where the two of them took up vigil before the sparsely filled wardrobe.

"We haven't much time," Larina informed her, staying her hand when she reached toward one of the dresses. "The other Ladies and Maidens have already begun to assemble and you still need to wash before dressing." She bit at her lip when Mahryn turned questioning eyes on her. "I'm sorry, my lady. Ceeda said we should let you rest, but I knew the head mistress would…"

"Ceeda!" Mahryn practically hissed. That woman would revel in the humiliation and downfall of any and all, congratulating herself for having a hand in the process.

"I waited until she was busy helping the others…"

"Thank you." Mahryn smiled at her before quickly

turning back to her closet. She sighed. There wasn't a dress one in there that would allow her to have her hair up, which it would have to be if they were to dress it wet. They would all show the scar on her upper back.

"If I may... I have a dress that... I believe might work."

Mahryn could tell by the halting way Larina spoke that the other woman was trying to offer assistance without offense. Fortunately, only she and another older woman had been available to help Mahryn with her bath times and in dressing. Those two alone knew of her scars—except for Redahn. She closed her eyes, thinking of how he had traced his fingers across the ugly marks, had kissed each one with fury burning in his eyes at what she'd had to endure, and how that fire had been replaced with the unmistakable glow of passion...

She shook her head to clear the memories, then nodded, confusing poor Larina. With a soft laugh, Mahryn asked if she might see the gown.

Together, they made their way to the bath chamber where Larina got her started before going to fetch the dress, leaving Mahryn soaking in thankfulness that at least one of them was thinking with a level head. With Larina's help, she just might make it to the Gathering with at least a shred of her dignity intact.

Jaw muscle flexing, Redahn let his eyes run over the women in the Great Hall for probably the hundredth time in the thirty minutes he'd been there. Ignoring the smiles and other posed expressions of those attempting to catch his attention, his scowl deepened along with the tightness of his lips. Where was she and why wasn't she there?

A low growl had the man to his right turning startled eyes in Redahn's direction. One of the others in the tight group that had yet to make their way toward the Ladies chuckled and clapped the King's great grandson on the back.

"You have the look of one who has had his prized possession stolen, man. What could possibly have your britches in such a bunch with all these fine maidens before us?"

Redahn looked around again. His companion was right. There were beautiful women for the taking—willing women.

Only none of them were the one he wanted to see.

It was time he put a stop to her monopolizing his mind. Shoving away from the wall, he moved off from the other men and crossed the floor with a determined stride that took him toward a small gathering of the few remaining unspoiled maidens. "Ladies," he greeted them with a bow and a smile. As he straightened, they began their expected tittering. Looking back toward the group of men he'd left and wondering why, his attention was captured by an angel. She was dressed in gossamer cream over yards and yards of delicate lace, the blond/brown streaks of her hair forming a perfect halo atop her head and he couldn't take his eyes off of her.

The vision, her arm looped with another of the Ladies, a woman very nearly her same size, drifted across the floor toward a smaller group, not far from where he stood. Almost as if she was drawn by the heat of his gaze, she turned her head toward him, offering a slight smile and barely perceptible nod before her blue eyes darted away from his face.

Redahn watched as one of his fellow warriors changed his direction and turned toward her. He gave a low whistle of appreciation, his eyes lighting with desire as they traveled down Mahryn's body. Before the two ladies had even stopped, more men began to flock toward the space occupied by the ethereal vision, and Redahn stiffened. His nostrils flared, lips pressed tight, he made to step away from the group.

"Don't go." The small voice coming from his right checked his departure. He looked back, his dark eyes locking with those of a hopeful maiden. His muscles jumped beneath his shirt when he felt her fingers settle on his arm, just above his elbow. Eyes dropping to her bare neck, he smiled, especially seeing the beginnings of a blush creeping up from the top of the bodice of her dress. Tomorrow night, this maiden would wear the same neckpiece he'd noticed fixed around Mahryn's delicate neck, indicating she had moved from the status of Maiden to Lady.

The maiden before him returned his smile, and he knew she thought his look of desire was put there by thoughts of her. She had no idea how badly his heart pinched when hit with the reality that Mahryn truly would warm the bed of some other warrior that night while he was forced to endure companionship that would do nothing more than ease his tension for a while—tension that grew stronger with thoughts of the lady he'd had the night before.

Sweet laughter floated to his ears—laughter that had been his. That sound had filled his dreams while he'd napped throughout the day, trying to escape the strange feelings that had begun to assault him when he'd left the Chamber of the Ladies earlier that morning.

He could feel his jaw beginning to flex again, realized he had missed bits of conversation directed at him and looked down into eyes that begged for affections he could not give. Turning, he motioned toward one of the warriors who had earlier occupied space next to him. The man made his way across the room to accept the hand of the young woman, without question, when Redahn removed it from his arm and placed it within that of his friend. The maiden frowned, her lips quivering slightly when Redahn shook his head. "I'm sorry," was all he offered before turning on his heel and marching away from the group, knowing he was about to do something he had never done before.

"Ladies." He bowed when both Mahryn and her companion stepped back, turning to face him as he made his way into their group. "Lady Larina! How nice to see you again," he greeted the woman who had walked in with Mahryn. He recognized her as one of the Ladies whose favors he had enjoyed a time or two while she'd acted as companion to his brother's wife during Elenya's last pregnancy. "You're looking lovely, as always."

Larina blushed. "As are you, my lord." Her blush deepened when he chortled at her telling him he looked lovely.

Smiling, he touched her flaming cheek. "You would make a fine companion for a worthy man, my lady..." His eyes instantly snapped to Mahryn, her face unreadable as she watched him. Hesitating only a moment, he patted Larina's shoulder then, without preamble, he held out his hand to Mahryn. She stared down, her brows drawing tightly together before she looked back at his face. With their eyes locked, he waited for what seemed like an eternity before he felt the silky touch of her fingers rub against his palm. Sighing inwardly, he lifted her hand, grazing her knuckles with his lips. With a gentle tug and a tipping of his head, Redahn stepped away from the group, leading her toward the doors of the Great Hall. Neither spoke as they walked into darkness beyond.

Chapter 12

"You've worn your hair up," he said, breaking the silence at last.

Mahryn nodded. "I'm afraid I fell asleep and had little time to prepare for the evening," she confessed.

Redahn chuckled. "That makes two of us."

She smiled. "I'm fortunate Lady Larina had a gown that would meet with the head mistress' demands while covering…"

Redahn's eyes went to her mouth, knowing her lower lip would be caught between her teeth. "The look becomes you," he told her, continuing to stare at her mouth, biting back a groan when she released her lip and her tongue darted out to moisten the soft curves. Just a few steps off the main road and into the trail leading to the gardening cottage, he stopped and turned her to face him. She didn't speak, her only response a noticeable shudder when he traced the dress' neckline that dipped low between her breasts, while scalloped fanning hid the scar on one side. "You look like an angel," he whispered, wrapping his arms around her waist and pulling her to him, his mouth instantly covering hers, desperate to taste her.

The flesh on her back enticed him, beckoning from the lace-framed diamond covered in sheer gossamer that hid the scar that zigzagged between her shoulder blades. The heat beneath his hands intensified the desire that had been building long before he'd seen her again.

When he broke away, kissing her forehead where it rested against his chin, she tittered. "If I am not mistaken, my lord, I believe your intentions for me this evening are anything but angelic."

He pulled back to look down at her, knowing she was wrong. The night he'd spent with her had taken him closer to heaven than he deserved—close enough to make him break his own rule and choose the same woman for a second night during the Dremis Gathering. *I'm not falling*, he told himself. He'd simply enjoyed her more than most. It was silly to try to replicate that with someone unknown, untried, when he would be assured of mutual pleasures with Mahryn. Never mind the fact that he'd thought of little else since their parting and the mere sight of those other men looking at her had him wishing he'd had a sword lashed to his side so that he might close their eyes with the removal of their heads.

He breathed in, exhaling loudly before turning them toward the cottage. He had a feeling he would have to be diligent to keep from losing his own head where this woman was concerned and that thought bothered him more than just a little. *Just this night*, he told himself. After this evening, he would walk away, his desire for her satiated, and tomorrow night, he would leave the hall with someone else and her to whatever fate life had in store—a life that didn't include him.

But for tonight... he looked down at the angel currently his, and intended to enjoy all that she had to offer.

Unlike the previous night, they rose well before the moonlight faded from the sky. Redahn returned her to the castle gates without any words being spoken. No promises were given, no expectations were voiced.

The short walk from the cottage having been made hand in hand, Redahn simply squeezed her fingers and offered a sweeping bow before turning Mahryn over to the guards who usually escorted the returning Ladies back to their wing. Just before she entered the large wooden doors across the drawbridge, Mahryn glanced back, her eyes resting on the dark haired figure who stood talking to the remaining guards. She could hear them laughing at something one of them had said then, without acknowledging her in any way, Redahn turned and walked away. Stepping clear of the opening door, Mahryn slipped through.

"Thank you," she told the guard, her voice soft, clogging with emotion. "I can see myself back from here."

His lack of response had Mahryn questioning whether he was going to heed her desires, then without ado, he offered a bow that rivaled Redahn's and left. Mahryn exhaled a held breath, thankful for a few moments alone before she had to face whoever might still be awake within the Chamber of the Ladies. Although they had observed the mistress' rules and ended their night before the sunrise, she had remained in Redahn's arms far longer than propriety deemed reasonable for a man to satisfy his desires.

"To hell with propriety," he'd said as he'd pulled her close to him and the coverlet over them both before his eyes had drifted shut. *Yes,* Mahryn had thought, *to hell with the rules and demands of other*s. She'd pushed away an image of her father, content to revel in the feel of her lover's heart beating against her back as she'd closed her eyes and joined him for a couple of hours of sweet slumber. Only two nights, and she'd already come to realize no rest compared to what she'd found wrapped in strong arms after being well loved. The comfort rivaled only by the security she'd felt as a child in her mother's loving embrace.

"I miss you, Mama," she whispered, confusion creasing her forehead when her mind jumped to thoughts of Dara. She was glad the woman's husband, Zanak's gardener, had been the one to welcome her and Redahn back to the cottage. She didn't know why the woman unsettled her.

Her mind reached for something—a feeling of familiarity, arms other than her mother's wrapped around her... and an unmoving Hahna.

Sucking in hard, Mahryn shook her head, trying to clear the vision, willing her mind to recapture the serenity that had washed over her while she'd slept in Redahn's arms.

Another knock, much more forceful than the one the day before, acted as Mahryn's wakeup call once again. The light streaming through her window attested to an earlier hour.

Without the courtesy provided by Lady Larina, the head mistress bustled in, her frame seeming even larger in the confines of the small room. Lips pursed, she frowned when Mahryn made no effort beyond struggling to a seated position on the bed. With a shrug, she tossed the envelope she'd been holding onto the coverlet and Mahryn stared at it, then looked back up at her mistress, her hands remaining clutched beneath her chin.

"Are private invitations not usually declined during the Dremis, my lady?" Mahryn hated the smallness of her own voice as she spoke.

The head mistress nodded, her scowl deepening. "The

royal seal cannot be denied."

Mahryn looked at the envelope, then nodded, her eyes cast down, teeth working her lower lip. "When?"

"As soon as we may ready you, so I suggest you rise. It would not do to keep him waiting."

No, it would not.

"How long will I be staying? Do you know?"

The head mistress stared at her, through her and Mahryn knew she should open the correspondence and find out for herself. But she simply couldn't bring herself to break the seal, even the thought of the words sending a surge of queasiness through her middle. *The honor of your presence*, it would say. Honor! There was no honor in any of this.

With a sigh, the older woman answered. "The courier said I might expect you to be away for one night only."

Mahryn closed her eyes, inhaling deeply before nodding. She thanked her mistress with a breathy exhale. "Forgive my asking, but have you any idea why..." The older woman was already shaking her head, even as she turned toward the door.

"Some things you simply do not question." Smoothing her hand over her perfectly coiffed hair, the woman swept out the door, leaving Mahryn to wonder on her own. She reached for the invitation, her fingers absently tracing the raised design of the wax embossed seal.

After a moment, she forced herself to rise and pack a small bag for her overnight stay away from this place she'd been told to consider home.

"What games are being played here?" she asked the empty room. Wasn't there anyone who truly valued her as a living, breathing, feeling being? How long would they continue to play with her life?

Chapter 13

Looking around at the other occupants of Zanak's dining table, Redahn's pleasant countenance was replaced with a scowl. They had all stopped speaking when he'd made his third light-hearted jest and had focused their attention fully on him.

"Ill-mannered lot! Stop staring at me." The brunt of his harshness drew direction toward his mother who actually had the nerve to laugh at his outburst.

"Oh, son. We're simply surprised to see you so..." Her words dropped off at his deepening scowl.

His older brother, accustomed to the dark countenance, and fearless of any potential backlash from Redahn's ire, quirked a brow. A lazy smile drew his mouth upward on one side. "If it weren't a known fact you have no heart, Brother, I'd say you've been scorched by the fires of blooming love."

"Lov..." Redahn's growl, complete with snarl-curled lips had the other guests looking away, most of them hiding their mirth behind lifted hands or down-turned heads. Redahn saw only his brother, his eyes never leaving the face so nearly like his own. "Tahruk, you're mad, man. You know that's not in the stars for me, especially since you're right about one thing. I have no heart to give." He shrugged away when his aunt, sitting at his right, tried to lay her hand on his arm. Looking around at those sitting closest to him— his mother on his left, his brother across from her, he shrugged and pushed back his chair. "If you'll excuse me," he said, standing and moving behind his chair. "I have a Gathering to prepare for. The *Dremis* Gathering," he emphasized looking first at his father's empty seat and then to the one beside his brother. "Perhaps you all may remember it, though my sorrow swells for you when I think how tightly strapped you have become because of such. Tied by honor and blood, while *I* continue my greedy indulgences thanks to a court that has seen fit to provide me with a week's worth of maidens—a fresh one every night just clamoring for my touch.

"Not at the table!" his mother chastised, though Tahruk's snorted laughter overrode any threat Lady Neria's words might have held.

Nodding, the older brother's lips curled upward. "Which is why you've chosen the same maiden, or Lady now, I should say, for the past three nights? Hmmm?" He laughed at Redahn's surprise, not bothering to temper his mirth, even faced with the stormy look that flashed in his brother's eyes.

"Two nights. *Two!*" Redahn repeated the number, his voice low, menacing. "Though it's none of your concern with whom I spend my nights. Not that it matters now. I am done with her anyway."

With that, he turned and walked toward the door.

"Brother."

Tahruk's use of the endearment, spoken in a tone steeped with the sibling bond they'd held even as rivaling children, stopped him, though he didn't turn back. He stood still, staring at his toes.

"The fires of lust will never compare to the continual heat that engulfs once love's flame ignites."

Redahn stood at the threshold a few moments longer.

Finally, shaking his head, he answered, "Love cannot settle where there is no heart. I shall enjoy my fires only in a bed of lust."

He walked away wishing he felt the satisfaction usually found at shocking his family, but it didn't come. The only thing he felt was a burning need for the Dremis moon to reach her full height so he could go and find someone to share his fire—someone who didn't have soft tresses streaked with brownish-blond, and no gold flecks in her blue eyes that dared to attempt to penetrate his soul and rid him of the shadowed darkness inside.

Redahn seemed the very essence of the life of the party during the first hour of that sixth night of the Dremis Gathering. He cajoled his fellow warriors, and flirted with Maidens and Ladies alike, truly seeming to be enjoying his time. Only someone who knew him well would have sensed the agitation that had begun to fester beneath the cheerful facade, would have known his tension grew with each passing moment. The light in his eyes darkened as he made the rounds, his target of interest remaining conspicuously absent. He'd wanted to show Mahryn, as much as anyone, that he had no need of her, that he could be fulfilled by any of the numerous other warm, feminine bodies that beckoned.

"Your jaw works too hard for a man enjoying his sport, Brother."

Redahn jerked around at the sound of Tahruk's voice. A slow, mirthless smile lifted the corners of his mouth. "I see my talk of honor and denial brought you to your senses, *Brother*. Though I doubt your Chosen will let your actions go unpunished when she finds you have exercised your right to take a Second during her time of… infirmary."

Tahruk simply chuckled. "I have no desire to search for comfort beyond my own bedchamber. In that understanding, I have come to my senses and boast of being a wiser, more contented man."

A single brow lifted, he shrugged. "What then? Why else would you be here, other than to check up on me?"

"Precisely." Tahruk guffawed at his younger brother's thinly disguised disgust.

Redahn moved to walk away, growling in annoyance when Tahruk followed. The men's expressions, one dark and one uninterested, turned away the hopeful maidens who approached, eager to garner the attentions of either member of the renowned pair. Neither spoke again until they'd reached the curved side of the wine table. Redahn grabbed one of the goblets and glared at the liquid inside.

"You may as well drink, Brother. It's not like you'll find anything stronger here, at least not tonight."

Redahn's head snapped up at his brother's words. He'd found himself wondering if Mahryn's Drille was responsible for the liquid, though he doubted it was the same fine stock found in the cellars of Zanak. He tossed back the contents of his cup then turned to survey the Great Hall's inhabitants once again.

"She's not here, the maiden who has your emotions so misaligned?"

"Lady," Redahn corrected before cursing himself under his breath. "I took care of that two nights ago." He turned the slip into a callous joke that only made his older brother shake his head and eye him with a look of pity.

There was a time the brothers would have laughed about such, each congratulating the other on their abilities to *transform* so many of the maidens without having their own hearts conquered. Tahruk, firstborn son of Renaine Sharanis of Zanak—son of the King's oldest son, who was no longer living, making their father a viable contender for the throne—had always known his wife would be chosen for him. That's how their system worked. The *Chosen* were ceremonially injected with altered blood from the firstborn sons of the King's elite forces who all descended from the royal bloodlines. The ritual was intended to assure strength, the breeding of a superior fighting class, as well as to forge a lasting bond. After all, what man would not be drawn to something that was part himself, and what woman would not be swept away with the romantic notion that the man had been a part of her since she was a mere child of three? But that bond didn't always form, didn't ensure the uniting of hearts, regardless of that being the desired effect. The warriors were raised as fighters, not lovers. And each woman, removed from her family at the age of eighteen, was forced to begin a new life in the arms of someone she'd never met before, in the arms of someone who, too often frightened her or, worse yet, didn't even want her.

At least for those not affected by the marking, there was choice. For the men anyway. Too many within the Kingdom still believed it a privilege and an honor to send their daughters to this Gathering, where those young maidens found themselves suitably matched, chosen as a Second by a warrior whose wife had not produced an heir or simply no longer pleased him, or ended up as one of the Ladies of the Courts. While as a Lady, she might end up being chosen as a wife or second, most often she would find herself being used to pleasure any one of the warriors at his discretion, or invited to act as companion or servant to those whose elite status ranked higher than her own.

It had never mattered to Redahn. He'd taken what was offered, what he'd considered his right as one of the men who fought to protect the Kingdom, while choosing to remain unharnessed. He cursed Tahruk's Chosen under his breath for putting ideas to the contrary into his head. For nearly two years now, Elenya had been working to change perceptions, to shed light on what was really going on, and let others know it was not all right. And she'd done it one ear at a time, support for her cause growing, especially since she had the ear of the King. Redahn allowed himself a smile. Damn if she hadn't charmed the old man into giving her audience. Hell! Even *he* liked Elenya and had stopped to think about what she had to say. It hadn't changed his actions, as evidenced by the fact that he was at the Dremis Gathering, but he had listened.

He looked around at the people within the Hall. By the number of women marked with the special neckpiece worn to show she'd moved from Maiden to the state of belonging to the Ladies, it appeared the number of actual maidens was dwindling, as it always did. Those still unclaimed would find themselves chosen, no doubt, by the end of that night or the next. Never before had he seen a maiden go unclaimed. He thought of Mahryn and her ill-conceived notion that she would persevere.

Squinting, he continued scanning the Hall. Smaller groupings had broken off as usual. In several, there were couples flirting, some already preparing to leave for the evening. He watched the men moving about among the women, men hungry to continue feeding on the frenzy that had begun six nights before. The women giggled and batted their lashes, smiling from behind fans or gloved hands, doing whatever they might to flame any fires of desire that could take them away from a lonely night, or even lead to a better life. Desire ran rampant within the Hall, desires of many kinds. He also glimpsed something else. Sorrow and desperation. Why had he never noticed the misery within the eyes of so many before? Elenya was right. This was no way of life for anyone.

Setting the wine goblet back down on the table none too gently, Redahn turned and stormed from the Hall without a word to anyone. Not even to his older brother who watched him with a knowing smile.

"I wish to speak to the Lady Mahryn."

The man seated at the tall table just inside the doorway that led to the Chamber of the Ladies scurried to his feet when Redahn burst through with enough force to slam one of the doors into the adjoining wall. The watchman wasn't a large man, but in Redahn's presence, he seemed to shrink even more.

"The... La... La... Lady is un... unavailable mmm... my lord." He took a step back when Redahn placed his hands on the table and leaned forward, the latter man's jaw working, lips pressed tightly together, and his eyes narrowed.

"Make her available." Redahn's voice was low, silky. His body hummed with the threat of action for unmet demands.

With a halting shake of his head, the other man stammered again, "I ca...cannot, my lord." His sentence finished with a squeak. His eyes traveling to the ripple of preparing muscle beneath Redahn's shirt, he rushed to continue, "She is not here."

Redahn just stared at the man, his words making no

sense.

"I suggest you get me the head mistress before I tear this place apart to find the Lady myself…"

"No need, my lord, though I am afraid the Lady you seek truly is not here."

Redahn turned to see the head mistress bustling in from another chamber. Her state of readiness indicating someone else had gone to fetch her, most probably the moment he burst in. She stopped several feet from the table where he stood.

Arms crossed, emphasizing his broad chest and thick biceps, he eyed her, probing in his determination to find out whether she was telling the truth. His raised brow and unwavering glare spurred her on.

"She received a private invitation, my lord, and agreed to accept it." The head mistress held his gaze. Her unwillingness to say more was evident in the tightness of her lips and the way she drew her body to full height, her shoulders back and chin up.

With an incoherent mumble, he turned and stormed back out the doors, threatening to unhinge them with the force he used to pull them open.

Inside the antechamber of the Ladies' hall, the head mistress shook her head, her shoulders drooping with relief as she turned to watch the man melt into his seat.

"We may need to put in a request for additional guard," she said, turning to walk away.

Outside the castle, Redahn stormed past the guards, ignoring the words of men who had once fought beside him. He walked toward the Square, past the Great Hall, and turned onto the road leading to Zanak.

"Cursed woman! Curse them all," he growled into the dark night, realizing for the first time he was again doing something he had never done, and all because of Mahryn. Never, in all his years of attending the Dremis Gathering, had he gone home alone.

Turn back. There are still willing maidens. There's still time, his mind sang. He didn't stop, didn't turn. Instead, he kept moving forward, the clenching behind the wall of his chest an unwelcomed unknown. He didn't have a heart, he reminded himself. And even if he did, he wasn't going to let himself be controlled by it or by some woman attempting to lay claim there. Perhaps she was a witch, working her magic on him. It certainly seemed as if he was under some spell. Enchanted, that's what he was. Enchanted, not falling in love.

He continued to think all this while his feet took him home. Alone.

Chapter 14

Night seven, the last night of the official Dremis, loomed. The next night would be the introductions of the marked with their mates as well as the pairing of those Ladies who had been chosen by the lesser warriors as wives and seconds. Redahn lay in bed, where he'd been since the night before. He stared at the ceiling, fighting the urge to rise to prepare to go. Somewhere within the dark hours he'd decided to forego his rights and stay away from the cursed event. That was the only way. If he went and she was there… He blew out a loud breath. Worse yet, he felt sure, would be finding out that she was not. How many times during the night had he pondered who it might have been that had asked for Mahryn and received a confirmation to a private invitation?

His insides churning, Redahn rolled over to take in the desolate state of his garden area outside the room. He thought of the garden that sat adjacent to his brother's chambers. Its loveliness seemed to have increased with Elenya's presence. His mind roamed to another heavenly scent—the sweet fragrance that had wafted into his room at the cottage when he'd slipped from the bed and opened the door that first morning with Mahryn. He supposed one might expect such a showcase beyond the walls of a home inhabited by a gardener, but Redahn had never really paid it much heed before then. It wasn't that he hadn't noticed. More, all his senses seemed heightened when she was around.

"The dinner hour is well upon us and here you lay, wearing the same britches you wore last night and looking none too prepared to meet the lady that has your heart pining so."

Redahn had turned away when his brother's figure loomed before him in the garden entryway. "I can't be pining. You said so yourself, we all know my chest cavity is empty," the younger man grumbled, pulling the coverlet over his head. "How did you get into my chamber anyway, and what business of yours is it how I spend my time?"

Tahruk laughed, eliciting a muffled growl from beneath the blanket. "Your wing of Zanak mirrors mine, Brother. Have you forgotten that? I could get in here in my sleep, no matter how many bars you placed on the door."

"And you have opted to grace me with your presence because…?" Redahn rolled over and pushed himself to a sitting position. Unaware of his actions, he rubbed the scar that ran across his right shoulder and upper arm. Cutting his eyes in his brother's direction, he caught a glimpse of the pity that flitted across Tahruk's face and pulled his hand away, letting it drop to the coverlet beside him with a muffled thud. "So, you are here because…" he asked again.

Moving further into the room, Tahruk scooped up a disheveled pile of clothing from a chair at the foot of the bed and tossed them to the top of a nearby trunk before sitting down. "Your actions grieve our mother. I might be willing to let you rot in your own discontent, but not her."

Redahn shook his head. "So that's what marriage does for a warrior, sets him to fulfilling the mission of women's entreaties."

Tahruk didn't rise to the bait, simply relaxing into the back of the chair and propping his booted feet on the end of

Redahn's bed. Both actions garnering him a glare that intensified by the moment. Thick arms crossing over broad chest, the older of the two chewed his lower lip as he returned the stare.

"Tell me, brother, what is it about this lady that has you fighting your feelings so? If you enjoy her company, why not continue to enjoy it until the desire to do so passes? There's no rule that says you can't take up with her as often as you'd like." When Redahn didn't answer, choosing instead to look away, Tahruk chuckled, though softly enough not to further stir his brother's ire. His words, however, had a much different effect. "I believe you're afraid of this lady, my brother. Who is she that she has such power over you?"

"What the..." In a momentary flash, Redahn had scrambled to the foot of the bed causing Tahruk to rise in a flourish of motion. The brothers, two bodies strengthened by genetics and training, squared off at one another.

With his chest rising and falling in rapid succession, Redahn squinted at Tahruk who hadn't moved since he'd stood. "She is no one. A Dremis Maiden who happened to catch my fancy. Nothing more. She'll *never* be anything more and the sooner each of you understands that, the better for us all," Redahn ground out.

Nodding, Tahruk pushed his brother back to a sitting position on the bed with a hand on his chest. "Take it easy. I didn't mean to goad." That garnered a raised eyebrow from the younger man and a snort of laughter from the older. These two men had been at each other since before the younger was even able to understand what was happening. It was merely the way with them. At least the comment managed to dispel some of the tension, allowing them to both laugh a little before Redahn's head lolled forward and he placed it in the vice-like grip of his own hands.

"Women are nothing but trouble."

"I'll concede and give you that. But I'll also remind you of how much they have to offer as well." Tahruk paused but Redahn said nothing, not even so much as a groan. Leaning forward, making him closer to his brother, Tahruk asked in a quiet voice, "Who is she?"

Redahn shook his head, leaving Tahruk to believe he was not going to answer. The stretching silence added confirmation before he finally cleared his throat and spoke.

"Tedran's daughter."

"What!" Tahruk almost choked. He straightened in his seat again, his mouth drawing down. He stared off into the desolate garden. "The mousy girl who lurks in the corners?"

Redahn sat up as well and nodded. "Only she's not mousy now." He paused, his eyes darting about as he thought about the castle mouse, as they'd called her. "I rather doubt she ever was. More we just couldn't really see her there in the shadows. Though... there are peculiarities. For starters, the reasoning for her being thrown into the maidens."

Tahruk nodded. "Nothing in connection with Tedran's personal life is any good. He's steeped in too many levels of conspiracy. He may be good at what he does for the King, but that man is definitely hiding something."

"And his daughter is his puppet." Redahn looked back at his brother then away again. "She's too pure and simple to be put through these roles in whatever game it is he's playing."

"Sweet, is she?" Redahn missed the upward curve of Tahruk's mouth, but his brother's suggestive tone and words had him swinging his head back toward his older brother whose features sobered for all of three seconds before he laughed. "Come on, Brother. I meant no harm," Tahruk told him, his hand once again holding his brother at bay. "So," he began after Redahn had settled. "May I tell Mother you'll be joining us for dinner before you head out to the Gathering?"

"I'm not going," Redahn snapped. "I've lost my desire to attend."

Another knowing smile from Tahruk had Redahn scrambling back under the covers.

"Have it your way," Tahruk told him as he pushed to his feet. "Any words you would have me take to the Lady?" he asked before moving to the garden doorway.

Redahn was sitting up again before his brother's foot even crossed the threshold. "What are you doing? Where are you going?" Anger and concern streaked across his face.

Tahruk shrugged as he walked out, his voice floating back through the open door. "To protect your interests as any good brother would."

Redahn listened to the footsteps fading into the distance, then fell back into the soft matting beneath him, pondering his brother's words.

Mahryn's nerves had begun to get the better of her long before the Ladies were ushered into the Gathering Hall. The likelihood of Redahn asking for her again that night was as nonexistent as one of the other warriors taking her as a wife or a second. Neither of those two options was particularly appealing, though anything less would put her at the mercy of the whimsical desires of the warriors of Dorengar on a first-come-first-served basis. That scenario was the most appalling of all. And it was unfortunately the most probable, especially after her *private invitation* had kept her away from the gathering the night before. Not only did her absence lessen her ability to show these men that she might be a worthy candidate for a wife, the old out-of-sight-out-of-mind adage would have come into play.

She looked around, careful that enough hair remained over her bare back to conceal the scar. Not that it mattered. Her fate was pretty much sealed. Between her keeping the men at arm's length for the first few nights, and Redahn occupying her the others…

Redahn. Try as she might, she couldn't keep him from her mind. The feel of his hands on her, his lips—the impression of him was forever imprinted on her skin. How many times had she wondered last night who he was with, whether he had noticed she wasn't among the Ladies? She wanted to know, and yet she didn't. What had the head mistress told her? Hearts and emotions had no place in their world. She looked around again, still unable to find him amidst the crowded hall.

"As I was saying…"

With a start, Mahryn realized she'd completely tuned out the others around her. Not the best decision, considering one of these men might well be her future. She looked around at the others in her small group. Eight ladies and five men. Not the most favorable odds, yet they were all she had. Why, she wondered, did the river of life never quite flow in the right direction for her? Why was it the one man she craved, the only one who knew her intimately, was also the most likely never to settle down? Her heart had tried to tell her otherwise, that his asking for her twice was an indication that he cared. But her head—that logical side knew better. Quickly surveying and sizing up the men around her, she turned her smile to a young warrior who gazed with unguarded hunger at the view of ample cleavage offered by her dress.

"Please forgive me, my lord. I failed to catch your name," she told him as she moved a step closer. His eyes snapped up to lock with hers, eyes close in color to Redahn's, though not nearly so sharp or mischievous. She swallowed hard and re-pasted her smile, pleased to have noted an air of interest within his amber depths. He was not bad looking, though young. She'd guess maybe a couple of years older than herself. He possessed an eagerness, which he probably took to the battlefields as well, provided he'd actually seen a real battle yet. She tried to calculate the timing of his training versus their last skirmish. It didn't matter. Regardless, he'd make a good husband. No doubt he'd be an excellent father, and most probably a passable lover. She sighed. Passable. She didn't want a passable lover, she wanted...

As if conjured by her thoughts, she saw the dark hair and unmistakable features materialize at the very edge of her peripheral vision. She felt her heart speed up, her mouth and throat becoming suddenly parched as she slowly turned toward him.

"My lord, I..." Mahryn stumbled back a step, surprised when her eyes met the dark blue depths in the near-familiar face. His hand suddenly beneath her elbow, the older warrior steadied her, bringing her closer to his side. The younger warrior's supporting hand on her other forearm barely registered, even when she found herself softly patting it while she gazed up at Tahruk Sharanis.

"Lady Mahryn?"

Without answering, Mahryn just stared, taking in the differences in the two brothers. Redahn was taller by at least two or three inches, which seemed surprising to her since he was younger. She also noted he was not quite as broad as his brother, though not a man of little stature by any means. The younger of the two also carried the look of an unsettled man, one who might be deemed reckless, daring. It was part of Redahn's charm, if one might call it that.

Realizing she had not answered, Mahryn nodded. She dropped in a slight curtsy, her eyes still fixed on Tahruk's face, moving slowly from the full lips lifted slightly higher on one side, past cheeks freshly shaven, to eyes filled with laughter. Was he laughing at her? Uncertain why she was so stunned she couldn't speak, Mahryn finally found her voice and asked, "Why are you here, my lord?"

Tahruk's snort caused many to look in their direction, though Mahryn didn't notice, having dropped her head. Her cheeks burned slightly when she looked back up at him. His finger trailing down the side of her reddened face caused another suffusion of heat. "Is it not my right to be here, my lady?" Up went the single eyebrow—another reminder of his brother.

Striking, she thought. Where Redahn was roguishly handsome, this man was just plain beautiful, without flaw—on the outside, at least.

Mahryn frowned. "Of course you have a right, as does any man loyal to the King's service. It's just… your *wife*, my lord. She's such an advocate against all this." She waved her hand in a small circle in front of her, her eyes darting about their surroundings.

Tahruk nodded, his face lighting with mirth. He leaned toward Mahryn, causing her to stiffen, her eyes wide. "And yet she is my wife because of *this*." He mimicked her circular motion, his brow lifting again along with the corner of his mouth. He laughed when she frowned. "Perhaps what she doesn't know will not hurt her?"

Her mouth falling open, Mahryn drew back from him, bumping into the young warrior who had remained at her side. She glanced at him, surprised he was still there. Had she not been so disgusted with Tahruk, she would have basked in the warmth that built quickly in her belly thanks to the younger man's obvious interest.

"Surely having spent time in my brother's company you didn't expect a gentleman when I walked in?" He crooked that brow at her again.

"My mistake," she said dryly, making him laugh once more. His obvious pleasure at her discomfort made her wonder what kind of people raised these men. They certainly hadn't inherited any of the gentle nature possessed by their great grandfather, the King.

With the verbal banter continuing between them, Mahryn missed the arrival of another warrior until the familiar scent assaulted her senses from directly behind her. Her words freezing mid-sentence, she swallowed hard and pressed a hand to her chest, willing her heartbeat to slow. A sense of warmth spread quickly, seeming to flow over her in an invisible veil, threatening her ability to breathe. Glancing up at Tahruk, noting his eyes no longer on her, she steeled herself then turned slowly to greet his brother.

Redahn glared across her, his hard stare trained on Tahruk. "What are you doing here?" he asked through lips pressed tight beneath his frown. Mahryn felt the young warrior at her side take a step back, though gave him credit that he didn't excuse himself all together.

Tahruk answered his brother with a chuckle, and although he was behind her now, Mahryn could almost see a single side of his face lift with a smile and an arched brow. "How alike you are," he told his brother with a head nodded in Mahryn's direction. "Your lady asked me that very question…"

"*My* lady?"

"*His* lady!"

Mahryn and Redahn answered at the same time, Redahn locking eyes with her for the first time. She could hear another rumble of laughter from behind her, the sound deepening her frown. Redahn's brow hitched upward, making Mahryn's tighten. She couldn't read him, was completely unsure of what he was thinking.

"Proof I am correct." Tahruk smiled and clapped his younger brother on the shoulder. "Settle down, my brother. I was just leaving anyway. I believe *the* lady has all the attention she needs now." He stepped back to provide her with an exaggerated bow to which Mahryn was obliged to follow with a deep curtsy. He was already moving away when she rose, though he stopped after a few steps. "I wonder how many men within these walls will allow wisdom to be his kinsman tonight instead of stubbornness, pride, and just plain lust?" he asked, quite loudly, to no one in particular. With a shrug, he moved on and pushed out into the darkness beyond the doors of the Great Hall. Mahryn heard feminine sighs echo through the Hall. She smiled, knowing without a doubt he was headed back to Zanak and the woman who had changed his mind to the wisdom found in love.

"He has to be the most annoying man to walk the grounds of Riandus."

When Mahryn laughed, he narrowed his eyes at her. She quickly forced her features into masked acquiescence, speaking quietly under her breath. "You are near mirror images, especially in that."

The silence that settled between them began to grow uncomfortable as they continued to stare at one another. His lips still taut, his eyes roaming over her face, he finally swallowed with difficulty and found the words to speak what was on his mind.

"Did you enjoy yourself last night?" His tone was hard, accusing.

"Last nig...?" Dawning could not keep the joy from touching Mahryn's eyes, making the corners of her lips dance slightly. He'd noticed her absence and he seemed a bit... jealous. She dropped her eyes and chewed on her bottom lip. She'd love to tell him she had enjoyed the evening, just to see his reaction, but lying wasn't Mahryn's first choice. Instead, she looked back at him and answered with her own question, even though it was one whose answer she didn't want to hear. "Did you?"

The dark glare he settled on her had Mahryn shrinking back slightly, only his hands now on her upper arms, kept her before him. With a near snarl, he let out a low growl. "You border on insolence in questioning me." He tightened his hold on her arms, making her wince.

"Forgive me, my lord." His grip loosened, no doubt the result of the single, startling tear that sprung up in the corner of her eye. She blinked it away, wondering at this new range of emotion that seemed beyond her control. The head mistress was right. She was going to have to do better if she expected to endure this portion of her life with her sanity intact. One thing was certain, she hadn't expected to kindle Redahn's wrath. She'd expected him to throw his conquest from the night before in her face. She simply didn't understand these games. "Forgive me," she said again.

Redahn released her and stepped back, turning his attention, for the first time, to the other man within their little group. They exchanged casual pleasantries, evidently already acquainted. Several others joined them—two couples, three ladies obviously searching for their night's companions, and at least half a dozen warriors, no doubt doing the same. Mahryn forced herself to smile, nod, and answer when spoken to, though her thoughts fluttered between potential escape to her tiny room and the silk-covered bed she'd shared with Redahn. She closed her eyes, doing her best to keep them from finding him across the tiny circle.

"May I have the honor of your company this evening, my lady?"

The unexpected timing of those words caused Mahryn's eyes to open widely. She glanced at the hopeful young warrior who had remained by her side, the one who would make a fine husband and a passable lover. He could offer her a way to get away from the Courts, was hers for the taking, she was sure.

She looked back in Redahn's direction and down to his outstretched palm. He wasn't asking for forever, just for that one night. She closed her eyes again, feeling another bout of sudden teariness, and willed herself to do the right thing, to make the choice that would allow her to take the reins of her own life.

Instead, she placed her hand on the familiar palm, biting her lip as Redahn's fingers closed around hers and he turned to lead them from the Hall. Head down, she didn't look back at the younger warrior whose name she never got.

Their silence intensified the sounds of the night as they walked, hand-in-hand, toward the gardener's cottage. Her head down, Mahryn tried not to let her mind dwell on what she was doing. She didn't want to think, only feel. She'd made the wrong choice, she was sure of it. And yet it was the only choice she could have made. Her life had never been easy. She'd never chosen the path of least resistance. Why should she start now, especially with her need for Redahn burning out of control inside?

The thought caused a quiet snort, bringing her head up when she felt Redahn's eyes on her. They stopped, close, she knew, to the clearing surrounding the cottage. She studied his face, the moonlight accentuating the shadows, adding to the veil of mystery that surrounded this man. Reaching up, she traced a finger down the side of his face. *What do you want from me?* She wanted to ask. Instead, she placed her palm over his heart and waited.

Redahn stared down at her for several seconds before covering her hand with his. Wrapping his fingers around hers, he lifted her hand and kissed the inside of her bent wrist before looking away. "We're almost there," he said, their hands dropping to their sides as he began to lead her once again.

Mahryn nodded into the darkness. Yes, they were almost there. But just exactly where was this night going to take them? Her future seemed more unclear than ever.

Several minutes later, ensconced in Redahn's arms, Mahryn no longer concerned herself with what would happen to her after that night. Her life, her thoughts revolved around that moment only and how right she felt when he was beside her.

Chapter 15

Redahn had been both rough and demanding of Mahryn at first, and it wasn't until he'd realized he was trying to make her pay for her absence the night before that he curbed his anger and treated her as a lady should be treated. Satisfaction at the hunger that blazed in the depths of her peculiar blue-gold eyes spurred him to take her to heights that surpassed both of their expectations. She'd missed him every bit as much as he'd missed her. That's what her body and lips told him, even if her words did not.

Breathless from their third climb to the mountaintop, he collapsed against her, his head resting above the luscious peaks of her full breasts. He closed his eyes, listening to the steady hammer of her still swiftly beating heart.

"Where were you last night? Who were you with?" The words came out unexpectedly, not that he hadn't wanted to know. But why they chose that moment… The *why* of many things concerning Mahryn made no sense to him. Her held breath lifted his head, then dropped it with the whooshing of air before she answered him.

"No one," she finally said.

Lifting his head, he glared up at her. "Don't toy with me, Mahryn. Tell me," he demanded.

She shook her head. "I tell you the truth, my lord. I received a private invitation. A command really… to go to my father's quarters… but…" She shrugged and looked away. "He never showed. I was told the next day to return to the

Ladies' chambers."

Redahn stared a moment longer, nodded, then lowered his head back, enjoying the smooth softness of her bare skin against his cheek. He traced his fingers up and down her belly, chuckling slightly at her attempt to keep from flinching from his touch. Flattening his hand, he covered the scar on her side. "That man is evil," he whispered.

The rumble of laughter beneath his ear surprised him. "That man is my father, my lord."

"No fault of your own, dear lady." That comment had them both chuckling before another burst of passion had them clinging to each other once again.

"Would that he was not," she whispered as they broke apart and he turned her to where he could snuggle against her backside. "But I am who I am." The last words were spoken on a breath as she drifted into much needed sleep.

"As am I," he told her, knowing she didn't hear him, even though he'd lifted up to press a kiss just below her ear before speaking. Rubbing his weathered cheek against the softness of her own, he kissed her again before settling fully behind her. He breathed in the fresh scent of her long hair that pillowed beneath his head, hating the rightness he felt being with her. It didn't matter. This was their last night together before the imposed week of waiting began. Surely that week would cool this craziness that churned his blood where she was concerned.

Surely, Redahn thought, as he followed her into the land of Sleep where thoughts of Tedran robbed him of full rest. Whatever that man was up to concerning his daughter, it was bound to be no good. Redahn had to remind himself that it was also none of his business. No matter what, he had to guard against the urge to care, for caring opened the doors to the heart and he was too set in his bitter ways to allow himself to find out now that he actually had one.

The morning light was met with a knowing certainty that time was not on their side. The ladies all had to be returned well before the sun reached its midday mark. Both Redahn and Mahryn kept the atmosphere light between them, engaging in playful banter and as much laughter as each could muster. The only time they'd been serious was when Redahn had pulled her to him and taken his time to memorize every inch of her young body and had allowed her to do the same when she'd shown interest in following suite. Fully sated, they'd laid together, the air thick with what each of them wanted to say. In the end, no one spoke, both swallowing their words when the shadows through the windows warned that they had to rise. Silently, he kissed her one more time before leading her from their cottage hideaway. With a last look back, a bittersweet smile lifted Mahryn's love-swollen lips. So much had changed for her inside that house. So much... and yet so little. She stifled a sigh, not wanting to alert Redahn to the crush of sudden emotion that threatened her.

They walked back to the Centrehead much the same as the night before—in silence, though the passing of others demanded courteous interchange and certain smiles.

"Good bye, my lord," she told him at the castle's gate, dropping into a curtsy when he stepped away and bowed. She rose once he had and turned to walk across the path that led to the lowered drawbridge, making sure to school her features into a pleasant façade for any who might be watching.

"Mahryn."

The smile froze on her face when she turned back to

him. The rise of her chest stilled and he swallowed hard, there was no way she could know how badly he was trying to tamp down the knot attempting to form in his throat. Even knowing what he was about to say could very well break her heart, he refused to provide her with false hope. They hadn't talked about a future, though each of them knew there was still time for him to ask for her before the ceremony that evening.

"These three nights... they're no indication of what's to come. I'll not call for you outside the strictures provided by the courts. You know that, yes?"

Her lips curved higher into the same smile she'd worn that first night of the Dremis Gathering, the well-rehearsed one that belied her sincerity. She tipped her head at him, her eyes not quite meeting his. "Believe me, my lord, I have not taken lightly the stories of your reputation shared within the walls of the Ladies Chambers. Callous disregard and use are the only expectations one should have when dealing with you."

Redahn's response died on his tongue, his mouth slightly open as he stared at her. Mahryn laughed at his surprise. Her words had certainly surprised her. Without waiting, she turned and walked quickly across the boards and through the door, barely nodding to the guard who opened it for her. Once inside, she sprinted to the Ladies wing, ignoring the call of the head mistress. She needed to get to her room before the flood of tears overtook her. It wouldn't do for anyone to see her crying over *any* man, especially one as hard and uncaring as Redahn Sharanis. She'd been warned he was not the kind of man one should set her sights on for anything lasting. If only she could convince her traitorous heart.

Redahn remained rooted to the spot where Mahryn had last seen him until the sound of his name being spoken jarred him from his pensive state. He stepped forward for a better look, almost smiling at the familiar face. Instead, he glowered at the man who walked at his great grandfather's side.

"I thought that was you," the King told him, forcing Redahn's eyes back in his direction. "I'm assuming you have just returned your Dremis night companion, though you don't carry the look of a man pleased with his lot. Did you not enjoy your chosen young lady?"

Redahn's snort and disdainful glance at Tedran had the other man swallowing hard and fidgeting to a degree that made the King look between his great grandson and his second in command. "My companion was perfect." Redahn's raised brows rung a challenge that Tedran was not about to accept. "It's the whole of these gatherings that I object to, Grandsire."

The King tsked. "Now you are beginning to sound like your brother." He chuckled. "Perhaps Lady Elenya has asked for audience in your presence too often as of late as well. She is most persuasive in her arguments and not at all hard to look upon. She reminds me so of…" For a moment, the old man seemed far away, a look of remembered longing crossing his features before he reined them in and shook his head. He shrugged and smiled again. Seeming to ignore the issue of Redahn's sudden dislike of the yearly festivities, he asked, "No chance you'll be making a match before the evening's ceremonies then?"

The long pause before Redahn answered had Tedran tensing up and he considered lying just to watch the man squirm. He still had no clue what game Tedran was playing.

He knew Tedran knew he was the one seeking out his daughter throughout the Dremis. He also knew Mahryn's match to anyone, especially to a man within the direct line of the King, would have been met with opposition from the King's closest advisor, though his reasons were not clear. *Why are you so opposed to her happiness?* He wanted to ask. Instead, he shook his head. "No. There is no one."

The old King laughed again. "That's right. I'd almost forgotten you believe yourself without the heart required for sealing such a fate." He tapped Redahn on the chest. "One day," he warned, then laughed again. "Will we at least see you at the Ceremonies?"

"Of course. My disapproval has not so muddled my head that I would care to deny myself of the pleasantries only a King's Gala can offer. My only complaint is that you refuse us the company of your fine Ladies after a week of indulgence. Surely as a man you must understand the hardship this action places on your warriors, my lord?"

The guffaw from the older man ended in a coughing fit that had Redahn patting him on the back. "Release your concerns, my dear boy," his great grandfather told him. "My time has not befallen me. I have high hopes of holding on until your father might become the next king. Ah! My words surprise you. Shenai is a wonderful man and would make an outstanding king, make no mistake about that. I do have doubts as to the line beyond him, however. My son chose well in his bride. His sons... not so much. But this is not the time for such discussions." He punctuated his words by waving his hand in the air. "I am not about to die anytime soon, and we have a ball to consider. As for your need of women, my handsome great-grandson..." King Andorak lowered his voice and leaned closer to Redahn. "We both know you have access to any number of lovely young maidens beyond those residing within the halls of my castle. Your bed need never be empty on account of protocol." Patting his great grandson on the arm, the old King motioned to Tedran that he was ready to move on.

Redahn chuckled. His great grandfather was right. He had his pick of any number of maidens. His smile faded as he watched the two men walk away. There was just one problem. The woman he wanted the most, the one whose absence filled him with emptiness and longing only moments after she'd left his side... she would be sequestered within the Ladies wing of the castle for a full week. As he turned to start back home, he wondered how he was supposed to wait a whole week when she continued to envelope his every thought? He would surely be a madman by then, unless he could find another to ease what felt very much like the hint of a forlorn heart.

Chapter 16

Mahryn was thankful the head mistress chose to leave her in solitude for the majority of the afternoon. She couldn't say she wasn't surprised, though even that couldn't stop her from hoping she might somehow be spared the humiliation of the evening's events. She'd witnessed the Parade of Ladies many times before, only from outside since she had never before been invited to the event. She remembered wondering, even then, how the women could hold their heads so high when they'd been relegated to a life no better than that of a common harlot.

That wasn't true. At least the Ladies knew they would have a fine roof over their heads and bed down with only the best of the King's warriors. Some would be whisked off to other duties as corisans, tending to a variety of needs of those whose social standings ranked above their own. Marriage was also still an option open to any one of them, though if a Lady of the Courts was found to be with child, she would be removed to the waiting chambers until three months after the birth. She would then be allowed to visit her child as often as desired, even though he or she would be raised by the nursery staff. And if the mother remarried, it would be up to the man to determine if she would be allowed to take her child into his home. Most of the children remained within the Castle and were trained as corisans or any number of other positions within the royal walls, including warriors who proudly served the King, since they still had royalty in their blood.

Her hands straying to her mid-section, Mahryn splayed her fingers across her stomach. She closed her eyes, trying to sense any life within. The thought of carrying Redahn's child both exhilarated and terrified her at the same time, the latter being the stronger of the emotions. An unhappy smile lifted the corners of her mouth. She'd taken measures, accepting the special herb concoction offered to her in secret by one of the corisans before she'd left her father's household. The woman, a comely blond most likely in her late twenties, told Mahryn too many heartaches had already been suffered by Ladies forced to leave their children behind. Conception during the Dremis was always heightened, and only the fortunate slipped through unscathed. The fortunate, and those like her who were willing to help themselves.

A loud knock on the door had her jumping to her feet, all hopes of deliverance from the evening dashed when she heard the head mistress clapping her hands and calling for the fifteen minutes to preparation time. With a huffy breath, she dragged herself across the room to pull open the doors of the large wardrobe. At least tonight she would be dressing for the King, she thought, running her hand down the trailing silk toile sleeve of the finest burgundy embroidered with gold thread.

"Tis a beautiful dress."

Mahryn whipped around to face Larina, a soft smile replacing the slack-jaw of shock. "I didn't hear you come in," she told her, turning back to the wardrobe. Try as she might to disguise her tone, she was sure the heaviness of her heart had to be seeping into her words. She bowed her head, the weariness of the day, the week... the last six years overwhelming her.

Gentle hands covered her slumped shoulders. "You're a strong woman, my lady," Larina whispered. "In spite of what you think, you've a lot to offer." She paused, no doubt choosing her next words. "And… your father is known and revered. You'll not stay here for long. Were it not for Lord Redahn's attentions, I have no doubt you'd already be gone." Larina sucked in hard. "Oh, my lady. I'm so sorry."

Biting her lip to help hold back the dam of tears suddenly welling in her eyes, Mahryn nodded. She knew Larina had been trying to help and that she really should be pleased to know someone would want her. She supposed that should be something to look forward to. Perhaps even someone like the nice young warrior she'd turned down for one last night with Redahn…

A tear slipped down her cheek. Then another. She shook her head, slowly. She didn't want to stay within the Ladies Chambers. The thought of the life these women lived with their heads held high sent chills of humiliation crashing through her. She wouldn't live that way, she couldn't. Yet how could she go on with someone else?

Always before, Redahn had reveled in the close proximity to the King his family's standing afforded him at the final ceremony of the Dremis. With an unfettered view of the Ladies that remained unbound, he could choose which of those women he'd enjoy the most before easing back to his favorites—those who knew their place and made no attempt to snare him.

This year he wanted to be anywhere but wedged between his brother's pregnant wife and his Aunt Nema in the front row of a box set back slightly that afforded him a view of Tedran's profile. He'd never liked the man who had served his great grandfather for many years, but now intense anger burned within as well at the thought of Tedran's treatment of his beautiful daughter.

He turned his scowl in the direction of his brother's wife when he felt her hand on his arm. She merely chuckled and leaned toward him.

"You could have saved yourself some misery and been able to quell your anger while igniting his, you know," she whispered, tossing her head in Tedran's direction.

"Minding everyone's business but your own, as usual, Elenya," he snapped out, his hard stare fixed on the beauty at his side. "Why are you here, anyway? I thought the physician relegated you for the duration of your term to the hardship of lying about in bed?"

Elenya only laughed and shook her head. "You know as well as I the delight it provides Andorak to have all his family in attendance at these gatherings. Were it not for the happiness of an old man, believe me, I would not be here."

Given Elenya's open disdain for the ritual of the markings and the Dremis gatherings, it rather surprised Redahn that his great grandfather still adored her as much as he did. He knew, even in her state of ordered bed rest, that the two of them still managed to meet at least once or twice a month. On more than one occasion recently, he'd seen his grandsire leaving his brother's chambers. The older man always looked refreshed after one of their meetings, which didn't make all that much sense to him. He'd been on the receiving end of Elenya's banter and knew the woman had a gift for making her opponent come around to her way of thinking. How many times had she beaten the truth into him with one of her verbal attacks? Silver-tongued witch, that's what she was.

The trumpeter sounded the call, alerting the guests of the King's arrival, commanding all to stand. Redahn watched the procession across the arena, his heart filling with pride knowing he shared the blood of the great man who had proudly led Dorengar for so long. Behind him, his only living son, Shenai, was followed by Renaine and the other eldest sons of his deceased children. Climbing into the boxes held for the King's direct descendants, the men stood before their seats, their right hands over their hearts. After a few moments of King Andorak looking over the throng of his people, taking in their salutes of adoration, the old man lifted his right hand to his mouth and kissed the open palm before clamping it into a fist that he placed over his heart. A deafening uproar of shouted approval filled the arena. Redahn noticed even Elenya was smiling. Few people in this world did not adore his great grandfather.

With a nod of his crowned head at the trumpeter, Andorak gave the order for the beginning of the festivities and the crowd began to quiet with the man's tune. The occupants of the arena took their seats and a herald announced the procession of the marked ladies and their warriors, each couple stopping before the King to drop into a brief bow and curtsy. Redahn glanced at Elenya, wondering what she was thinking. She and his brother would have been the first couple presented to the King just three years ago had the Dremis Gala not been cancelled due to unrest in neighboring Corigan spilling into their Kingdom. They'd had a shaky start, her and his brother, yet here they sat, their hands clasped, her belly growing rounder by the day with their second child. His brother had been very much like himself, so sure he'd never fall in love. But he had. There was no doubt whatsoever that Tahruk and Elenya loved each other.

Movement from the upper tier of the arena behind the King had the warriors in proximity of the old man moving into position to keep him safe, and halted the procession. Redahn had quickly moved to the far end of the line where his immediate family sat. He watched as the warriors relaxed and allowed the runner to move forward and kneel before the King. After commanding the man to rise, and listening intently, Andorak nodded, patted the young man on the shoulder, and motioned to several of the warriors around him. They returned the nod and turned to leave. Frowning, Redahn watched the men, led by his father, march toward the top of the arena and walk away. He moved back to his seat and lowered himself into it, his eyes never leaving his brother who was doing the same. When Tahruk looked in his direction, Redahn quirked a brow. Tahruk shrugged before leaning across Elenya toward his brother.

"The men have returned from the north. They have information," Tahruk whispered to him.

"Important enough to disrupt the Gala procession? It must be something." Redahn's sarcasm wasn't lost on his brother who shook his head before leaning back in his seat and looking out at the arena as the King motioned for the procession to continue.

Elenya shrugged as well before turning back to watch the procession. The unmarked ladies and the warriors who had chosen them began to enter the arena. Redahn fought to swallow the knot he felt forming in his throat. His thoughts were torn between the information his father would be studying and the activity before him, though thoughts of a certain Lady won out. This procession would end with the presentation of the new Ladies of the Court—the women assembled to satisfy the whetted appetites of the King's warriors. He closed his eyes then opened them again in an attempt to push away the picture of Mahryn in the embrace of one of his fellow warriors. He could have changed all that for her, changed this night, and their lives.

Shaking his head, he fixed his stare on the beauties that filed past and commanded his heart to be still. He'd never been ruled by any feeling, save one, and that wasn't going to change. Mahryn was just another of these lovely ladies... he couldn't deny that the strength of the allure she'd held for him was something he wasn't used to, but it didn't mean anything. She'd merely been intriguing because she was different than the others. Nothing more.

Redahn hadn't even realized he'd crossed his arms over his chest, or how tightly drawn his mouth and brows were until he felt Elenya's hand on him again and he turned to look at her. He could see the concern etched in the light lines of her face and smiled slightly in an attempt to alleviate them. He leaned toward her when she moved in his direction, lowering his head so she could whisper in his ear.

"Which one is she?" she asked, her voice so quiet he could hardly hear her.

"What?" He scowled at her, disbelieving she would ask him to point out the woman whose innocence he'd taken without regard or promise. In the end, she hadn't needed him to tell her, his brother's alert to their mother when the maiden approached the King's box enough for Elenya to know. She smiled again and looked back at him.

"She's quite lovely, Redahn..."

Redahn didn't hear the end of her sentence or whether she even said anything more at all. When Mahryn stopped before the King, the broken warrior could see no one but her, until she rose from the deep curtsy and turned slightly to face her father. As was customary with the kin of those within the King's inner circle, she placed her fisted hand over her heart and waited for Tedran to return the gesture. The man stared down at Mahryn, his lips pressed tightly together, nostrils flared. Only when the King fisted his hand and placed it over his own heart and began to turn toward Tedran did the man have the decency to acknowledge his daughter through the same gesture.

Redahn heard a low growl and realized it was coming from him when heads, including the King's and Tedran's, swiveled in his direction. Tahruk's arm pinned Elenya to her seat in an attempt to press Redahn back into his chair. The low murmur that ran through the arena had Redahn biting into his own lip in an attempt to quell a verbal outburst. He pushed Tahruk's hand away and settled into his seat, his eyes straying first toward Tedran, who had the audacity to smirk and shake his head, and then toward the burgundy clad figure expecting to see a lowered head and slumped shoulders. What greeted him instead was a woman with her chin held high, her back straight. Her face was, perhaps, a bit reddened, but other than that, she showed no outward distress at her father's snub.

How strong you are, he thought when their eyes met briefly. Without a hint of acknowledgment, she turned and followed the Ladies who had gone before her. "What?" Redahn asked when he looked over to see Elenya smiling up at him. Feigning innocence, she shrugged and patted his arm before turning her attention back to the remaining Ladies.

He turned to look at his Aunt Nema, surprised that she'd been so quiet through the ordeal, though this was probably the only night of the year that woman was ever particularly quiet. She was another woman who possessed an abundance of strength. He wondered if she was thinking of her first night before the King. She'd been marked, a maiden from neighboring Corigan. Her match was meant to unite the two kingdoms. And it had, though she'd renounced her position when she was unable to produce an heir. She'd stepped down, relegating herself to Second while her younger sister was bound as the wife of the man she would never stop loving. Redahn turned the other direction and looked down the row at the seat his father had vacated and to the woman who sat one chair over. Neria—Nema's sister and his mother. What a crazy, mixed up system those in charge had foisted on their world. At least he wasn't as much a part of it as some of his family members… or even as much as Mahryn. Even though he was one of the King's elite warriors, still considered so in spite of his injury, he had choice. How funny. He'd always taken that choice, and the rights that went with it, for granted. Tonight, he didn't feel entitled. He felt grateful.

What had changed? There was only one answer.

Mahryn.

Mahryn didn't look up when she heard footsteps coming her way. She didn't care, beyond a flash of irritation that someone would bother her seclusion. No doubt it was someone coming to demand she do something other than what she desired, which was to sit alone for a bit. That was all.

"There are plenty of seats closer to the festivities, my lady. You're welcome to join my family's table if you don't wish to throw yourself into the midst of the others."

She hadn't expected *that* voice. "My lord. I surely did

not expect to see you this evening. Well, not that I didn't think I'd *see* you. Of course I would, your family being who they are and all..."

Tahruk chuckled and she shook her head, her eyes remaining on the liquid she swirled in the goblet in her hands.

"Are you not concerned about ruining your gown? It's a beautiful dress." He lowered himself to the grass beside her, adjusting his back against the smooth bark of the tree where she leaned.

She turned to look at him and then down at the ground where he sat. A quiet snort escaped her before she turned her attention back to her cup, her other hand sliding across the material of her gown. "It really is a fine dress, though I doubt I shall ever wish to wear it again."

Tahruk nodded. "You share my Elenya's sentiments to the Dremis."

She was silent for a moment, using the silence to take another drink of her wine. "So I am told." Another sip and a sigh followed. "Only she ended her Dremis with the warrior of her dreams." She cut her eyes and looked at him.

Tahruk laughed. "She didn't believe so at the time," he assured her, relaxing a bit more, his head lolling back against the tree. "In fact, she was quite sure the Masters had made a grave mistake."

"And you? Did you think they had?"

Turning his head to look at her, Tahruk's grin said it all. "I thought the truth... that I'd inherited a hellion." They both laughed. "She had no choice but to be high spirited since she had my blood mixed with her own."

Mahryn nodded, wondering if it would have been easier had she been a marked lady, like Elenya, knowing her mate was already chosen, the blood they shared causing him to have an undeniable affinity towards her. She thought of Hahna, of the man she was to marry. Her sister hadn't been marked since Tedran wasn't the oldest son in his family, but her marriage had already been arranged. Or so their father had said. He'd also thrown it up to her from time to time that the same man had refused, as was customary, to accept Mahryn as his betrothed after… "No," she whispered, willing her mind not to go there.

"Are you all right?" Concern etched itself into Tahruk's creased forehead urging Mahryn to force a smile.

"Yes, my lord. I was just thinking… about our system, your wife's disdain for it, and my own."

Tahruk picked at a tuft of grass, pulling one of the blades free and rubbing it between his thumb and fingers. "I'm glad the Dremis brought her to me, and I'm afraid I freely partook of the favors of the young maidens and the Ladies throughout the years before." He studied the piece of grass before continuing. "But having gone through it, living the turmoil and angst that can accompany the union… not to mention seeing it from her side, and the thought of my child participating… I can't imagine what I would be feeling had my firstborn been a girl." He paused again then looked at Mahryn who was nodding. "It's different even for you, is it not?"

Mahryn was surprised by his question. It took her a minute before she could answer with a nod.

Tahruk leaned closer and whispered "And you had the misfortune of capturing my brother's attention."

Sighing, Mahryn sat up, leaning away from the tree. "And of being born to the King's second in command." She drained her cup, replacing it with another that sat on a small tray to her other side. She laughed when Tahruk made a face. "This is not a night I wish to remember, my lord. I had thought to secret myself away over here, outside the scrutiny of others, and yet still close enough that I would not be reprimanded for leaving before the head mistress gave her approval. We aren't allowed to venture out with anyone tonight, so I'm not sure what our purpose is in being here. But I'm also not one for rattling a biting dog's chains either, if you know what I mean."

"It appears you are destined to have your plans turned over by the Sharanis men." Tahruk chuckled, taking one of the goblets she offered him as an afterthought. "I'm sorry about your father," he added quietly.

"Me too," she answered just as quietly before downing a sizeable amount of the liquid in her cup.

They sat in silence for a few more minutes before she turned to him. "Do you think your wife will ever find success in changing our system? It's how things have been done for century upon century. What makes her think she can make a difference?"

"It all has to start somewhere." Tahruk shrugged. "Every change begins with one person. She has the passion, and she has the King's ear." He smiled. "He has a penchant for redheads." He laughed and Mahryn joined him, the wine finally working its magic to loosen her up.

"I heard he fell in love with one of the Daughters of Damalenya before his Chosen arrived. Is that true?" she asked, knowing the question was somewhat brazen, but no longer caring.

Nodding, Tahruk stared off in the distance. "We've never been as close, the old man and I, but Redahn used to sit at his feet and listen to him regale in the past and what it was like. He told me of our great grandfather's love for a young maiden, one he could not act upon because she was marked for someone else. I think he sees her in Elenya. It's part of why he listens to her."

"He was also there when her kin was sentenced to execution and her Drille sent into exile because the Aleone man acted upon his desire for one of Zanak's women... a marked member of your family."

Tahruk nodded slowly. "Not many people know that."

Mahryn laughed, polishing off her current glass of wine and reaching for the last of her filled goblets. "Ah, my lord. It pays to lurk in the shadows of the castle as I have for the past few years. After... after things changed, my father brought me here, moved me from the home I'd shared with my mother and sister to live here full time within his chambers at the castle. It was just the two of us left, so it made more sense."

"What kept you there... before."

"My mother. She didn't want to leave our family home. Don't misunderstand. She was so very proud and pleased for my father and that he had achieved such a high position. She just... she didn't like the royal life any more than I do."

Tahruk patted her arm when her voice broke. "What happened? To your mother, I mean? And to your sister? You mentioned a before. What... happened?"

Mahryn was already shaking her head before he finished talking. "Not tonight, my lord," she whispered. "I do not care to go there." She shuddered, finished her drink, and stared into the bottom of her goblet. "There's not enough wine to take away the agony should I allow myself to return to thoughts of that time. Not even this wonderfully enchanting concoction from my home Drille that is deemed worthy of the royalty within the Centrehead. I cannot change the past, especially by dwelling on it. I can't even change the future, but I *can* change the present." She smiled at him and began to push herself up. Tahruk jumped up to lend her a hand and she giggled when she felt herself wobble a bit. "Presently, I need more drink. You took one of my cups."

"Then we must remedy that," Tahruk told her, tucking her hand into the crook of his arm and leading her toward the table loaded with drink within the center of the Gala festivities.

"Ah! Lord Redahn!" Mahryn greeted, her voice more jovial than it should have been, when they met up close by the table. "Did you enjoy the ceremony? Was my father not in rare form?" Her giggle did little to mask her hurt at her father's unpardonable actions as far as Redahn was concerned. He frowned, watching as she took a glass of bubbling wine spirits and downed half the glass. He looked at his brother, his brows inching upward in question. Tahruk just shrugged and mumbled something about checking on his wife before he bid them a good evening, and walked away.

"The refreshments seem to be of your liking, though perhaps you might leave some for the rest of us." He tried for a nonchalant tone, not wanting to appear accusatory, even with his attempt to sweep the goblet from her hand. She stepped away, sloshing some of the liquid onto her gown when she pulled it out of his reach.

Her mouth turned down in an exaggerated frown, she looked at the spot on her dress and then at him. "You've ruined my lovely gown. I do believe I should demand resisisution." Her frown deepened. "Restisiut..." She waved her hand in the air, dismissing her inability to say the word.

Her antics made Redahn chuckle. "I was merely going to offer to refill your cup, my lady." He lied. "Though, since

I am not the one who did the spilling, no *restitution* will be forthcoming."

Her scathing glare brought out a full out laugh and caused several heads to turn to see what was so funny. "Come," he whispered. "Let's walk away from these wondering eyes."

Mahryn began to shake her head, the action so exaggerated she nearly spilled more of the drink. "I am not allowed. I shall not suffer the head mistress' wrath, even for you. Not that one more night with you would not be worth whatever punishment she might rain down. Because I never imagined being in the arms of a man would be quite so…" She stopped talking and clamped her lips tightly together, her eyes growing comically round. She looked from the wine goblet to Redahn, then back again. "Cursed drink." She handed the half empty glass to a passing server and refused another from his tray, instead lifting her skirts and turning to walk away.

Redahn caught up with her after a few steps. He noticed she was heading directly toward the arena's entrance. "Where are you going?" he asked, keeping pace with her steps while his hands remained at his sides.

"Do your eyes not work, my lord? I'm leaving, of course."

"Yes, I can see that. But why?" And had she not just told him she could not leave without consequences?

She stopped, swaying only slightly, and turned to look at him. "I thought to use drink to salve the sting of this night. Yet now I find I do not wish to make an even greater fool of myself by professing suppressed feelings I may have for you, knowing I would regret that when the effects of the wine drain away." She threw her arms up, then let them fall limply to her side before she shrugged and turned to walk

Linda Boulanger

away, leaving a smiling Redahn to catch up to her again.

"You cannot leave, my lady," he whispered, pulling her to a stop with a hand on her elbow that she quickly jerked from his hold.

"Pray tell, why not?" she demanded with a tap of her foot while turning a steely glare on him.

Redahn lifted his hands in surrender. "The head mistress has not yet released you. You would be just as much at the mercy of her wrath should you walk away alone as you would should you leave with me."

As if they could round any more, Mahryn's eyes did just that. She blinked a few times, sobering more, the realization that Redahn had just saved her from a consequential blunder evident in her expression. He watched the delicate movement of her neck as she swallowed before she forced her eyes up to meet his. "Thank you, my lord."

Leaning toward her, a wicked tilt to his mouth, Redahn whispered, "You can thank me when this week of hellish separation has ended."

A tiny gasp escaped Mahryn's lips and she began to fan herself with her hand.

"Are you okay?" Redahn asked her, knowing full well the thoughts his words had evoked.

"Tis the drink. It makes my head swim."

Redahn knew the turmoil that raged inside the woman before him, knew firsthand because he felt it too. He stepped forward and tucked her arm into his.

"Come, my lady," he murmured softly. "Come and walk with me. We'll stay within the perimeter of the Gala and not risk the ire of the head mistress. You'll feel better then."

Mahryn's compliance was accompanied by a chuckle. She was thinking of Tahruk's comment about the Sharanis brothers always interfering with her plans. Unlike Tahruk, Redahn didn't try to find out why she was laughing. He just pulled her along at his side. Unfortunately, it was a place Mahryn found all too comforting—just another thing to add to all she shouldn't let herself think about tonight.

"I don't suppose we could have just one more glass of wine?" She looked up at Redahn with a hopeful smile. He just chuckled and shook his head, motioning the approaching tray bearer to keep on going.

They walked along in silence for some time. It wasn't uncomfortable, but Mahryn could still tell her companion was wrestling with whatever he wanted to say. Prickles of concern began to shoot through her and she was startled by the sound when he finally cleared his throat and started to speak. It made them both chuckle when she jumped, though Redahn quickly sobered again.

Patting the hand that was hooked in his arm, Redahn told her he was sorry her reception from her father had been less than noble. "He's a pious, arrogant ass."

Mahryn nodded, her head remaining down as she thought how to answer, or even whether she should. "I embarrassed him," she finally said.

"Of all the ludicrous…" Redahn stopped and turned to look down, studying her face. "How many years has that man been in attendance at the King's side? He knew what would happen this evening."

"Of course he did!" Mahryn looked away, her face pinched. She blinked swiftly to ward off unwanted moisture forming in the corners of her eyes. "I… I won't pretend to know what his plan was or is, but I do know my walking into the arena alone, as one of the Ladies of the Court, was not a part of it, though I didn't realize that until I stood before him." She shook her head. "I suppose he expected to see me married off and out of his life. He doesn't understand my lack of appeal to men." She sighed, and looked up toward the heavens and the stars that blinked above their heads. "I've never been able to please him. Only Hahna could do that." She took a deep breath before whispering, "She should have been the one to live."

Redahn grasped her upper arms so firmly that she winced. Looking up at his face, she was aware just how incapable she was of reading the thoughts and emotions lighting his dark eyes as she was her father's.

"You are wrong about so many things, Mahryn."

Mahryn's brows drew down, tightening between her eyes. She didn't understand the thickness of his tone. She watched his neck rise and fall when he swallowed, found a strange, though no longer foreign, tingling shooting out from her middle when her eyes again rose to his and found his gaze on her mouth. She moistened her lips with the tip of her tongue, sucking in a breath when his grip on her arms tightened even more. As he closed the distance between them, she closed her eyes, expecting, anticipating the feel of his mouth covering hers. Instead, he laid his cheek against hers.

"Every man at the Dremis knew you were to be mine, Mahryn. They dared not touch you until I'd had my turn," he whispered.

Her lips were bereft of his kiss, though the softness of his breath blowing over her ear still had her swaying into him. Only when his words finally sunk in did her eyes snap open and she pull back, trying to make sense of what he was saying.

"I am just as much at fault for your future as your

father, I fear. Believe me, you will have no lack of callers once this week is over. And I have no doubt you would have made a match that final night had you not chosen to go with me. I shouldn't have…"

Mahryn placed her fingertips against his mouth. "You have ruined me and saved me at the same time." The bittersweet smile she offered reflected her words perfectly. She was thinking of how angry she'd been at him for foiling her chances of remaining untouched through the week, when in reality, it seemed his interest had kept other men at bay. Would the attention of those other men have kept Redahn from ever coming to her? She tried to imagine life without having experienced the joy of being in his arms. She couldn't, no longer wanted to, even if it meant being at the mercy of other men when the week was over. "I wouldn't change what was."

Mirth shining in his eyes, Redahn teased, "I admit I have confidence in my abilities, my lady, but to think that would be enough to make you eager to serve…" Again she silenced him.

"On second thought, I recant my comment," she told him. They both laughed and he hugged her before threading her arm back through his and continuing their walk. When Mahryn laughed again, he asked why. "We still gather eyes, or had you not noticed?"

Redahn nodded. "It seems our relationship is of interest to many."

"Relationship? Is that what we have?" Mahryn kept her tone light, but the weight of her question was undeniable.

"Don't go there, Mahryn," Redahn answered in a tone as dark as hers had been light. "Don't be like everyone else, pressuring me, especially since I have found just how enjoyable your companionship is, both inside and out of the bedroom. Titles. What difference do they make?"

"No difference, my lord, and far be it for me to pressure. I was merely asking."

Redahn laughed when she set her chin and thinned her lips. After a moment, Mahryn was laughing as well.

She sighed. "I fear too much has been said this evening. Pray we won't remember it all when the light of the moon leaves us behind."

"I will remember, Mahryn." He leaned in and whispered. "This is a night, a week, I shall never forget. It has been a Dremis like no other." He had stopped them again, his eyes growing serious. "Because of you, I fear I am changed forever."

Mahryn stared at him, saying nothing for a moment before shaking her head. "But not enough." She searched his eyes though she already knew the answer. Slowly, he began to shake his head.

"*I* am not enough," he whispered, then hastened her toward the spot where his family sat, along with the King and his closest confidants, which included her father.

"*You* are wrong, my lord," she said under her breath before quickly turning to drop into a deep curtsy before the King, giving Redahn no chance to respond.

Chapter 17

"Lady Mahryn!" The King greeted her, his still sharp eyes dancing with obvious pleasure at her presence. "Rise, my dear. Come and honor this old man with a kiss to the cheek and let me look upon you with delight."

"I believe it is I who should be honored to look upon your greatness, my King," Mahryn flattered. "How are you?" she asked, gracing him with a smile filled with fondness before she leaned down to press her lips against the aged cheek, whispering something in his ear that made him chuckle and grasp both her hands in his as she straightened.

"I'm well. Better now that you're here," he told her, briefly bringing her hands to his lips. "I am surprised to see you among the Ladies, though." He lifted a brow and cut his eyes in the direction of his top confidant. "One would have thought a good match would have been secured for you instead."

Mahryn's smile never faltered, even when she glanced at her father. Bringing her attention back to the King, she answered, "Sometimes life chooses a different path for us than what we might expect."

His old head nodding, the King chuckled. "And sometimes, even when you believe your path is straight, you find out there are many twists and turns along the way." While everyone laughed at his comment, both Redahn and Tedran remained serious and silent. Andorak's brow raised again. He paused to study the face of his kin while ignoring his old friend. "You doubt my words, young man?"

Redahn shook his head. "No, Grandsire. Your wisdom far surpasses any knowledge I have of life, that's for certain." He looked from his great grandfather to Mahryn. "Though I am already old enough to have the wisdom to guard against certain attractive *curves* life can throw in unexpectedly." She took in a shaky breath when his eyes began to travel down her shapely body, a deep stain creeping up her neck and settling into her cheeks.

Mahryn's smile wavered only slightly before she replaced it with a rather devious grin. Bending again toward the King, she whispered just loud enough for all to hear, "I believe the majority of his curves are ones he could easily maneuver around without trouble should he decide to do so. I happen to have first-hand knowledge of that extending to those he finds within his bed," she half joked.

Snickers surrounded them while the King worked to fend off a hearty belly laugh. It was obvious that Mahryn's time in the King's presence had afforded her the opportunity to pick up on his sense of humor—a plus for her, though Redahn wasn't quite sure what it meant for him.

Her smile faded the moment she lifted her head and looked in her father's direction. The scowl on his face let everyone know just what he thought about it. Mahryn quickly schooled her features into the perfect picture of a well-trained lady, only softening slightly when she looked back at the King.

"It's been a lovely Gala and Dremis week, Lord King. Thank you for providing such for your steadfast subjects," she told him, her words and stance indicating that she intended to take her leave.

"I am honored to do so, my lady, though surely you do

not intend to run off so quickly?" With one corner of his mouth rising slightly, he added, "And certainly not with him." Nodding in Redahn's direction, he chuckled when the younger man frowned, especially when he continued, "He is much too much like me for his own good, you know."

Mahryn quietly echoed his chuckle before nodding then shaking her head. Redahn was momentarily lost in the motion that caused the few loose tendrils of her hair to caress her neck. His mouth watered remembering the sweetness of her flesh there…

"… time for me to take my leave… not with him… though I really must."

His retrospection had caused him to miss all but minor snippets of her answer. He watched her turn to walk away, just like that, finally ending this week they'd shared.

And he did nothing to stop her.

"If you please, my lady…" His brother's voice came from somewhere beside him. He turned toward the sound, as did Mahryn. "Before you go, I would like to introduce you to my wife."

Graceful as always, Mahryn nodded her head slightly before looking back at his brother. "I'd be honored," she told him, stepping forward to take the arm he offered. She smiled up at him as he led her toward the tables that seated Redahn's immediate family, not far at all from the King. With a silent sigh and shake of his head, Redahn followed, wishing he'd been the one to garner such a sweet smile from the lady in the presence of others.

"Please, do not rise on my account, my lady," he heard Mahryn tell Elenya when they reached the table. He couldn't tell what Elenya said when Mahryn dropped into a low curtsy before her, though it had them clasping hands when Mahryn rose, and Tahruk offered his chair and walked away.

"I suggest you claim her for your own or find diversion elsewhere before you drive yourself to the brink of insanity, Brother."

Redahn glared at his brother's whispered directive as Tahruk came to stand beside him. "Too late for that, *Brother*. I feel certain I crossed that line the day they took away my sword."

Now it was Tahruk's turn to glare. "No one *took away* your sword."

The two brothers stared at each other for a moment longer, the muscle along Tahruk's jaw twitching, Redahn's eyes beaded and his nostrils flared before he turned on his heel and marched away. Without looking back, he walked through the gates of the arena, crossed over the very path Mahryn had been forced to walk a few hours earlier, and pushed out the far entrance into the darkness of the night.

Back at the Gala, Mahryn gave herself a mental shake, attempting to return her thoughts to the conversation with the redheaded beauty who might just have the power to effect change in the world they lived in. She smiled when she felt Elenya's hand cover her own, though she didn't look in her direction for fear the few tears that had welled in the corners of her eyes might spill over. She had no idea what had transpired between the two brothers, she only knew one had marched off toward the refreshments table, while the other, the one who caused her heart to constrict every time she thought of life without him, had walked away without ever looking back. How fitting, she thought, grateful for Tahruk's return with a full glass of wine.

"I believe I owed you one," he told her as he handed the goblet to her.

With a slight nod of appreciation, Mahryn tipped up

the glass and drained it in one go. "Ah!" she said, paying little heed to the concern on the faces of those around her when she finished and placed the glass on the table, thankful her slightly exaggerated movements hadn't snapped the stem. "It appears the head mistress is summoning her Ladies. My Palatial suite and a week of pampering and rest awaits." Her laugh was hollow, making her look down at her lap for a moment before turning embarrassed eyes on Elenya. "Forgive me, my lady. I fear this week has tested my endurance."

Elenya leaned forward and wrapped her arms around Mahryn, a gesture that was almost the younger woman's undoing. "I'm on your side," she whispered before giving her one last, tight squeeze and releasing her.

Mahryn nodded and thanked Elenya before standing to offer a curtsy to those around her.

"Lady Mahryn." Elenya's words halted her as she began to move away. Mahryn turned to look at her, waiting without speaking. She was sure words would fail her. "It only takes a small ray of hope to bring light to a dark room."

Mahryn sucked in sharply, then bit her bottom lip to still its quivering. She dared a glance in her father's direction and found him glaring at Elenya, his brows drawn down so sharply it made the crease in his forehead look painful. Had he recognized the exact sentiment her mother used to make? Without comment, she turned and walked away, her mind focused, wondering what form that potential ray could possibly take for her.

Chapter 18

Mahryn was thankful the Ladies were allowed to sleep to their content the next morning, though the noise in the hallway and in the courtyard outside the window of her chamber told her the majority of the women had chosen to rise much earlier than she had. She groaned, covering her throbbing head with her pillow, praying the weight of the packed feathers would drown out their merriment. A knock on her door had her gritting her teeth before squeaking out a whispered "Come in."

Balancing a tray on one hand, Larina pushed the door open and stepped in. "My apologies for disturbing your rest, my lady." Her tone was hushed, the tilt of her head and sweetness of her smile brimming with sympathy. "Lord Sharanis has sent a gift that I was told to bring to you immediately."

At the mention of Redahn's surname, Mahryn pushed herself up in the bed, a gesture that had her groaning and clutching her head before moving one arm down to press against her churning middle.

Larina groaned in sympathy. Placing the tray on the nightstand beside Mahryn's bed, she poured out a cup of water from the chilled carafe and measured out exactly four drops of liquid from a tiny decorative bottle that was more vial-like in its appearance.

"What is it?" Mahryn asked, barely opening her eyes when Larina handed her the glass and told her to drink it.

"It's something from the Sharanis' aunt. She dabbles in potions and concoctions and her medicinal herbs are said to be quite good." Larina chuckled at Mahryn's exaggerated groan.

"I suppose it can make me feel no worse."

Larina laughed again when Mahryn looked at her with only one eye open.

"Perhaps if I am fortunate, it will kill me."

Larina tsked at her and began to tidy up the discarded clothing from the night before while Mahryn worked to swallow her drink. It certainly wasn't going down as smoothly as the wine had, though after just a few sips her stomach was already beginning to settle and the sound of Larina opening and closing her wardrobe door was no longer taking off the top of her head. If it wasn't for the terrible ache in her chest, Mahryn might have believed herself capable of moving on with the life that had been foisted on her.

With a gentle squeeze to Mahryn's shoulder, Larina reached behind her to fluff the pillow, then stood quietly beside the bed, her hands clasped before her, head tilted, a sweet smile lifting the corners of her mouth. Again Mahryn wondered why some warrior hadn't snatched her up. She seemed so... perfect. It was on the tip of Mahryn's tongue to ask when Larina clapped her hands together and began to spell out all the events the Courts had available for the Ladies throughout the week.

"A *reward* for our sacrifices, I suppose." Mahryn's voice was packed with sarcasm and bite that had Larina shaking her head, a sympathetic set to her mouth.

"Believe me, there are much worse places you could have ended up." She turned away quickly, but not before Mahryn saw the shine of a tear in the corner of her eye.

Larina cleared her throat, her voice once again chipper and coddling when she spoke. "Let's see what we can find for you to wear so that you may partake in these festivities. It helps keep the mind from wandering and wondering."

With a false smile, Mahryn agreed to Larina's assistance, putting away thoughts of the other woman's past just as she was trying to do to her own. What Larina was offering would at least keep her busy, and there was no denying she needed a good diversion. She wavered between wishing this week would last forever, and worrying that its end wouldn't come nearly soon enough. She hated the idea of what life had to offer, though the thought of the unknown was far worse. If only… She shook her head. Dreams were the only place where her happily ever after might possibly come true.

Many miles away the man that attempted to occupy Mahryn's thoughts was having a much harder time. No diversions had been laid out for him, and as he lay in his bed, all he could think of was the same thing he'd thought about all night long. A deluge of her scent, her taste, the feel of her… it all bombarded his senses. The sound of her voice teased—the way she said his name, the soft, sweet, incoherent words that formed on her lips in the throes of passion… even the way she breathed… It all ran through his mind, bringing his body to life, obliterating the numbness he so desired. He cursed her under his breath, then took it back to place the blame fully on himself.

"This will pass," he growled into the empty room before rolling over to try again to find some semblance of peace in sleep. It was not to be his, especially when he dreamed of Mahryn curled up against him, her body fresh, covered in a translucent film of white silk. He badly wanted to touch her, needed to feel her, though even as his hands slid over the fabric and he could feel the warmth radiating off her, he could find no opening in the material that would allow him full access to her.

Frustrated, he thrashed about in his bedding until the tangled mass began to restrict him and he woke. With a groan, he rolled over and checked the sundial he could just see from the garden door that led from his room. It was not yet noon. Not even a morning had passed of what promised to be a week more hellish than any he'd ever known.

Throwing back the covers and swinging his legs over the side of the bed, Redahn sat with a fluid-like motion common to the warrior he'd once been, and pushed himself to a standing position. With all the wine he'd consumed the night before, he was surprised his head didn't hurt. He wondered how Mahryn was faring. She'd had far more to drink than someone her size should have attempted.

Too bad for her, he thought. She wasn't his responsibility. She'd have to answer for her own actions. Just like everyone else. Besides, what could he do for her anyway? He wasn't even allowed near her for a full week. Even if he'd wanted to help her, which he didn't, he couldn't.

His face set in a deep grimace, Redahn pulled on a pair of soft pants and a plain shirt, ran his fingers through his dark hair, and made his way into the tunnel system of Zanak. Mahryn's plight may be out of his hands, but he could certainly do something to stop the rumbling of his midsection. A noonday feast would be laid out by the time he reached the dining hall. He hoped quieting the grumbling beast in his belly would help settle the one in his head. That bothered him the most because it was trying to make him think a heart resided behind the wall of his chest. He refused, *refused* to be sucked into thinking there was any way he could be falling for Mahryn.

The problem was, he was afraid there was a chance he already had. And that was a *huge* problem as far as Redahn was concerned.

Voices fell silent when he entered the dining hall, the majority of eyes turning in his direction. Ignoring them, Redahn glowered at the spread of food laid out on the buffet table near the burning fireplace on the far side of the room. Feeling his temperature rising along with his ire, Redahn turned his wrathful thoughts to his mother, wondering why she always insisted the fire be lit, even on days that needed no chill chased away.

"Son!" His mother seemed to walk from his thoughts and he looked at her with a frown. "Are you not well?" she asked, tentatively reaching for his arm.

Pulling back, Redahn continued to stare at her until she stepped back.

"Just because your night didn't go well doesn't mean you have to take your mood out on the rest of us, Brother."

Redahn looked down, biting the inside of his mouth to hold back the anger that threatened to spew out at the sound of his brother's voice. A false smile lifting the corners of his lips, Redahn finally looked up, his eyes dark and without humor, trained on the owner of the offending voice. "Don't you have a wife you should be catering to, *Brother*?"

Tahruk chuckled. Redahn smirked when he realized the others in the hall had moved a respectable distance away. It was good to see they'd all learned their lessons, knowing neither of these two boys had been opposed to throwing a fist at the other to punctuate a moment of irritation. He shouldered into his brother when turning to the buffet and Tahruk chuckled, though it was his continual head shake that irritated the younger man more than it would had he actually thrown a punch or grabbed him.

"What? I suppose you pity me because I had no woman in my bed last night?" He practically growled the question, his fists clenching and unclenching at his sides.

Tahruk shook his head. "No, my brother. I happen to know what you're going through, though I don't pity you at all. You made your own choices, and you have to live by them. Just see to it they don't affect those around you." Tahruk stepped in front of him and filled a plate that he handed to his mother before filling a second. No doubt he was preparing food to take back to Elenya. Thinking the conversation was over, Redahn moved in line behind him.

When Tahruk had finished piling a platter full, placing it on a tray someone had finally produced for him, the older brother cleared his throat and waited for Redahn to turn to look at him. Hand poised midway between his plate and the bread tray he'd just scored a huge roll from, Redahn froze and turned a stony face in Tahruk's direction.

"Just so you know, I think... *we* think you've made a huge mistake in letting her go. You need to reconsider." Tahruk's affirmation of what Redahn refused to believe he was feeling was the younger man's snapping point. He released his hold on the bread, then dumped the platter he held in the other hand, sending its contents to mix with the other dishes on the table. They'd be inedible anyway since he dropped the platter as well and it shattered, sending shards of glass into the family's midday meal. Amidst protests and reprimands, Redahn turned and stormed from the room, not caring about the wrath that would be directed at him once his father caught wind of his ill behavior.

A half hour of pacing about his quarters was about all Redahn could take. His anger had yet to subside. Damn his brother for speaking his mind. There was obviously no way he was going to be allowed to lay low and let his wounds heal among his family. Traitors!

He didn't really believe that. He knew they loved him and only wanted to see him happy. But what did any of them know about *his* happiness and what it would take to get there, if it was even possible. He'd felt it when he had Mahryn in his arms, or at least he'd felt closer to finding it than he had in a very long time. Mahryn, Mahryn, Mahryn. How was he ever going to push her out of his thoughts if every turn brought him back to thinking about her? He needed to stay busy. It was the only way.

Sleep and mindless activities brought an end to the torturous week. Unable to shake his need for Mahryn, Redahn reasoned that it was his right to enjoy her if he wanted. He looked at the sundial in his unkempt garden. Almost noon. Visiting the Ladies during the day may not be considered *normal*, but it wasn't exactly taboo either. Not that Redahn cared. This trip could wait no longer.

Dressing with haste, he practically ran to the stables and pushed the old groom out of the way when he offered to help with Redahn's horse. How many times had Redahn had to ready the beast in a hurry during battle? This may not be a war, but his body was every bit as charged, and he managed the task in record time, preparing to leave Zanak without even letting his family know. He'd been so horrid throughout the week, he was sure they'd just as soon he stayed away. Besides, they'd be preparing for the noonday meal now, and what he hungered for certainly couldn't be found at his family's dining table.

He chuckled and leaped up into the saddle, turning the eager warhorse toward the stable door opening and giving him rein to take his leave. It had been too long since he'd ridden and it felt good to be astride again. Redahn smiled. Yes, today was going to be a truly great day.

With the horse's hooves gobbling up the distance between Zanak and the castle, it didn't take long for Redahn to arrive. He actually smiled at the castle groomsman, flipping an extra coin in his direction when he released the reins to him and slipped off his mount. Whistling a soft tune, he strolled toward the Ladies' chambers, his cordial smile remaining in place, even as the man at the desk stared at him as if looking at a madman.

"I know it's early in the day, but I wish to take the Lady Mahryn out, if you please." When the man didn't move, Redahn's brows hitched upward and he added, "Is that a problem?"

The man shook his head, though he still remained silent.

"Then. Get. Her," he demanded, his smile turning to a menacing grimace. When there was still no action on the deskman's part, Redahn leaned toward him over the table and the man finally acted, leaning back as far as he could.

"She... she's noh not here, mm my lord," he stammered.

"What do you mean *not here?*" Anger surged through him and he mocked the man's words. This had her father written all over it. Reaching across the table, Redahn grabbed the assistant by the shirt ties, all the while mumbling through gritted teeth, "That miserable blackguard! Where has he taken her?"

"To Zanak, my lord," the man squeaked out.

"Zanak?!"

"Yes, my lord. She left late last night... with your father."

Chapter 19

Had the man actually hit him over the head with a heavy skillet, he could not have surprised Redahn more. Mouth agape, he stared blankly at the shaking attendant.

"Zanak," he repeated before shaking his head and leaning back across the table. "You expect me to believe that? Liar! Tell me the truth! Tell me where she has gone before I tear you to bits!"

The assistant had somehow managed to get out of his seat and backed away from his post, his eyes never leaving his crazed opponent, except for a quick glance around. Redahn figured he was looking for an escape route, though he didn't plan to give him one.

"Lord Redahn!"

The feminine voice cut through his madness, just enough to halt his advance on the assistant. He turned his wrath-filled glare on the head mistress instead. Her skirts swishing about her ample body, the woman approached, two rather large male attendants on either side of her. Someone must have alerted her that trouble was brewing. He glanced back at the attendant and growled, nearly laughing when the man squealed and slinked around the corner as quickly as he could.

But there was no humor in the situation that deserved laughter. The week had been torturous, and now they were keeping him from the one thing, the only person that could alleviate his agony.

"Where is she?" he demanded through gritted teeth.

The lady smiled, the action only serving to further plump her already rounded cheeks. "Who, dear? Which of my girls is it that you seek?"

Redahn covered the distance between them, stopping just far enough away that he'd have room to take care of her goons if he had to. "Don't toy with me. You know exactly which of *your girls* I'm looking for. You will either bring me Lady Mahryn or tell me the truth of her whereabouts, or I shall assure your removal from this posh position you have grown so comfortable in. *My lady*," he added with a menacing grin.

The mistress' smile wavered for a mere half second before she thinned her lips and stepped toward Redahn. Finger pointed at his chest, she spoke to him through gritted teeth. "Now you listen to me, young man. You may be one of the best warriors this kingdom has ever seen, and we all know you're a favorite of the King. Heaven help us that his blood is also yours and you most assuredly have the power to do exactly as you have threatened. But you will not come in here and act as some boorish brute and expect I would send any of my girls out with you. I don't know what your game is with Mahryn, but I can tell you, I'm glad to see her gone. That girl deserves far better than she will ever find here. And far better than you."

The two stared at one another for several seconds before anyone spoke again.

"Do as you will, but you've been told the truth. She's been taken from here to Zanak." The head mistress lifted her skirts and turned, leaving Redahn stunned for a second time.

"Zanak?" he called, still unbelieving. "Why?"

"Go home, Lord Redahn. You'll find what you're looking for there," she called as she exited the hall.

It was a good thing someone had been tending to his horse's daily need for exercise during his time of neglect or the poor mount may have expired due to the fast pace his rider demanded of him on their trip back to Zanak. Fury and his need for answers fueling his every action, Redahn urged the mount to move faster while his mind whirled, trying to light on some reason his family would have gone so far as to bring Mahryn into their home, *his* home. They'd meddled in his affairs before, but this time, they'd gone too far. Affairs of the heart had always been off limits.

Affairs of the heart? What was he thinking? He didn't love this girl. He was merely smitten by need. Lust was a dangerous opponent.

With those thoughts, he jumped from the horse, handing the reins to the closest person, not bothering to see if they were qualified to tend to the high-strung animal or not. His priority was getting to the place his long strides would surely take him.

"What the *hell* is *she* doing here?"

All heads turned in the direction of the voice that boomed from the doorway of the family's dining hall. Only his mother, Nema, and Mahryn moved.

Her eyes only switching their view from him to his mother, Mahryn breathed in—a deep, full breath that had her chest straining against the bodice of the simple dress she wore. "He was not informed, my lady?" she asked his mother.

Neria, swallowing hard, shook her head. Her lips tightly drawn, she glared first at Redahn, then turned her attention to Mahryn. "He is not the head of this household. All actions do not require his approval."

Nema had moved in beside Mahryn, actually

positioning herself between the younger lady and her nephew. "Neria is correct. The decision was made by the master of this house, the one who fetched you from the castle."

Mahryn nodded, her head bowing slightly. "Still. Perhaps I should leave."

Tahruk chose that moment to make his entrance, pushing in from behind his brother, bumping him in the process.

"You're behind this, aren't you?" Redahn ground out, grabbing Tahruk's shoulder.

Tahruk didn't even flinch when Redahn reared back, his fist poised to strike. He looked up at the raised hand and then at his brother. He shrugged. "Elenya needed a companion during these final months of bed rest. Lady Mahryn captivated her at the Dremis Celebration. It seemed a good fit. Besides," he added, lowering his voice and leaning in close enough so that only Redahn could hear him, "The Courts were no place for *that* Lady. We both know it. Only you were too fool-headed to do anything about it. So I did. Or... I had it done."

Prepared for the fist he knew would be thrown, Tahruk grabbed Redahn and spun him around, slamming him against the wall, though not before Redahn managed to hook a boot around his brother's leg. The men went down amidst screams and murmurs, plates and utensils clanking as the room's guests scattered.

"What in God's good name is going on here?" The voice that boomed its occupant's entrance to the hall had everyone freezing once again. His hand on their collars, Renaine hauled his boys off the floor, gracing each of them with a look that would have had the strongest of men quaking. They merely continued to glare at one another.

Their father thrust them in opposite directions, holding up a one finger warning to each before advancing on his wife. He glowered first at Mahryn, and then at Neria. Eyes squinted, nostrils flaring, he said directly to her, "And you thought this would be a good idea because…"

Breaking the stare down between Neria and Renaine, Nema stepped between them, gently pushing her sister back a few steps and gaining the concentrated scowl of the head of the household. "Your wife was merely looking out for the good of the mother of your heir's children, my lord. You should be pleased with her thoughtfulness."

"And my Chosen would do well to keep her opinions to herself," he growled at her, though his face softened, perhaps only visible to those who knew him well. Nema's lips twitched slightly.

"The young maid is a good choice," she said quietly.

"Then perhaps the young maid would better serve her Lady by being with her instead of treated as an honored guest within the family's dining hall."

Mahryn's chin lifted, her lips thinned, and she nodded her head before curtsying to the older man. "I shall be glad to return to my mistress' chambers, my lord."

"Why should she have to leave? She wasn't the one behaving badly," Tahruk piped in, speaking for the first time since his words to his brother found them on the floor like a couple of teenage boys. He challenged Redahn with his look of accusation. Fortunately, a raised hand from their father was all that was needed to avoid another wrestling match.

"Don't bother," Redahn spat out at the group, his glare honing in on a frowning Mahryn. "I'm leaving anyway." He spun on his heel and stormed from the room, leaving its occupants in stunned silence.

As the shock of the moment wore off, cleared throats and sighs signaled the relief. Mahryn, head still down, turned and placed her platter back on the serving table.

"I'm sorry, my lady. I seem to have lost my appetite. Perhaps I may lie down for a few moments before returning to Lady Elenya. If someone could just show me the way…" She turned away, not wanting any of them to see the tears that she was fending off. She closed her eyes. Damn Redahn! Why hadn't he stayed away like Neria had said he'd been doing, at least for her first day.

"I'll walk you back," Tahruk told her, his voice quiet and soothing at her side. "My mother can fix Elenya's meal and have someone bring it to her."

"Of course." Neria stepped to Mahryn's other side, rubbing her hand down the young woman's back. "I'll send something for you as well, dear. Just in case…"

Mahryn attempted to smile at her and offered her thanks as Tahruk led her away for what was a blessedly silent trip back to the chambers he shared with Elenya. At the door to the rooms she now occupied within his home, Tahruk cleared his throat and Mahryn steeled herself for whatever he had to say.

"I'd apologize for my brother's behavior, but we both know this probably isn't the last time, so I may as well save my breath. I only wish we'd steered clear of him until I'd been able to talk with him. I was late to the dining hall because I'd gone in search of him, only to have been told he'd left Zanak such a short time before that I never expected to find him there before me."

Mahryn's answering smile was hollow. Sadness clouded the light from her unusually colored eyes. "I have yet to fully unpack, my lord. I can be ready to go within the hour…"

"What?" Tahruk interrupted, his voice loud enough to cause Mahryn to step back from him. Frowning, he shook his head. "You misunderstand, my lady. Redahn's desires play no part in the decisions made by the rest of the family." He waved his hand in the air in between them. "I don't mean we don't take him into consideration. It's just... he can be a bit moody, as you've no doubt already learned."

Mahryn nodded, her shuttered eyes an indication she was still unsure of her place within the walls of Zanak.

"You've been hired as companion to my wife, not my brother. As long as you do that well, you have my invitation and my parents' approval to stay. Redahn will just have to learn to deal, or stay away." Tahruk laughed at the candid surprise that caused Mahryn's mouth to fall open for a moment before she remembered herself and clamped it shut again. "Now go and rest. I'm going to have lunch with my wife and she'll be needing your company as soon as her midday nap and visit with Rennie are over."

"Yes, my lord. Th... Thank you." Mahryn curtsied then turned to rush through the door to her new quarters with seconds to spare before fresh tears threatened. This time, there was no holding them back.

Tahruk stood on the other side of the closed door, staring at the vacant spot where Mahryn had been. With a deep sigh, he turned to make his way to the room he shared with Elenya. He'd been taking the noonday meal there with her for some time now, ever since Dr. Jorian had suggested extended bed rest would need to accompany the last few months of her pregnancy. Not that there was anything wrong, the good doctor continually affirmed. He merely wanted to be cautious after the trauma surrounding the birth of their son.

Elenya did well hiding the fears she had to be experiencing, chattering on about how different she felt this time around. He joked with her that it was probably an indication she was growing him a daughter to go with their fine son who was almost three. He actually hoped that was the case, loving the way Elenya's emerald green eyes lit up at the idea. There was no doubting that she loved their son considering the way she doted on him. But, a little girl...

Tahruk envisioned a smaller version of his beautiful wife and then frowned. As the second child, she'd be unmarked, just as Mahryn was, and there was no way he wouldn't work to assure her a good match, secured well before her eighteenth birthday. He tried to imagine how any father could send his daughter into the throng of the Dremis maidens, knowing she'd be used by the warriors for their sexual pleasure. Oh, he knew well enough that most of them were sent with the hopes they would garner the attention of one single warrior who would ask for her, assuring a place of prestige for both the woman and her family. How often did that really happen? It was more likely that those young ladies would find themselves in the very positions Mahryn had. A pang of guilt over all the times he'd been one of the warriors who had taken pleasure in an innocent Dremis maiden without offering her any future stopped him at his bedroom door. He shook his head, cursing himself first, and then Tedran. Elenya's love had assured he'd never be that sort of man again, and Tedran had him vowing he'd never be that kind of a father.

Inside the suite of rooms Mahryn had been given to use during her stay at Zanak, the tears flowed freely. They weren't all sad, some were tears of relief. She slumped against the door, sliding down until she sat in a crumpled heap just inside the door and thought about the night before—the moment of her salvation, even if it was only meant to last for a little while.

Chapter 20

The night before…

The rocking of Mahryn's body registered urgency even before her mind processed that she was being awakened.

"Mahryn, please. You need to rise and make ready. Quickly. You have a visitor." The head mistress' voice raised an octave higher than usual. Three other women bustled through the door of Mahryn's small room, all carrying items she'd need to do as the head mistress had commanded. No time was being wasted in her preparation.

Finally awake, her curiosity piqued and Mahryn sat up in her narrow bed asking the obvious question, "May I inquire as to the visitor's identity, my lady?"

Eyes narrowed to match the thin line of her lips, the older woman fisted her full hips and stared first at a blank spot on the tinted wall and then at Mahryn. "Lord Sharanis has requested your presence." Toe tapping an annoying rhythm, she continued, "I don't know what you have done, as he declined to discuss matters with me, but he seemed most vexed."

A frown wrinkling her brow, Mahryn wondered at the peculiar visit, even as the slightest thrill ran through her. It had to be just past midnight. The mandated week of refrainment would have been barely over. He'd wasted no time in coming to her. And yet it didn't make sense that he would be angry… unless he was mad because he found himself still wanting to be with her. It just made no sense. Then again, this was Redahn…

"The elder Sharanis!" the head mistress snapped.

"The elder?" Why would Redahn's brother want to meet with her? Tahruk had been most congenial toward her the final night of the Dremis Gathering, almost flirtatious, and again in passing at the Dremis Gala. Eyes widening, she slowly shook her head. Oh no. No, no, no. Surely she hadn't misread his kindness, or him hers. Oh, surely he did not plan to…

"I suggest you move, my lady. Believe me, you do not want to keep that old bear waiting any longer than you have to. I've seen firsthand how contemptuous he can be," Larina whispered to her while holding up a dress of blue taffeta overlaid with a shell of flimsy ivory gossamer for the head mistress' approving nod.

The chatter ceased as Mahryn slipped out of bed. Voices were replaced by the sound of bustling about in preparation for her meeting with Lord Sharanis. Mahryn sat quietly, her hands folded in her lap. She looked around the room. Certainly this was not what she'd expected her life to become, being forced to join the other Dremis maidens at Dorengar's Centrehead. She felt cheated of what should have been, of all she'd dreamed about as a little girl. She was never meant to be a Lady of the Courts.

Yet, there she was.

She contemplated what this meeting with Tahruk could mean. She supposed being chosen as mistress to the kingdom's finest warrior, whether he was the man she desired or not, was better than what she had. At least she would be provided with a home of her own, and her children would be raised with the knowledge they belonged to one man, instead of simply being one of the many

Children of the Courts who might become warriors themselves, or go on to serve as corisans or any number of better positions within the castle. She wondered what Lady Elenya would think when she found out. That Lady had a very staunch stance against many of the customs of the day, and she was sure sharing her warrior with another was not something she would take lightly. This was all so much harder because she liked Elenya. She sighed, earning a deep frown from the head mistress.

Her transformation complete, the ladies went their way with the head mistress barking orders for Mahryn to follow her. Arms crossed over her chest, she scanned her room one last time, rubbing her hands up and down to ward off the cold bite of an emptiness that went far beyond the sparseness of the space. Her eyes fell on the cross medallion lying on the small table next to her bed. A gift from her mother when she was very young, it served to remind her that a higher authority was in charge, that even in the most tumultuous storms of life, she must not allow the darkness to overshadow her because one small ray of hope could cause the clouds to break, the light chasing away the darkness. Wasn't that what Elenya had said as well?

Mahryn's mother had always been a dreamer looking for that silver lining—so sure that all situations would end well. Closing the door behind her, Mahryn said a silent prayer, hoping against hope that this time her mother was right.

The man stood with his back to the door studying one of the art pieces placed around the room to appease the temperament of lords awaiting the presence of requested ladies. Mahryn frowned, unsure of whose back she was looking at. This older gentleman, magnificent in his own right, was not the stately young warrior she knew Tahruk to be, though there was something oddly familiar about him. She was puzzled, even more so when he didn't offer a nod of confirmation or anything to show he'd heard her mistress announce her arrival. He continued to stare at the painting, even after the door closed and they were left alone. Mahryn felt her ray of hope dimming.

Just inside the doorway, she stood as still as any of the marble statues scattered about. Turning to face her, the man must have thought so too because his eyes darted from her to one statue in particular and then back again.

"You are Mahryn?" he asked, foregoing any semblance of formal introduction.

"Ye, yes, my lord." Her voice wavered slightly and she quietly cleared her throat in nervous anticipation of answering additional questions from this unknown man. Attempting to appear courageous, she tried to maintain eye contact, but the intensity of his stare made her look away. She cast a furtive glance at the painting over his right shoulder and her face reddened. Of course it would have to be Goridano's *Faded Boundaries* depicting the scene of an older man seducing a much younger maiden. She glanced back to see mirth lighting his dark eyes, even if it didn't make it to the rest of his features. Unnerved, she turned away, garnering a snort from the older man.

"What my son sees in you I am not quite sure. Though I'd agree you are not hard to look upon, I still would have expected a more assertive woman, given his nature."

His words grabbed her attention and she turned back to him, though it was less their abrasive nature as it was their use in identifying who he was.

"Redahn is your son, my lord?"

"*Lord* Redahn is, yes." He quirked a brow at her improper addressing of his son.

"Beg pardon, my lord." She dropped a stiff curtsy from her position across the room before employing her own blunt manner. "Please, may I inquire as to your reason for wishing to see me?"

The older man snorted again. "Perhaps I judged you prematurely." He crossed the room in few steps, moved her away from the wall with a fingertip pressed against her back, and walked around her, assessing her much as one might a piece of livestock. It was no wonder his sons acted as they did, and it was on the tip of her tongue to tell him so when he silenced her with a finger to her lips.

"Smooth your ruffled feathers. I'd like to offer you a proposal."

Standing in the confines of the waiting room, his finger still against her mouth, her blue eyes locked with his near blacks, Mahryn felt as if the world around her stood still as they began to spin. *A proposal*? She willed him to speak.

"I would like you to accompany me to Zanak Drille."

Mahryn's raised brow gained another snort, making it quite obvious he was not inviting her into the most elite household outside the castle for his own sake.

"My oldest son's Chosen is heavy with her second child. Extended rest has been advised…"

"Perhaps you have been misinformed. I am not a corisan, my lord."

He was already shaking his head. "She doesn't require someone to tend her needs. Lady Sharanis believes she needs a companion of sorts. Someone closer to her own age who might sit with her, read with her, perhaps engage in needlework or…" he waved a hand about, "whatever it is you women do."

He raised a brow and turned away, seeming to study the closest art piece. His agitation showed in the set of his strong shoulders and fists clenched at his sides.

"Why me?" she finally asked.

Lord Sharanis turned to stare at her again, his frown leaving her fearful he might recant his offer. Heaven knew, no matter the reason, it was a far cry better than finding herself on her back beneath different men at their discretion and forced to act as if it was an honor to do so. She was fortunate that, presently, Redahn… *Lord* Redahn had been her only lover.

"Forget I asked, if you may. I would be honored to accept your proposal, my lord," she told him with a low curtsy.

"Good. Now make haste, girl, and gather your belongings so we may be on our way. I'm weary and made more so by this larking around that has kept me from my home far longer than I have cared to be away."

His impertinence got the better of her and she answered him with her own question. "Are you aware that I am Lord Tedran's daughter? Would it not be fitting for you to address me as a lady as well, my lord?

He turned to her, eyes narrowed. "The King's advisor?" He shook his head. "No, *my lady*. He doesn't speak of having children. Perhaps *you* are mistaken."

Mahryn's laugh was sadly hollow, her expression wistful when she looked at him. "Whether he speaks of me or not, I am indeed his daughter. You have but to look at my eyes if you need to be convinced."

The elder Sharanis did just that, bending close, turning her face toward the light with a finger beneath her chin. Surprise flickered in his own eyes as he recognized the faint flecks of gold within the blue, known so prominently to belong to the man heralded as the King's closest confidant.

"Are you ill-gotten then?" he asked as he pulled his hand away.

Mahryn's lower jaw dropped at the question of her legitimacy. She clamped it back shut to glare at him with thinned lips. Seconds ticked by before she answered. "I am *not*! In fact, I am Tedran's second daughter. His oldest, my sister, was killed..." her voice broke and she remained silent.

The older warrior studied her, his expression giving away nothing of what he might be thinking or feeling. With a curt nod, he turned and opened the door for her. "I shall remain here while you gather your belongings," he told her. "Be quick, my lady. My patience has been sorely compromised this evening."

Mahryn left him to return to her room. She was quite sure his lack of patience began long before he came to visit her. And why his visit couldn't have waited until the morning was beyond her. She could only hope it would all come together and make sense.

There it was again. Hope. The one thing she'd been able to rely on through her whole life. She lifted the metal cross from the bedside table and slipped it over her head. She seldom wore it. Its size alone made it impractical most of the time and Mahryn had found she more enjoyed laying it about where she could see it. It brought her a sense of comfort and peace, much like the woman who'd given it to her.

"Never stop believing," her mother had told her as they sat together beside her grandmother's deathbed. "Dreams belong only to those who believe they exist." It was then she'd handed her the cross.

Mahryn frowned. Why didn't she remember Hahna being there? Even with all she still didn't remember, she knew her grandmother had died before her sister did. It was an odd thing to remember since she had so few memories from her childhood. She shrugged and turned back to shove the last of her belongings in her case.

"I hope you are right, Mama," she whispered before lifting her bag and walking through the door that would lead her to who knew where.

The sun peeking through the carelessly drawn drapes had awakened Mahryn the next morning. She'd turned, barely able to open groggy eyes until awareness hit her and she bolted upright in the oversized bed fitted with the softest of linens. She'd looked around the room and fell back, laughing, overcome with giddiness at the finery that surrounded her. If only her father could have seen her... Her stomach had clinched. What was the likelihood her father would allow her to remain once he found out?

A knock on the door had pulled her from her revelry, though she'd found herself elated when an invitation to join Elenya had been presented to her on a silver tray. An *invitation*! Not a command! At least for that moment she'd chosen to forget about her father and his silly games and simply enjoy being where she was for however long life deemed her worthy to remain.

Of course, that was all before the face-off with Redahn had taken place.

Dragging herself up off the floor, she crossed the room and picked up her medallion. She studied it, then sighed and returned it to the table beside the chaise where she'd envisioned herself reading while the breeze blew in the fragrant smells from her hosts' lovely garden. Mahryn longed for a peace she hadn't felt since the passing of her childhood days. It was a time she may not remember well, but she knew somehow that there had been times of great contentment. She'd felt that same sense of contentment for a few brief moments when she'd awakened that morning in the Sharanis household, and again when she'd first entered their dining hall and been greeted fondly by Redahn's family.

And then he'd shown up.

She closed her eyes. Even if by some miracle her father stayed away, there was absolutely no way Redahn would ever allow her to stay.

Chapter 21

Mahryn spent the next few hours feeling as if she was living on top of a case of eggshells. She felt the need to tread softly as she paced around in her new rooms, no longer seeing the beauty surrounding her. She jumped at every sound. Even her own breathing felt too loud and the time for her to return to Elenya's side could not come fast enough. The rap on the door indicating her lady was ready for her had Mahryn's heart sputtering within her chest. She stood in the center of her room, hand pressed over her heart, until the second knock came. She'd been expecting it, so why had it startled her so? And why did she feel such a sense of letdown that Redahn had not sought her out, even knowing for him to do so would surely have been for the sole purpose of informing her she'd been turned out.

Mahryn knocked softly on the door to Elenya's bedroom, then quietly pushed open the slightly cracked door when there was no answer. Peeking inside, she saw Elenya sitting in the bed, even larger than the oversized one she'd slept in the night before. Inside, Mahryn sighed. The Lady really was the beauty everyone claimed she was. Propped up with overstuffed pillows all around her, Elenya leaned against the cushioned headboard. Her red hair cascaded in waving curls down to cover her chest on both sides. Mahryn touched her own straight hair. She'd always found it dull. Who would ever want someone with a streaky dark blonde mop when there were women like Elenya with a crop of silky cinnamon-honey that most assuredly smelled like heaven as well?

The object of Mahryn's envy opened her eyes, green eyes as deep and beautiful as a perfect rock spring emerald. It was said her hair and eye coloring were the answer to a prophecy that freed her Drille from a century long exile, that she was a perfect replica of the Princess Damalenya— the daughter of the King's sister when the exile was decreed. It was the Princess' son who had caused Elenya's Drille to be exiled to the far Eastern shores of Riandus, though that was all Mahryn could remember of the lore as she fell under the kindness of her Lady's stare.

"I… I'm sorry, my lady. I didn't mean to interrupt your rest. I was told…"

Elenya waved a hand before her and smiled. "No! I'd asked that you come. I spend too much time bound by sleep. So much so that I fear my mind will turn in on itself. It's why I asked for a companion. Among other reasons," she added so quietly it was nearly inaudible. "Come," she said, her smile widening. "I had Tahruk move the chase closer to the bed so you could sit and relax as well while we wile away the hours with silly talk and whatever it is we women are supposed to do when we're together." She mimicked the motion the elder Sharanis had made in the castle room the night before and both women laughed. When their laughter subsided, Elenya motioned again to the chaise. "Sit down and let's begin this journey to a great and lasting friendship."

Mahryn thought her heart would burst and had to blink to keep unexpected tears at bay as she moved to settle on the chaise close to Elenya's bed. Friendship. She couldn't remember ever having a friend... except for Hahna.

"Tell me about yourself, Mahryn... things I don't already know. And let us dispense with that tiresome Lady business. From here on, except when we are in company that would require such, I am merely Elenya, okay?"

Mahryn nodded. At least that part of her Lady's request would be easy since she was quite certain she would not be allowed amongst company other than Elenya's."

Mahryn couldn't believe how quickly the afternoon passed and was surprised to find herself actually relaxing and enjoying her time doing little more than talking with Elenya. Never being one to talk about herself much or to open up to others, she'd fallen under the spell of Elenya's kindness and actually told the Lady things she'd never told anyone else. It was odd to find her confessions refreshing and she wondered if this was what friendship was really like.

Elenya's cleared throat brought her back to the conversation. "What of your relationship with Redahn?" she asked, a single brow lifted in indication she may have asked the question more than once. A soft smile slightly curved her pink lips as she waited for an answer.

Mahryn lowered her eyes. Biting at her lower lip, she thought of the best way to answer. She wanted to tell Elenya the truth—that she'd lost her heart to a man that would never return her love. But she couldn't.

With a sigh, she shrugged her shoulder. "I believe relationship is too bold a word for what we've shared. His behavior during the Dremis was most peculiar, but..." She shrugged again.

Elenya laughed. "Redahn is a quandary, even to himself." Silence punctuated her words. "Don't give up on him, at least not yet."

Mahryn stared at her, eyes squinted slightly, her forehead wrinkled.

"I've heard he behaved most unseemly this week away from you, Mahryn, even more so than usual. And I saw the way he looked at you at the Gala." She nodded when Mahryn scoffed. "I've known him long enough to know he's suffering over this, whether even he realizes it or not. He is. He needs someone who is strong and stable, someone like you."

This time, Mahryn could not hold back her choked laughter. Strong and stable? Her? "After all I have told you, how could you possibly think I would be the one he needs?" She stood and walked to the door leading out into the immaculate garden. With a deep breath to steady herself, she added, her voice still quivering, "There is so much of my past I can't remember. And what I can recall is filled with such unpleasantness... I thought I would die when I learned my father was forcing me into the midst of the Dremis Maidens. And then there was Redahn." She paused for a lengthy period, her voice barely a whisper when she continued. "I found both heaven and peace in his arms, though both are nothing more than memories now, cruel reminders of what will never be mine."

The rustling of the bedcovers had her turning back, her own concerns put aside when she saw that Elenya was trying to rise from the bed.

"My lady, no!" She rushed back to Elenya's side, eyes round, fear seizing her. "You mustn't jeopardize your life or that of your baby. You have to stay in bed."

Elenya pushed her hand away and used the side table and frame of the bed to steady herself as she got to her feet. "I am no less fit to wander around than I was a week ago." She rolled her neck and stretched the muscles of her back. "Sitting or lying grows insufferable after just so long. I rest when I'm tired and listen to my body. Believe me, I want everything to go right as much as anyone, probably even more. I haven't forgotten Rennie's birth, though I fear my body and muscles will grow lax and forget how to function if I do nothing but sit."

The determination in Elenya's eyes had Mahryn stepping back. "I cannot forbid you, my lady, though I must voice my concerns to you. Are you not fearful of what your husband might do should he find out you have disobeyed?"

"He's already aware of her stubborn defiance."

The deep voice that sounded from the garden door had Mahryn whirling about. Her eyes widened as did the sick feeling in the pit of her stomach. If the debacle in the dining hall wasn't going to get her sent back to the Castle, this surely would. Her father was right. There was very little she could do right.

Tahruk laughed, his long strides taking him quickly across the floor to Elenya's side. "You remind me of my Chosen when she first arrived at Zanak, Lady Mahryn. I seem to recall my brother commenting that Elenya had the look of a lady concerned about a great many things." He leaned down to kiss his wife's cheek, then nuzzled her neck, his large hand over the roundness of her belly. "My child is restless today." He pulled back, a dreamy glint in his eyes as he gazed down at his wife.

Elenya smiled, drawing herself up to kiss his chin. "*She* grows tired of sitting as well." There was no mistaking the determined set of her chin. "Please, my lord, walk us to the main garden and back to expel some of this energy. I fear she feeds off my need to move."

Tahruk's stance stiffened and Mahryn thought he was going to deny his wife's request. Instead, he bent to whisper something in her ear that had her giggling and pushing him away. "You forget I have a guest," she told him, though there was no mistaking the flirtatious promise glowing in her eyes.

"Vixen," he growled before turning to Mahryn, not bothering to wipe away his mirth. "Would you care to walk with us to the main gardens, my lady? It would allow you to see a bit more of Zanak."

Mahryn wouldn't have minded tagging along, though seeing the love that passed between them constricted her heart. She shook her head. "I believe I'll use the time to continue unpacking my belongings, if doing so would be acceptable to you both." She looked at them, unsure of the look they gave each other. Elenya finally nodded and Tahruk let Mahryn know he'd return his wife to their quarters within half an hour. Elenya added that she didn't have to hurry her unpacking, casting Tahruk a wistful look when she suggested he might deposit her in Mahryn's rooms and they could return to the room she shared with Tahruk once Mahryn was done.

Tahruk gave her a stern look and shrugged before nodding his approval, making Mahryn wonder if there was anything he wouldn't give his wife. She wondered what the possibility was that she'd ever have that kind of relationship.

Not much, she thought as she walked back to her borrowed rooms, alone.

Chapter 22

Unlike her earlier break from Elenya, Mahryn actually went to work removing her meager belongings from her case and putting them away. Additional gowns had also been delivered, both from her wardrobe closet back in the Lady's Chambers and new ones she hadn't seen before. Gifts from her hosts, perhaps? She'd have to ask and properly thank their provider.

Mahryn was so busy she didn't hear her visitor when he entered from the garden door. It was only after he cleared his throat that she jumped and turned in that direction. Staring at Redahn from across the room, Mahryn tried to slow her breathing, holding the garment she'd been about to put in the pulled out drawer against her heaving chest.

"Lord Redahn." Her whispered words came breathlessly and she stepped back, placing a hand against the door of the wardrobe to steady herself. "Wha... what are you doing here?" Eyes rounded, she glanced around her room, feeling a prickle of apprehension at the fact that they were completely alone. Redahn's snort further unnerved her, especially when accompanied by the hungry way he looked her up and down.

He threw his head back and laughed when she wrapped her arms about her torso. "You're a bit too late to protect your virtue, I'm afraid." He laughed again and she flinched, staring at him for a moment more before turning away. She'd meant to keep him from seeing the tears that stung her eyes, though he must have thought her motion an act of disrespect. He crossed the room in few steps, grabbing her by the arm and spinning her roughly back to face him. Lips pressed tightly together, he glared down at her, their faces mere inches apart. "I don't know what kind of games you're playing, Mahryn, or what you think your little escapade into my home will accomplish," he ground out between clinched teeth. "I've already told you where I stand, so you have nothing to gain by being here."

Mahryn could barely breathe. She knew there was no way Redahn could not feel the way her body shook, especially as he pressed her more tightly against himself, and had to will herself not to faint.

"Please, my lord…"

"Please, what?"

"No please about it. Get the hell back from the lady, Brother, lest I leave you without the ability to stand!"

Tahruk's roar as he ripped Redahn away from Mahryn had her whimpering, though it was Elenya grabbing Tahruk's raised hand, keeping his fist from connecting with his brother's face that caused her concern to shift from herself to her newfound friend.

"My lady! No!" She wedged herself between Elenya and the scuffling men, lost her balance, and found herself falling to the floor. Elenya squatted to put an arm around her, and both women watched the standoff between the brothers. For the second time during the first day of her stay at Zanak, these two brothers had come to blows over their disagreement as to whether she belonged there or not.

"Stop this!" she demanded, unwinding herself from Elenya's embrace and pushing herself up. She glared at the two men who had, to her surprise, frozen to watch her. She reached a hand out to help Elenya to her feet, and with a deep breath and trembling voice, she spoke quietly to the Lady.

"I'm sorry Lady Sharanis. I should have known to accept this position with you would have put undue hardship on certain relationships within this family." She sent a scathing glare in Redahn's direction, then turned back to speak to Elenya. "I apologize for imposing on your time and want to let you know I am forever indebted to you for your generosity, and for allowing me these few hours to dream my life might yet end up beyond the shadows others have demanded I walk within." Her gaze falling to the floor, she sniffled, unable to contain the tears, even with her eyes closed. "Please, give me a few moments to compose myself and I will gather my belongings…"

"You miserable ass! Get out of my chambers and don't ever disgrace us with your presence again. You are a sorry excuse for a human being."

Tears streaming down her face, her head snapped up at Tahruk's command. She'd expected him to be disgusted with her, but the use of such language…

Only he wasn't looking at her. He was facing his brother, held back only by the gentle urging of Elenya who held tightly to his arm. Several steps across the room, Redahn stood, watching her, his expression unreadable. Without comment, he turned and walked from the room.

Mahryn stared at the spot he'd vacated for several moments filled only with the sound of his footfalls and Tahruk's angered huffs. She shook her head and, closing her eyes, sunk to the floor when her legs gave way.

"Tahruk…" Mahryn heard Elenya urging her husband to go, fully expecting her to go with him. It wasn't until the door closed and Elenya sunk down beside her and pulled her head to rest against her shoulder that she realized, no matter what happened from here on, she had a friend who intended to stick by her.

Chapter 23

Mahryn opted to spend the next few days within the confines of her hosts' wing of Zanak. Her rooms alone were large and lavish, though she'd been given permission to move about without reserve. Her days were filled with time spent in Elenya's company, and during the hours her mistress chose to be alone with her husband, Mahryn enjoyed the outdoors within the safety of their secluded garden. After the... confrontation with Redahn, Tahruk had assigned a corisan to be present whenever he was not. Mahryn was grateful for the corisan's discretion, barely noticing the man whose size rivaled that of these mighty warriors of Zanak. She still doubted he would be much of a match should he come against Redahn. Even with his strength compromised by his injury, she could not see his pride ever allowing him to be bested.

Standing from her seat by the table she'd moved closer to the doors leading out to the garden, she sighed and picked up the tray with the remains of her meal. Elenya and Tahruk had invited her to share her lunch with them, but she'd declined. Too soon, Tahruk would have to return to the training fields, leaving fewer hours for the two of them to spend together. Already, he was away quite often, and only his concerted effort to break away from other duties brought him to Elenya's side every chance he had. Within her home back in Bander, and even living in the Centrehead castle, she hadn't realized the extent of all these warriors did beyond their time on the battlefields. She knew there was plotting and conferring, and of course training to keep the warriors strong, but even while a large majority of the warriors took their leave during the week of the Dremis and the two weeks that followed, the kingdom could not be left unguarded. She thought of the stories Elenya had shared about her own Dremis, three years prior. Not only had Elenya found herself bound to a man whose family was a sworn enemy of her own, but unrest had erupted, taking Tahruk away from her for an extended length of time. That time period and battle were recorded as among the worst in recent history.

Mahryn stepped into the hallway and deposited her tray onto the table outside her door. She smiled at the sound of childish laughter that rang out from the direction of her mistress' room before returning to her own to gather up the toy she'd been working on for little Rennicus. Another thing her mother had given her during their time together beside her grandmother's sickbed was a love of using a needle and thread. While she enjoyed needlepoint work and stitchery, this time, she'd tried her hand at creating a stuffed ship. Next, she intended to toy with a horse, and perhaps a rider to go with it. She placed her hand on her own midsection and her smile faded. Grabbing the ship, she slipped out into the garden. No doubt that's where she'd find her mistress, the nursemaid, and Zanak's next generation. She shook her head, working to shake away the disappointment that carrying Redahn's child would never be a dream that would come true for her. Try as she might, she simply couldn't imagine wanting to be the mother of a child fathered by anyone besides him.

As the first week dragged into the next without incident, Mahryn began to settle into her new life, even beginning to venture out to the family gardens with Tahruk and Elenya most afternoons, at their urging. Nema, the aunt who had created the concoction sent to ease both her head and her stomach the morning after the Dremis Gala, seemed to enjoy sharing with her a love of all things growing. The older woman was showing her a rare rose she was nurturing under a rather ingenious tent devised to protect it once the nights began to cool. That's when Mahryn's world went cold—when Redahn blew into their midst. Her stomach lurched when she heard his voice, and she attempted to remain crouched beside the odd greenhouse contraption to avoid notice.

Only the faintness that came with his presence prevented her success, especially when she found herself falling backwards, taking down a pole holding a potted plant in her wake. The watering bucket that flew from the nearby table when the pole and plant hit it, soaked both her and Nema, and she found herself pulled up by strong arms. The feel of him was almost more than she could bear and she buried her face against the chest she knew intimately, breathing deeply to avoid the threatening tears. *God*! What was wrong with her?

"Let me walk you back to your chambers, my lady," he whispered, his breath tickling her ear.

Mahryn felt her legs go weak. How she wanted to accept his offer, wondering how far that walk back would take them.

But, she couldn't. Shaking her head, she stepped away

from him, willing her legs to keep her upright. Without looking at anyone, and with a mumbled apology to Nema, she turned and fled from the garden.

"I'll be out in a moment. I'm changing," Mahryn called when the knock sounded on her door, hopeful the trembling in her voice wasn't too noticeable. She also hadn't actually begun to remove her wet clothing, but hoped to buy herself a little time with the admission. No such luck, she thought when she sensed more than heard the door opening.

Whirling around, her hands on her hips, she leveled her best glare at the offender. "No," she whispered, her hands going up to cover her mouth as she watched Redahn gently closing the door then turning back to look at her. Why hadn't she slid the lock into place when she'd returned from the gardens?

When Redahn crossed the floor to stand before her, she didn't move. She looked down when he took her hands.

"Look at me, Mahryn," he commanded quietly. She did so, silently cursing the fact that he hid his emotions so well behind his schooled features. *A warrior's mask*, she thought. He'd spent his whole life perfecting skills such as these in order to best his opponents on a field of battle. It was no wonder he was such a perfectly horrid person, considering the future he'd anticipated had been ripped from him.

New tears welled in her eyes and she attempted to look down only to find his hand beneath her chin. As she turned her eyes up to his, the tears began to spill one at a time. He watched one of the droplets trail down her cheek, and when he looked at her mouth and moistened his own lips, she could stand it no more. She closed her eyes when he bent to kiss away a tear that had collected at the corner of her mouth. Something between a moan and a sob broke from her throat and when he covered her mouth with his own, she could do little more than cling to him.

"Tell me to go and I will," he managed to eke out between panted breaths, never stopping the assault on her mouth and face.

Mahryn shook her head and he groaned while moving down to taste the sweetness of her neckline.

"Good," he mumbled against her throat. "I'm not sure I could have."

Mahryn tried to smile, confusion railing her when she felt more tears coming. Clamping her mouth and her eyes closed, she willed them away, wanting nothing more than to savor the moment. Suddenly, it didn't matter whether he was planning to offer her forever or just the here and now, she still wanted him with every fiber of her mixed up being.

Neither of them noticed the outer door to her chamber softly closing, though satisfied Mahryn was not being coerced into doing something she didn't want to do and hopeful this... excursion might cause his brother to come to his senses, Tahruk left the scene that had made even him wax a bit nostalgic. Had it only been three years since his Chosen had come to him and he'd tried to deny his feelings for her? He hadn't had the option of walking away, a *greater cause* having joined them together when she was only three. He couldn't deny the bond formed by having his blood mixture altering her chemistry, but he'd sure tried to refuse to give her his heart. For a day or two, at least. He chuckled to himself as he walked back to the room he shared with her. Even without the marking he wasn't sure he'd have been able to resist Elenya. Either way, there was no denying that he loved her with every fiber of his being… spirit, soul, and body.

Chapter 24

Pushing the door to her bedroom closed with his foot, Redahn settled Mahryn's feet back on the floor. He kept her pulled close, his fingers deftly working the buttons that ran the length of her back while she tugged his shirt free from his pant waist. He had to close his eyes when she ran her fingertips up to his chest beneath the material. He worked faster. Too much still separated them. He had to stop her for a moment when she reached for the button on his britches once she'd managed to free him of his shirt, and he had done the same with her dress. At the rate they were going, he wasn't sure he would last long enough to satisfy her.

He frowned, surprised at how much her pleasure concerned him. Longer than he'd known Mahryn, longer than the occurrence of his wound even, life had always been about him. With a shake of his head, Redahn pushed away all thoughts beyond those of the beauty who stood before him. An involuntary shiver ran through her when he pushed his fingers into her hair. He didn't stop until he firmly cupped her bare bottom in his hands and crushed her against him. Lifting, he pulled her up and she wrapped her legs around his waist. No hesitation. Since the moment he'd kissed her in the outer chamber, there'd been no hesitation. She was his for the taking. She'd always and only been his. Possessiveness took over, and with a primordial growl, he moved them to the bed and softly fell on her, devouring her like a hunter with its prey.

Their first union was fierce, neither of them able to deny the hunger their separation had caused. Like a fine battle, their bodies collided, working at each other until they melded into that peaceful harmony that drove them higher and higher. Redahn fought to hold on while unable to slow his pace. The feminine panting and mewling sounds coming from his partner didn't help, though they did spur him on, knowing she was as close to the edge as he was. When she urged him to go faster, he gave up trying to hold back, his roar of satisfaction echoing through the room when he felt Mahryn's body tighten around him and he met her as their worlds exploded into sated bliss. No moment in time had ever felt as gratifying. Had he not been so consumed with emotion, Redahn might have laughed at himself for thinking if he died right then, he would surely die a happy man.

Staring down into the face of the woman who had so completely consumed him that he'd been unable to find satisfaction with another since she'd come into his life, Redahn frowned. "I haven't changed," he lied, trying to make himself believe his words.

"Shhh." Mahryn shook her head and surprised him by placing her fingers on his mouth.

Neither of them said any more. No promises were made, no futures discussed. They merely shared an evening and a night drifting in and out, enjoying what might very well have been mistaken for love.

Mahryn stretched her arms above her head, a contented sigh accompanying her waking act. She breathed deeply, the scent of the garden floating in, reminding her of another morning and another garden.

Redahn.

She turned, opening her eyes to find herself alone and

her heart quickly plummeting.

No! She chastised herself with a stern reminder that she'd promised to take whatever he was willing to give her and demand no more. Of course that promise was made during the heat of a passionate moment. She'd have done or said anything to have assured what had followed.

Smiling, she inhaled the sweet fragrance. Floral was something she'd never have used in a description of Redahn Sharanis, and yet she'd always associate it with him, especially the distinct scent of fine peach roses. She started and sat up when her eyes came to rest on the simple bouquet lying on the table beside her bed. Peach roses in various shades lay on top of a note with her name scrawled on the front in a hasty man's hand. Mahryn stared at it, pulling her knees up to her chest and wrapping her arms around them. Rocking slightly, she contemplated what it might say. Was Redahn so calloused he would tell her goodbye in a note?

She shook her head. He was a calloused man, but he *had* left a note, taking the time to gather flowers, and obviously placing it where she would see it all upon waking...

"Please be no bearer of bad news," she whispered, grabbing the note and holding it against her heart. Eyes closed, she worked to steady her breathing before folding back the page and peeking through a lash shielded squint to see that he had written his name inside. *His name*. That was *it*. Collapsing against the padded headboard, she closed her eyes, her hands falling limp at her sides, the paper clutched in one fist. *His name*! What was she supposed to make of *that*?

A knock at the garden door of her room had Mahryn nearly jumping through the roof. Her hand back on her heart, she reached for the thicker coverlet as the knock came again and Elenya opened the door and peeked in.

"Good morning! I was hopeful you were up." Her mistress' smile did little to ease the tension caused first by the note and then by Mahryn's immediate apprehension when she realized how blatantly insubordinate she'd been.

"Oh, my lady! I am so sorry..." She leaned toward Elenya with her hand out only to have Elenya wave off her concern.

"Are you kidding? To see Redahn roaming through our garden, whistling whilst he clipped the stems of my favorite roses..."

Mahryn groaned and fell back against the mattress, covering her head with the thick coverlet. She peeked out when Elenya's sweet laughter accompanied the feel of the bed dipping when her mistress sat down.

"You're... not angry with me for shirking my duties? Or for..." Trying to actually phrase what she and Redahn had shared proved too much and once again, Mahryn covered her head and groaned.

"Mahryn! He was actually *whistling*! A not half bad, happy little tune, too. I've *never* seen him like that." She pulled the blanket off Mahryn's head and nodded then laughed at the way Mahryn cocked her head.

"Really?" she asked, her brows popping up toward her hairline when Elenya nodded. "I don't know what to think. I just... I don't... I... Wow!" She couldn't help but smile when Elenya dissolved into a fit of girlish giggling, and it wasn't long before she joined her.

And that's how Redahn found them. Two women— one clothed only in the bed sheets, the other heavy with child—chatting and giggling, though they both stopped to look at him when the hinge on the door squeaked.

Linda Boulanger

"Lord Redahn," Mahryn whispered, pulling the covers higher and tighter. Redahn chuckled. It wasn't as if he didn't know every inch of her luscious body. He looked down the covered length of her, then raised a brow when their eyes met. If the stain growing on her cheeks was any indication, she was remembering too.

"I'm assuming you'd expect no other, my lady," he finally answered. "Though I have to say, *you've* surprised even me, Elenya. I certainly didn't expect to find you here."

Elenya said nothing, just stared back at him while beginning to work to push herself up from the bed.

It was on the tip of Redahn's tongue to make a comment about always knowing Elenya harbored a secret desire to share his bed, but held his tongue for Mahryn's sake.

Pointing a finger, Elenya scoffed at him. "Don't think I don't know what you're thinking, Redahn. I've been around you long enough to practically read your mind." She looked at Mahryn. "I'd tell you to run as fast as you can, Mahryn, though I know firsthand how futile it is. These Sharanis men... once they get in your blood, they're irresistible." Pausing for a moment, Elenya giggled. "In your blood," she repeated, rubbing over the markings not far above her wrist on the inside of her left arm. All *chosen* women had them— a subtle reminder at the injection site where they'd received their future mate's genetic altering blood concoction. "Oh, dear." She rolled her eyes then glared when Redahn did the same.

Mahryn's titter broke the stare and made Elenya smile before she added, "It must be the baby. Be forewarned. These wee things change you. Maybe even more than a marking." She was already turning to go, missing the momentary look of horror that passed across both Mahryn's and Redahn's faces at the mention of children. "Anyway, it looks like Redahn has decided you need sustenance by the look of that laden tray. Be careful. He never gives anything without expecting something in return." She turned at the door and stuck her tongue out at her brother-in-law and had to duck to miss the roll he threw in her direction. "Don't worry about me today. I have a good book..." she called back as she waddled through the door. Moments later, they heard her whistling—a not half bad, happy little tune that grew faint as she moved further away from Mahryn's room.

Redahn sighed loudly and rolled his eyes again before shaking his head and moving to the bed. Carefully settling the tray on the coverlet next to Mahryn, he lowered himself to where he sat facing her on the other side. "That woman has to be the most annoying creature on the face of this earth," he mumbled, "but she is right about one thing." Studying the tray, he finally grabbed one of the lush, ripe strawberries and, bringing it to Mahryn's mouth, he traced her lips with the sweet fruit before pushing it through. Watching her slowly chew it, he swallowed hard and leaned across the tray, his hand on the back of her bare neck coaxing her toward him where he sampled the lingering sweetness. Whether that sweetness was from the fruit or just plain Mahryn, he didn't know. To be honest, he really didn't care. "Eat, my lady," he whispered as he pulled away from his softly panting partner. "You're going to need your strength for what I have planned for you today." His hand trailing down her front solidified his promise.

"Yes, my lord," she answered with a dreamy sigh. No doubt food was no longer the only thing she was hungry for either.

Chapter 25

The next few days settled into her nights filled with Redahn and her days spent with Elenya. Mahryn couldn't remember ever feeling so happy, though she tempered that with a fear that something so wonderful truly couldn't last. It never had in her life. At least in the parts she could remember.

"You're deep in thought today," Elenya interrupted. They'd been sitting in the garden, reading... or rather holding books as they relaxed in the last of the warmer days before the coolness of an approaching winter began to settle in.

Mahryn closed her book and laid it on the table beside her. She breathed deeply and let it out with a sigh before pulling her knees up and wrapping her arms around them.

"I've loved being here with you..."

Elenya stopped moving her legs around on her chaise—a byproduct of the restlessness of latent pregnancy and an imposed sedentary lifestyle. "You're... you're not planning to leave me, are you?"

"No!" Mahryn swung her legs over the side of her own seat. "I'm sorry. I didn't mean to cause you concern."

Elenya laughed and motioned Mahryn to sit back down when she began to rise. "I'm fine, other than being selfish and overly emotional." They both laughed.

"Rightly emotional, perhaps. Though selfish isn't a word I could ever see being associated with you."

Elenya smiled at Mahryn's words and held out her hand. "I'm glad you're here. You've saved my sanity and you salve my ego. That's not a strong trait in the Sharanis men, as you well know by now."

Mahryn chuckled softly, squeezing Elenya's hand before she sighed again. "I'm not sure that's a trait found in many men."

"Are you troubled by Redahn? You've seemed so contented..."

"Oh, no. Redahn is fine. I mean, he's Redahn, of course." Elenya agreed and Mahryn continued. "It's just... Have you ever had that feeling that things were about to change?"

Placing a hand on her swollen belly, Elenya laughed. "Every single day!" Both young women laughed before Elenya sobered and nodded. "I know what you mean. I get that feeling almost every time right before Tahruk gets called back to the battlefields. I never fully understand it until they come and he tells me he has to leave, but I feel it, often days in advance." She squeezed Mahryn's hand again.

Mahryn turned to look off toward the corner of the garden. "There's a cloud about to snub out my sunshine," she whispered. "And I don't know how, or who, or why, but I know it's coming. I feel so defenseless..."

That cloud materialized a few days later when she, Elenya, and Tahruk were making their way back from a slow stroll through the family garden. A ruckus from the hallway that led to the courtyard and Zanak's exit had Tahruk moving his wife behind him and motioning Mahryn to slide in beside her. He lifted his hand and three very large corisans appeared seemingly out of nowhere.

"Do not leave them," he commanded the men before taking several steps toward the hallway.

"I demand to see my daughter!"

"Oh, no," Mahryn whispered.

Tahruk groaned and continued forward to intercept the animated figure who stormed down the hallway toward them. "Lord Tedran," he said, bowing slightly then turning to mouth to one of the corisans to go and get his brother. The man hesitated only a fraction of a second before departing as told. Two more corisans joined them to replace the one, and Mahryn noticed her father was no closer to her than he was moments before. She frowned when three more men joined them and her skin prickled. Tahruk was expecting trouble.

Attempting to peer around Tahruk and the large men who flanked him, she heard her father huff, knew the vein along his temple would be bulging and the top of his ears would be turning a bright pinkish shade of red. "Why are you keeping my daughter from me?" he demanded.

Tahruk clicked his tongue several times in succession. "Hmm. Now, let me see. You somehow found it necessary to storm in with your own guard by your side and barge into our private family quarters instead of asking properly to see your daughter, and I'm supposed to think what, exactly?" Mahryn could see Tahruk's broad shoulders raise and lower. "My guess is you expected to find her alone with my wife. Then what, Lord Tedran? Would you have allowed her to remain or demanded she return to the hell you sentenced her to when you chose to serve her up to the men of Dorengar?"

There was silence, interrupted when her father finally cleared his throat. She still couldn't see him, but knew the look he would be leveling at Tahruk with his next words. She found herself holding her breath when he began to speak. "She is *my* daughter," he ground out. "You have no right..."

"We have every right to invite her into our home as a paid companion. The Court's Ladies are taken into such positions every day. Why not your daughter, Tedran? What has you working so hard to change the rules of the game for her?"

Mahryn cringed at Tahruk's challenge. She started to step forward, to go to her father, when she felt Elenya's hand on her arm. She looked into the green eyes that implored her to remain. With a deep breath, Mahryn attempted to relax, only to find herself tensing up again when she heard the fast-moving footfalls that could only signal Redahn's arrival.

"What's going on here?" A voice boomed, only it wasn't Redahn's. It was Renaine's. Mahryn groaned. The last thing she wanted was to anger the master of the house. There was no doubt by the glare he sent her way when he passed by that he thought her presence in his home was more trouble than it was worth.

Redahn, a few steps behind his father, winked at her when he went by, and even in her agitated state, she couldn't suppress the tingling sensations his look caused to shoot through her.

"Lord Renaine. Beg pardon, but I'd like to know why my daughter has been removed from the castle and brought here to... *take up* with your son without proper commitments being made. I have been informed she has become his mistress. Is this not so?"

"Tedran. Would that you had taken up your grievance through the proper channels, though if you must know, I personally solicited the services of your daughter to act as companion to my son's Chosen during her time of lying-in."

"Then you're denying she is cavorting with your son?"

"*Cavorting*?" Redahn chimed in with a chuckle.

Both Renaine and Tahruk turned to glare at Redahn and he immediately sobered and stepped up to stand beside his brother. His chest out, he drew up to his full height, making him stand out among them all.

"Well?" Tedran demanded. "Are you sleeping with my daughter or are you not?"

"There's not a lot of sleeping going on…"

"Don't toy with me, young man."

"Okay. Are we lovers? Yes. We are."

"Then you will declare for her or return her to the castle at once."

"She is here at my brother's request, not mine."

"I've had enough of this." Tedran moved to push past the men. "Come, Mahryn. I'm taking you home."

"I don't think so, Tedran," Renaine chimed in, moving to stand in his way. From her position, Mahryn couldn't see the brow Renaine lifted, but she could hear the menacing tone in his voice. "You would dare to defy the son of the King's firstborn? It is I who brought her here, so your grievance is with me, not my son."

Mahryn's father was silent for a moment, his tone low and menacing when he began to speak. "You'll be sorry for this. You have chosen the wrong man to stand against."

"Understood," Renaine answered. "Now, if you'll excuse us, we all have *important* business to attend to." Without hesitation, he turned and began to walk away, the trained guardsmen stepping in to close the gap left by his absence.

Mahryn closed her eyes knowing her father would not get any further into the family quarters, at least not during that visit. Even so, a queasy feeling began to grow inside her and was solidified when she heard him call her name from further down the hall.

"Someone will have to pay for your disobedience, you know. Of that, you have my promise." And with that, he was gone.

Sighs of relief sounding around her, Mahryn began to shake. "No," she whispered over and over as she backed up. Hitting the wall behind her, she slid down, crouching much as she had at the garden cottage that first night. Elenya, Redahn, and Tahruk were immediately at her side.

"He's gone," Redahn told her. "You have nothing to fear."

Mahryn looked at him with hollow, sorrowful eyes. "You don't understand what he is capable of."

For just a moment, she was transported back to a dark forest floor. Pulling her knees in, she covered her ears with her hands, trying to block out the screams and laughter. Shaking her head, she bit at her upper lip, trying to hold back the tears that refused to stay dammed. As they began to spill onto her cheeks, she again looked at Redahn. "You have no idea…"

Chapter 26

The nightmares that never seemed to surface while she was in Redahn's arms suddenly refused to stay at bay. That night, after her father's visit, she dreamed of that same cold forest she'd glimpsed in her mind earlier in the day. She was lying on the ground, her hand pressed against her side in a futile attempt to slow the flow of blood. Her dress was torn and muddied, and she ached all over. With nearly unbearable effort, Mahryn had twisted her body and turned her head until she could see the others—two bodies, lying lifeless on the ground not far from her.

Hahna. A tear slid down her face. Her sister had fought off the men who grabbed her and yelled for her to run, to get out and find help. Mahryn had tried. She really had, only part way back to the house, one of them had captured her, galloping up on his horse and scooping her up even as she ran with all her might. She'd been terrified, kicking and screaming and scratching at the arm that held her securely to his side. He'd merely laughed, telling her to keep fighting, that he liked that in his women. Crazy man. Could he not see that she was nothing more than a little girl?

That thought had dissipated when she looked back to see her mother running toward them, yelling at the top of her lungs as she followed them back to the forest. That's when he'd turned his horse around and, with Mahryn dangling helplessly at his side, had circled her mother then run the frantic woman down.

Oh, dear God! Mahryn's blood curdling scream had echoed through the forest, and suddenly there was yelling and action all around. Guardsmen from the house were crossing the open field. The ruthless men badgering her sister released her, and Mahryn screamed again when one picked up a rock. He slammed it against Hahna's head stilling the girl's flailing limbs and cries. Mahryn fell limp as well and that's when the pain had come. Searing, hot fire shot through her middle and she looked down to see the horseman pulling his dagger from her side. Her vision swam as she searched his leering face.

"Why?" she'd mouthed. He answered her with a derisive laugh and dropped her body to the forest floor before he and the other men rode off.

Someone always has to pay. Those words floated around her sleep-laden mind as the bodies in the forest began to multiply, to change. Forcing herself to look again, Mahryn screamed when she realized every one of them was a key member of the house of Zanak.

"Hey," Redahn's voice cut through her ghastly vision. His hands on her shoulders, she felt the gentle shake as he tried to wake her. "It's okay, Mahryn. You're just having a bad dream."

Barely able to see him in the darkness, Mahryn nodded. Somehow, even though she couldn't remember it happening in real life, she knew what she'd just seen had been much more than a bad dream, and things would never be okay. She didn't know how, but she was sure her father had something to do with what had transpired in the forest. And if he could do that to his own daughters and his wife, then what might possibly stop him from coming against a family he cared nothing about, especially since she did? "Why?" she mouthed again into the darkness.

Settled against Redahn's chest, Mahryn didn't expect sleep to find her again, and she certainly hadn't thought she'd find any answers in her dreams, but as she drifted off, the comforts of her old family home surrounded her. Alone, she sat beneath the window outside her mother's sitting room working to finish the needlework piece she'd been sewing on. Her goal was to complete it before her father left. He was going to the Centrehead of Dorengar, back to his position within the King's inner guard.

If she finished the piece in time, they would send it with him as an omen for peace and safety, her mother had told her. She looked down at the image of the golden shield with the thread lion in front of crossed swords emblazoned in its middle. So much time she had put into this piece. So much work, and still it wasn't done. There was so much more to do...

When was he leaving? Two, three days at most? She tried to remember what her mother had told her.

Among the voices of the guardsmen who had run out behind her mother, she heard a woman's cry. She looked at her mother, hopeful, all while knowing it couldn't possibly be her. Looking toward the clearing, she saw the woman running toward them and screaming. Over and over, the woman called her name.

"Mahryn," she called, her voice catching. She nearly stumbled and cried out when she came upon the body of Mahryn's mother. Though the noise she'd made when she saw the other woman was nothing compared to the loud sob that tore from her when she took in the smashed skull and lifeless form that had been Hahna. She went toward the body, then stopped and turned to stare at Mahryn. "Sweetheart," she whispered holding her hand out in

Mahryn's direction. "You're alive. Oh, baby. You're alive."

Mahryn blinked twice, trying to clear the dark spots that had begun to cloud her vision. She wanted to nod her head or raise her hand to the woman approaching her, but the effort was too great.

"Shhh. Be still, love. You'll be okay," the voice cooed, comfortingly familiar in its sing-song patter. Again Mahryn tried to nod only to groan when the slight movement caused the wound at her side to seize. She pressed tighter, her hand seeming a poor barrier for her life-force draining from the gaping hole. "Here," said the voice. "Let me help you."

The pressure exerted from the larger hand wracked her body with another wave of pain, though somehow Mahryn knew it was necessary to save her life. She closed her eyes and sighed before placing her own cold, sticky fingers over the woman's. She feared the effort was too late. She could feel herself slipping into a dark, dense fog and tried one last time to open her eyes to say goodbye. Her vision swimming, Mahryn blinked, closing her eyes tightly between lid lifts in order to squeeze out enough moisture to see. Desperately, she fought to clear her vision.

"I don't want to die alone," she croaked out. "Please, don't leave me alone."

"Be still, love. I'm right here."

A tear slipped out, followed by another one. The woman hadn't told her she wasn't going to die, only that she was there. Looking up at the tree diffused sky, visible now that her eyes were not so dry, Mahryn managed a weak smile. "Thank you," she managed to eke out then sucked in hard when she turned to look at the face of the woman who had tried to save her.

Dara! The woman married to Zanak's gardener. And she stared back at her with the same blue and gold flecked eyes Mahryn had only ever seen in herself and in her father.

"Who are you?" she asked, though before Dara could answer, Mahryn found herself falling through the thick fog and landing in the grass and flowers, just outside the window of her mother's sitting room. She looked down, wondering where the needlepoint piece in her hand had come from. Mindlessly, she poked the needle through the material and then pushed it out again. Pull, push, poke, pull—over and over again. The monotony began to wear on her, carelessness setting in and she poked her finger. Instinctively, she brought her finger to her mouth and sucked then pulled it back out to see the damage that had been done. Blood pooled on her fingertip and she watched, fascinated as the dark, circular shape grew before slowly slipping over the side to land right in the middle of her needlework project.

"Oh no!" The flow of blood increased, forcing her to wrap the cloth tightly around it. After a minute or two, she lifted up the stained material, her heart beating wildly when she realized her blood had smeared across the lion's mouth and along the blade of one sword. *What did it mean*? As she stared at it, she heard the door to her mother's sitting room slam, the thud indicating a forceful closing.

"I'll not discuss this. I already told you she's too young. This is foolishness. Why must you insist on this crazy scheme?"

Mahryn heard her father's unmistakable sigh, knew he was shaking his head before dropping his chin to his chest. "He's offered marriage, Saryn. Just marriage. Where's the madness in that?"

"Just marriage!" The shrillness of her mother's voice hurt her ears. "*She's only twelve years old*! Twelve. Have you even considered what the act of marriage would do to someone her age? She's not ready physically, and she's certainly not ready mentally. I won't have my daughter play any part of this. The conversation is *closed*."

"Then we'll send the older one. Surely a fifteen year old is ready. You were just sixteen…"

Saryn must have leveled a piercing gaze at him because Tedran fell silent. "What have you done, Tedran? It must be pure evil to have you offering up first your own daughter, and then a girl you have no say over. Are you forgetting, Mahryn isn't yours?"

Mahryn isn't yours. The words echoed around Mahryn's head, moving faster and faster until she felt dizzy, felt herself spiraling down a dark tunnel. She didn't fight the blackness as it swallowed her. No, she was thankful for the escape that it provided.

Waking with a start, Mahryn shot up in the bed, gasping and fighting for air. Redahn sat beside her, and after making sure she was okay, tried to comfort her by rubbing her back and whispering soothing words to her.

"Your father's visit?" he questioned.

Mahryn nodded not wanting to go into all the details of what she'd seen in her mind. Unsure of what was fantasy and what had been dredged up from the emotions of her father barging in, she wanted to talk to someone else first. At least she had direction—she would pay a visit to the one person who might have answers. At first light, she would find the wife of Zanak's gardener. Dara.

Please, she prayed as she lay back down next to Redahn, *no matter what it is, I need to know the truth.*

Chapter 27

A loud rapping on Zanak's private training room door caused both Sharanis brothers to turn their heads toward the offending sound. "Enter," Tahruk called out, continuing to press against the arm Redahn held high in the air.

"My lords," the wide-eyed corisan stepped in, then shuffled from foot to foot until Redahn dropped his left arm down and commanded him to speak. "It's the Lady Mahryn. She... she's left Zanak."

"What?" The man shrank back when Redahn stormed across the short distance between them.

Tahruk's hand on his brother's shoulder tempered him. "Who took her out?" he demanded.

The corisan shook his head and stammered, "N... no one, mmm my lord. Sh... she slipped out, alone."

"Bloody hell!" Redahn roared, pushing the corisan aside and taking off at a sprint toward Tahruk's wing of Zanak.

"He's going the wrong way, my lord." The corisan stood rubbing his arm where it had connected with the doorframe.

"She left out the front gate," Tahruk cupped his hands around his mouth and called to his brother.

Without missing a step, Redahn changed direction. At the front gate, he commandeered a horse from a guardsman just arriving and gave him an order to take to his brother. Tahruk scratched his head when he was told Redahn wanted him to gather a guard and meet him at the gardener's cottage. Shrugging, he called for a group of his men to assemble and wait for their horses to be brought around. He wasn't sure what was going on, but he trusted Redahn's judgment. With a sigh and a prayer, he went to gather his arms and to tell Elenya goodbye. He had a feeling this was going to be more than a simple ride across Zanak's outer territory.

Redahn wavered between anger and fear as he galloped at top speed down the roadway toward the gardener's cottage. So many questions ran through his mind, though the only thing that mattered was getting to Mahryn before Tedran's men. He wasn't sure just how he knew they'd been watching, waiting to catch her alone, but he did. What form of derangement would cause a father to harm his own child? Redahn laughed derisively. No, Tedran wasn't even man enough to do such a thing himself. He'd send in hired thugs to do the deed. The thought of what those men might do to Mahryn caused his gut to clinch and he dug his heels into the already flying horse, urging him to move faster still.

The area surrounding the gardener's cottage was heartbreakingly quiet, and even before his feet hit the ground outside the doorstep, Redahn knew Mahryn hadn't made it that far. Still, he burst through the unlocked door, startling Dara and her husband who had just settled in for their lunchtime meal. Both of them jumped to their feet and Dara came to him immediately, her eyes imploring then filling with tears.

"What has happened to her, Redahn?" she asked, taking his hand in hers.

Redahn stared down at Dara, his eyes rounded. "How did you know..." His words trailed off. Squinting, he took

Dara's chin in his hand and turned her face toward the light. How had he missed it before? Her eyes... they were the same peculiar shade of blue with gold flecks. Much like Mahryn's, only perhaps not as pronounced.

"Please," Dara whispered. "Go now. Go and find her."

Redahn nodded. "Where, Dara?"

The older woman lowered her head for just a moment, her eyes closed in thought. "Bander," she said at last. "Though I'm not sure that's where he'll stop. The men... those from her past... they were from the house of Voringlok."

Audible gasps were heard from both Redahn and her husband. "Thank you, Dara." He turned to the older man. "Someone should alert the King that treachery is at hand."

"Yes, my lord. Godspeed, lad." The two men clasped arms before Redahn turned to leave.

"Please tell my brother what you have told me," he implored them after they'd followed him out and watched him mount the borrowed horse. When Dara's husband asked him to wait, he had to temper his annoyance, especially when the older man ducked back inside. It was only when he returned with a sheathed sword that Redahn grew thankful. A fist to his heart, he saluted them with a slight bow of his head, then whirled the horse around and dug his heels into the animal's fleshy sides. He wished he had time to find the place where the men had grabbed Mahryn, to confirm they were, indeed, headed in the direction of Voringlok's Keep. But his instincts told him to ride, that the only way to save her was to intercept them and take them by surprise. God help him if he was wrong. God help them both.

Linda Boulanger

- - 191 - -

Chapter 28

The hooves of the warhorse sending clods of dirt flying behind them, Redahn kept his eyes forward. He didn't have time for covert maneuvers, choosing instead to slip to the little known trail on the other side of a tree-lined barrier from the more commonly followed path. It was a perk of living and training in these areas for so many years. Voringlok's men would care very little about remaining unseen now that they were outside the Centrehead, and Redahn knew he would lose the advantage of knowing the land the further North they traveled.

Redahn's lips curled into a snarl. What was Tedran doing getting mixed up with the likes of Voringlok? Whatever his game was, it went well beyond his disdain for his daughter. Voringlok was a power hungry bunch, lording over the northernmost part of the Land of Riandus. Their leader called himself a king, though Redahn would have placed them well below the vagabonds who ruled their own land given to them by his cousin, King Travensworth of Corigan. Teeth grinding together, he pushed the horse harder, wondering just how badly Voringlok's men, with the help of Tedran, had infiltrated Dorengar's ranks? And how did Mahryn fit into this game? That latter part was his true concern, at least for now. He had to get to her before nightfall. If he didn't... he couldn't allow himself to think what those savages would do to her.

Chest down, head up, he slackened his hold on the

reins, allowing the horse to set its own pace. The animal still flew, and would continue to do so for some distance. These beasts were bred for endurance, though even with their superior genetics, Redahn knew he'd have to find water for both of them and allow for a few minutes rest before long. Would that he had his own horse so he would know exactly how much the mount could handle. Time had not allowed for that either. He didn't care. He'd run if he had to in order to get to Mahryn.

He laughed at himself. The heart certainly had no problem sending its captives on fool's missions. Yes, he now knew for certain he had a heart, because it was surely breaking at the thought of losing the only woman he had ever fallen in love with.

Fallen in love? He laughed again, shaking his head. Damn, if his brother wasn't right. Double damn if it didn't feel good to finally stop pretending.

Another hour passed before he felt a change in the big horse's pace. Redahn would need to find a watering hole and a place for them to rest soon. Looking toward the distant treetops, it took only a moment to find the signs he'd been searching for. A dip in the trees and an increase in the bird's native to the area lakes flying overhead told him that's where he'd find their water. With a slight tug, he pulled back on the reins, letting the horse know he was, once again, in control. Within a few feet of the clearing, Redahn steered them off the path, knowing they may not be the only ones needing to refresh. He muttered a silent prayer of thanks when they stumbled across a small stream trickling away from the main body of water while still within the cover of the trees.

He tethered the horse where it could rest and drink freely before helping himself to the cool water. Gulping it down, he satisfied his thirst, then splashed the refreshing liquid over his face and hair. The temperature of the water, and even the air, told him they had already traveled much farther north than he'd thought.

With a last sip and a quick check to make certain the horse was secure, he began to follow the stream toward the main body of water, his ears and senses alert. Movement to the left had him freezing, then breathing out a near silent sigh. Deer. Four or five of them moved away from the lake. They moved as slowly as he did, the large buck merely glancing in his direction before continuing to lead his small herd away. Redahn surmised their lack of concern was most probably an indication that they were alone at the watering hole.

Stopping at the tree line, Redahn searched the perimeter of the lake. He saw no one, no sign. Except... His frowned as the sun caught something shiny a ways down the shore. He moved among the trees until he was parallel with the spot he thought he'd seen something. Continuing to scan the area, he moved out to grab the item. His heart soared while his stomach plummeted. It was the gold comb Mahryn had been wearing in her hair that morning. He'd watched her twist her gold-brown hair to the top of her head and secure it with a few pins and that very comb. And then he'd kissed her neck and breathed in her scent, and she'd told him the comb had been her mothers. His heart joined his stomach. There was no way she'd willingly part with it.

Clamping his mouth tight, he slipped the comb into the pouch at his waist and stooped down to study the tracks that surrounded him. How many? Five. Six at the most, not including Mahryn's. Six men, and no sign of struggle. He held onto that as he made his way back to his horse, though he was still troubled by one thing. The hoof prints led away in a direction other than the one he'd been expecting. Why would they be moving west? What would prompt these men to go into Warik territory? They'd have to move fast to get through there before nightfall.

Warik was a strip of land rich in game, but overran with criminals and vagabonds. While the vagabonds were manageable by day, thanks in part to a pact between them and Corigan's king, the criminals seemed to multiply in numbers at night, making it a place unsafe for anyone. Redahn had often thought it was too bad no one had been able to claim it, but he also knew it was a near impossibility to defend. And now he was headed into it.

He looked up as he untied the horse. Three more hours of daylight, maybe a little less. He walked them toward the lake's shore while digging into the saddlebag, hopeful the beast's owner had packed it full of the mandatory, standard gear. Relief came when he found what he was looking for.

Close to where he'd found Mahryn's comb, he placed several markers, then formed an arrow in the sandy sludge that pointed northwest. He closed his eyes for a second, offering yet another prayer that his brother would come this way. Even Redahn was smart enough to know Warik was no place to get stuck without reinforcements.

An hour or so in, Redahn pulled his mount to an abrupt halt, stopping to listen. He'd done this every so often since entering Warik, though it wasn't until now that he'd felt that familiar prickle. He patted the slathered neck when the horse tossed his head, his ears twitching, nostrils flaring. Whatever it was, they both sensed it.

"Easy, boy," he whispered to the horse, then fished a sugared cube out of the saddlebag and pushed it into the velvet-lined mouth. Loosely securing the mount's reins to a tree, he slipped away, moving toward the faint sounds that floated through the forest.

There! One, two, three... four. Depending on their number, one or two of them would be standing guard. He'd bank on two, and guessing from the narrowness of this section of the trail where they'd stopped, he'd put his money on them being a ways down at either end. Heart hammering, he watched as one of the men moved toward Mahryn. He was surprised to see her untied, though not at all surprised when she slapped away the hand that tried to press food to her lips. The man growled, and said something to her about keeping her strength up for what they had planned for her later. Redahn felt a surge of bile forcing its way to his throat, especially when she said something in return and the man grabbed her face in a vice-like grip, forcing her to look in his direction.

Patience, he thought. He'd be no good to her at all if he hurried in and found himself dead. But all that went by the wayside when the man attempted to kiss her, his hand working its way into the folds of her already torn skirt. In a flash, he burst from the woods, his sword unsheathed as he ran. Catching them off guard, it was easy enough to separate the head of Mahryn's offender from its neck, though that brought the other two to full alert.

"Mahryn. Go!" he yelled at her, tossing his head in the direction of his horse as he fought with the other two men. If he couldn't get them before the others returned... It was too late. They must not have been as far away as he'd thought, because one of them intercepted Mahryn. And from the other direction came not one, but five men.

The man he held at the point of his sword began to laugh and placed his hand on the blade. He raised a brow when he attempted to push it away and Redahn kept it, increasing the pressure on his jugular by a fraction.

"Lord Redahn. Why, I'm surprised. I guess the rumors of your feelings for this girl are true." He laughed again, the hollowness sending a chill down Redahn's spine. "I'll enjoy watching you while you watch my men enjoying her this evening."

Redahn tensed, his snarled growl having no more effect on the scumbag than did the point of his sword.

The man shrugged. "Kill me, and they kill the girl. And then you." He smiled and whispered, "Either way you lose."

Redahn still didn't budge, his battle instincts telling him someone was about to make a mistake. Whether it was going to be him or one of these men, he didn't quite know.

"Bring her," the man at the end of his sword commanded, and Redahn watched out of his peripheral until Mahryn and her captor stood to the side and a few steps back from his captive. The man in charge lifted a finger and the dagger blade pressed more firmly against Mahryn's throat. She sucked in a shaky breath, but didn't cry out. Redahn could feel her eyes on him, piercing him, waiting... He couldn't look at her, didn't dare. He needed his wits about him.

"Your sword for his, my lord."

Redahn narrowed his eyes. Did this man think him an idiot? He countered with a question. "Who are you working for?" he demanded, actually firming his grip when the main failed to answer. He saw Mahryn stiffen and knew the man holding her had also increased the pressure on her neck.

How much could her delicate skin take? Something had to happen, and fast.

With a loud sigh, the man in charge tsked at him. "I grow tired of your game, already…"

"As do I!" Redahn spat, ducking to avoid the man who had attempted to sneak up behind him. With a booted foot, he kicked the man's feet out from under him and rolled to a squat before pouncing on the second man who had joined in. That's when he saw his moment, when the man holding the dagger dropped his hand from Mahryn's neck to move her away from the action. He sprung like a panther, taking out two of the enemy's men when he grabbed them and clanked their heads together. Kicking back, he downed a third, and then ignored the others as he pursued Mahryn and her captor who dragged her struggling form to the far side of the path.

As he darted forward, his arms around her waist, he heard the caustic laughter of the leader and his few remaining men. It was the sound of victory.

It was also the last sound he heard as he and Mahryn crashed through the deceivingly small span of shrubs and tumbled over a cliff toward the treetops below. At least he had saved her from those men. He only hoped Mahryn would understand that his final act was one of pure love. God, how he wished he had told her…

Chapter 29

When Mahryn's world stopped spinning, she waited a few moments before opening her eyes. She may never release her hold on the man who'd held her tightly against him, shielding her body with his own as best as he could while they tumbled down the rocky cliff side. There was no doubt she'd have her share of scrapes and bruises, though they'd be minimal compared to his.

With that thought came a stomach-dropping rush of concern, especially when she realized he still hadn't moved.

"My lord?" she whispered. "Redahn?" She unwound herself from his hold and pushed herself up into a sitting position so that she could see him. "Oh. My lord..." Silent tears took the place of her words as she took in the mass and depth of his many scrapes. One wound in particular garnering her attention. Unable to blink back the unwanted tears, she rose to her knees, and reached up to wipe away some of the blood that was amassed around a rather nasty looking gash just above his temple.

Laying her head against his chest, Mahryn allowed grief to consume her, finding comfort at last in the steady thrumming of his heartbeat.

Mahryn froze, holding her breath while she listened to make sure she was hearing what she thought she was. Yes! Relief had her back up on her knees, her hands poised at his shoulders, ready to shake him, though she stopped herself just in time, common sense whispering that any movement when his injuries were obviously so bad could be even more detrimental. Leaning down, her mouth close to his ear, Mahryn whispered his name. There was no response. "My lord. You must wake up," she told him, her voice only slightly louder than it was before. "Redahn…"

Again, her words died on her lips and she lifted her head, straining to hear. Riders were approaching. She could hear the pounding of the horses' hooves growing louder by the second. Any moment, they would pass by or… They stopped. Right below the ledge where they lay.

Mahryn looked back at Redahn. Even though he hadn't moved at all, she slowly lifted her hand and placed it over his mouth before daring a glance down through the trees to the rider's path below. Gratitude washed over her. How thankful she was that they'd landed on this small ledge when they fell and that the ledge was at least partially obscured by the treetops.

Barely breathing, she listened, not fully recognizing the dialect of the men conversing below. She stared off, looking beyond the treetops. She'd heard that particular vernacular before. But when?

While her mind struggled to place it, she continued to listen, able to catch only bits and pieces of what they said to one another. Though, the last part came to her loud and clear.

"There be no way they could survive a fall like that, mate."

One of the men cleared his throat and spit, forcing Mahryn to suppress a gag.

"If we be wrong, Venderlay will have our heads, he will. And if not him, then Tedran. You remember what happened to those men who failed to get the chit back when she were barely out of diapers?"

Mahryn struggled to breathe, their words acting as a vice around her middle, cutting off her air. Her father? Her heart refused to lay hold of the treacherous ideas their words were forming in her mind. There was no way... and yet they knew of that other time...

"I agree with Giand," came yet another voice. This one she recognized from the men who had abducted her from the forest. "And if they're not yet dead, they will be. There be no way to tumble down that hill and still have the strength, or even the body parts, to fight their way all the way back to Zanak from the middle of Warik. I admit his lordship possessed great fortitude." Mahryn heard the men agreeing, found herself nodding her own head. "But should he live, he has to be greatly wounded. With the smell of death on him, the wild animals in these parts will quickly pick him to shreds, and if not... nightfall is fast approaching." They all laughed and she heard the murmurs of agreement.

"And what of the girl?" came a voice, smoother than the rest. She recognized him as the leader and the others silenced immediately once he spoke. "It seems unlikely she would have survived, though she looks to have a streak of luck surrounding her. One would not have expected her to survive the last time. The others didn't."

"Little chit seems to have thrived too. She be quite pleasant, to the eye at least. I would have enjoyed teaching her things that lord of hers surely hadn't." If her stomach hadn't already been churning, Mahryn was sure it would have with his last words.

"Ya. We could've all enjoyed her fer ourselves fer a few days afore shuttin' her up fer good." The men laughed, their comments turning raucous. She could hear them clapping each other on the backs and arms while they enjoyed their nasty talk at her expense.

"Brood of swine." The leader's voice barked out over the rest. "You wouldn't know how to bed a lady who doesn't smell like a used up whore. Now stop your yapping and let's ride out. We have to make it back to camp before nightfall ourselves and we've lost valuable time with all this diversion. Continue to keep your eyes and ears sharp," he commanded them just before she heard the unmistakable squeaking of men in saddles and boots against the flesh of their horses' flanks. Thunder ensued only to be quickly replaced with silence.

She looked down at her lover. Redahn had saved her. Now she needed to save him. But how? Frustrated, she laid her head back on his chest and tried to think.

"Psstt"

Mahryn's eyes fluttered. Despair was making her hear things. She'd thought she'd heard…

"My lady," the voice whispered from below. Not just any voice. This one belonged to a woman. "My lady." The woman's voice was louder, more insistent this time, and Mahryn decided to take the chance. Without help, there was very little hope of getting Redahn down. She maneuvered to where she could peer over without falling from the edge of the tiny ledge that barely held both of their bodies.

"Oh, thank God." The woman covered her heart with her hand. "I was beginning to think you hadn't survived. And what of Lord Redahn?"

Mahryn sucked in hard, the breath almost choking her. Her forehead tightly scrunched, she stared at the woman strangely dressed in a tightly cropped jacket and… man's britches. How did she know about them, know Redahn's name? "Who are you?" Mahryn whispered, wondering whether she had a choice in trusting her or not.

The woman's musical laugh floated up to them. "Forgive me for forgetting you would not know me, my lady." She swept into a low bow, her arm slicing through the air to curl about her own waist. "Christiana Durant, at your service." She stood up and pushed her straight, dark hair back behind her shoulders and looked up.

Mahryn still had no idea who she was, but her demeanor was friendly. She also knew she had little chance without help.

The woman turned to signal a group of men who had remained quietly in the shadow of the trees and they began to position themselves around the ground below the ledge, Christiana called up to Mahryn. "We need to get you down. How are you at climbing, my lady?"

"I'm quite sure I am better at falling," Mahryn answered, causing the woman and her men to laugh. She tried to smile and jumped when a rope swung down from above.

"My men will lower you down, though I suggest you push off against the wall with your feet, if you're able, to avoid additional scrapes from the brush and rocks."

Mahryn nodded then turned to look at Redahn. "What of Lord Redahn? He hasn't moved since…" Her voice broke and she had to take several deep breaths to regain some semblance of control.

"Once we have you safely out of the way, we'll lower down a stretcher and a man and they'll bring him down. Then we can assess how bad his injuries are before taking you both back to my cottage." When Mahryn didn't answer, Christiana added, "Does that make sense to you?" Mahryn nodded and, after she'd tied the rope around her waist as Christiana directed, the men slowly lowered her back to solid ground.

Even before the rope was untied, Mahryn had turned her attention to Redahn's rescue. She looked up to see a man now dangling above the ledge and watched as they lowered the stretcher before he moved into position to secure Redahn. Mahryn looked around feeling her world spinning as she contemplated the likelihood of them landing in that exact spot. The odds were astronomically improbable. It was so small.

Nausea engulfed her and Mahryn crossed her arms over her stomach, clinching tightly for a moment before illness won out. She turned and hobbled as quickly as she could toward a large tree just a few feet away and ducked behind it just in time for her stomach to relieve itself of its contents. There wasn't much. She hadn't eaten anything since breakfast, and even that had been light. She'd felt unsettled then as well, blaming it on her father's visit and the dreams. She stood, surprised to see Christiana beside her. Concern wrought the beautiful woman's features. "I'm fine," Mahryn eked out, then gratefully accepted the silken kerchief held in the extended, sun-bronzed hand.

"Come, my lady. They have him safely down and we need to be out of here before nightfall. Once the sun fades, even for me, these woods aren't safe." Christiana looked around. "We'll have to hurry as it is."

Mahryn scarcely heard her words, pushing past her and limping to the stretcher that held Redahn. A sob broke from her when she realized he was still unmoving.

She felt hands on her shoulders, and again found Christiana beside her. "He responds to touch in his extremities and torso. Once we get him to the cottage, we can apply cool compresses to his head. Other than his arm, and perhaps an ankle, it appears nothing more is broken, though we can't be sure of that. Mikail didn't think any of his ribs had snapped. That's definitely good."

Mahryn nodded and allowed herself to be lifted. She momentarily lost her bearings before she realized she was being dragged up into a saddle, a man's strong arms closing around her. Panic seized her for a moment and she thought to fight him, then remembered these were the people trying to help them. At least she hoped they were. At the very least, they had removed them from the ledge. She glanced up at it one last time, then back to where Christiana was supervising her men as they secured Redahn's stretcher between two horses. She'd never seen such a contraption and blanched at the thought of his body pressed between the two beasts. She quickly capitulated. What choice did they have? Christiana had said they needed to move quickly, and surely this would be easier on him than his stretcher being dragged behind. She felt a surge of awe as she watched Christiana climb into the saddle of one of the stretcher bearing horses. One of the smaller men climbed onto the other, no doubt to lessen the overall load of the two animals. With a silent prayer, she closed her eyes and let her head fall against the man who held her. Never before could she ever remember feeling so completely exhausted. Never would she ever have thought she could fall asleep in such a situation, but she did.

Chapter 30

Christiana's home was no cottage. It appeared to be the summer palace used by the wife of the former King of Corigan as indicated by its double walled grandeur and markings. Though Mahryn had awakened long before they crossed through the crested inner gates, she still had no idea who Christiana was, but she was definitely someone. She supposed she'd find out in time. For now, she was too weary to worry about anything but Redahn.

No sooner had they dismounted than another band of horsemen came through the gates. Her eyes wide, Mahryn sought Redahn and went to his side knowing her actions were silly since it wasn't like she could actually protect him. Watching the riders, surprise punched through her when she realized it was Tahruk, the relief weakening her already tender knees. She barely managed a weak smile and slight head bob before she felt herself going down. Her last thought was that this just hadn't been her day.

Hours later, Mahryn's eyes opened slowly to take in a richly decorated room which she assumed was inside the summer palace. Her body ached and pain sliced through her when she tried to move. Only her need to see how Redahn had fared kept her from snuggling back into the silk cocoon.

With a groan, she pulled herself free of the bed and limped across the room, thankful someone had left a small candle burning on a table near the doorway. Picking it up, she reached for the door handle and slowly turned it. Opening the door just a crack, she peeked out, expecting to see a darkened hallway. Instead, lamps had been lit along the corridor, and a woman sat dozing in a chair across from her room. Mahryn frowned. The small size of the woman told her she wasn't under guard. What then? She wished her mind wasn't so foggy.

The woman jerked awake when Mahryn stepped out of the room. She jumped to her feet and curtsied, her lips turning up as she rose. "My lady. You're awake." She stated the obvious to Mahryn who continued to stare at her, trying to make sense of everything. A pretty lass with long, golden hair and a bright countenance, she was much younger than Mahryn had first thought, at least two years younger than herself, if not more. She seemed confused by Mahryn's confusion, and bobbed again before continuing. "My mistress has asked that I take you to his lordship should you arise." The girl beamed when Mahryn nodded her head and she motioned in the direction they would be going, resuming the position of two steps back on the right side that was customary for the common and the royal. They walked but a few steps before she moved up to Mahryn's side. She'd been trained, Mahryn thought, though obviously her mistress didn't follow strict protocol. Mahryn was glad, actually. She'd never taken to the idea that some individuals were above or beneath others and she certainly wasn't one deserving of a place of honor. Who was she besides a common Court whore?

The thought caused her gut to knot and she crossed her arms over herself, the pressure helping to tamp down the roiling inside. *I just need to see Redahn*, she thought. Once she knew he was okay, she'd be all right.

"Your mistress… will you alert her at first waking that I am with his lordship?" Maybe talking would pull her mind from her distress.

When the girl shook her head, Mahryn cocked her head and frowned, causing the young lady to cover her mouth to suppress a chuckle. "There be no need, my lady. My mistress has remained with his lordship." Mahryn's frown had her rushing on. "The brother is there as well. And the King."

"The King?" Mahryn touched her temple. None of this was making sense. Did the King arrive with Tahruk? Fear gnawed at her. There must be more going on than she realized since the old King never went far from his castle anymore. She knew he visited Elenya at Zanak from time to time, but she doubted he went much further. Why was he here?

"The King of Corigan, my lady. He is… You do know he's the cousin of these brothers of Zanak?" They had stopped outside a door on the lower floor after a painstaking decent, and the girl's hand on the handle had Mahryn's mind whirling at top speed to process that thought. Yes, it was all coming back to her. Renaine's wife was the daughter of the sister to Corigan's current King's deceased father. So, technically, Neria was the cousin, and the men within the room were second cousins.

"And Christiana is… the King's sister?" Mahryn whispered right before the girl turned the handle. The young cheeks turning a light shade of red, the girl paused and shook her head.

"No, my lady," she whispered back. "My mistress… she is his mistress."

It took a split second for Mahryn's brain to decipher the two meanings of the word mistress, though she had enough time to school her features before the door swung open. She was thankful, especially when three sets of eyes turned on her, even before she had stepped over the threshold. They all stood and Tahruk came toward her. He held out a hand and she took it. Looking up into his wearied face, she noted the whispered tones in the room and tears sprang into her eyes.

"Is he... is he not all right?" She could barely choke out the words.

"Mahryn?"

Her name croaked from across the room had her pushing past the strong mass of Tahruk's body and moving as quickly as her battered limbs would allow. She fell to sore knees on the stool at Redahn's bedside.

"Hey," he whispered again, slowly lifting a hand to thumb away one of many tears that streamed, unchecked, across her cheeks. His hand remained against her face, and she rubbed her cheek against it. Her own, small hands encircling his wrist, she turned to kiss his palm. He smiled and groaned. His eyes fluttering as he labored to breathe. "They told me you were resting."

"I was," she whispered. "But I needed to see you. Oh, my lord. I am so, so sorry."

"Shhh." Before he could say more, a fit of coughing wracked him and Mahryn had to move back while Tahruk and another man lifted him slightly. When they moved away, he held his hand out and she went back to him. He looked awful. His face was scraped and bruised and a layer of compresses covered his forehead and the top of his temple. His right arm was held firmly to his side, undoubtedly broken. Mahryn's heart plummeted. It was his sword arm. Again. She reached for the sheet that had slipped down when they'd lifted him, and pulled it up over his bare torso. He grabbed her hand and held it to his heart. He smiled. "My heart's still beating. That's what is most important."

Mahryn smiled and leaned in to kiss the spot above where their hands lay. He moaned and she pulled back, concerned she'd hurt him. He was grinning at her, staring at her through half closed lids.

"My lips could use your healing touch as well, my lady."

Everyone in the room laughed.

"That man will be looking for your touch on his deathbed, I fear," Tahruk joked.

"But that is not today," Redahn confirmed, placing his hand on the back of her neck and coaxing her to where he could brush his lips against hers. "This is not my deathbed. I can assure you of that."

Tears again welled in Mahryn's eyes and Redahn frowned, grimacing at the effort. She blinked them back, cursing herself for her weakened emotional state. How many years after Hahna's death had she refused to cry? And now...

"I promise you, I'll be okay," he whispered to her before devouring her lips in a kiss that sealed his words.

A knock on the door had Mahryn reluctantly pulling away, her heart pounding when a breathless man stumbled into the room. He bowed at the King, who she latently realized she'd yet to properly address, then the man moved toward the house mistress. Christiana bid him to speak and he alerted them that the inner gates had been closed to a group of riders that included a man claiming to be a Lord Tedran from Dorengar. Mahryn stiffened at her father's

Linda Boulanger

name. She closed her eyes. He wasn't going to stop until he had what he wanted. The others may not understand, but she knew that about him. Anger flashed through her and, ignoring her battered body's protest, she pushed herself up from Redahn's bedside like a coiled snake leaping to strike.

"What are you doing?" Tahruk broke away from the group where he was conferring with Christiana, the King, and a handful of other men, and caught her by the arm just before she reached the door. She attempted to jerk away, flinching when his grip tightened.

Her eyes flashed with the anger she felt toward her father. She glared up at him and then at the others in the room, avoiding eye contact with Redahn, who was now being held down by his cousin.

"I have to go," she hissed. "Don't you see? There's no other way."

Tahruk shook his head and spoke quietly. "If you go, he has won already."

The seconds seemed like hours before she finally forced herself to relax. Dropping her chin to her chest, she shook her head. The reality was that her father's victory had been sealed years ago. "Fine," she said, her head snapping up. "But I need to see him. I need to know why."

"It may be unpleasant. He won't have come through the gates alone or unarmed... there may be bloodshed." He had grasped her shoulders, forcing her to look at him. His face sobered as he stared back, making sure she understood that he didn't intend the blood to be theirs.

A hollow laugh tore from her. "Would that it could be me that plunged the dagger," she ground out before wrenching herself from his hold and turning toward the door.

"Tahruk!" Redahn's voice stopped her and they all

looked at him. "Remember the tunnels and Elenya?" Mahryn had heard of Redahn risking his life to save Elenya from a would-be kidnapper several years back. She watched as Tahruk nodded his head, certain the look that passed between these two brothers held more words than anything either of them could say. Redahn returned the nod, the effort causing him to groan. "I'm counting on you to keep her safe." He concluded his statement by placing the fist of his good arm over his heart. Mahryn's own heart ached at the scrapes and bruises that covered him. Turning back to Tahruk, she noticed he had done the same thing—his fisted hand momentarily touched his chest before he reached for the door handle.

Christiana and the King fell in behind them, though King Garrick stopped to give orders to a handful of men who occupied an alcove just outside the room. She hadn't noticed them or the alcove before when she'd come down from the upper level. She paid them no heed, other than to notice they scattered in different directions. She also saw the young woman who had escorted her earlier slipping in the door to Redahn's room. A momentary pang hit her. Jealousy? She had no right to that emotion where Redahn was concerned. It wasn't as if he'd professed his undying love for her. He'd saved her life, just like he'd saved Elenya. It was what he did.

She felt the delicate touch of a woman's hand on her arm and looked to see that Christiana had moved up beside her, all of them having to rein in the desire to move quickly in order to accommodate Mahryn's slower pace. Her body protested the movement as it was. Unable to muster a smile, she nodded at the woman who had saved her and Redahn, and fleetingly wondered how old she was. Her years couldn't be too many beyond her own, and yet she held a wisdom in her eyes, in the way she walked and carried herself, that said she knew far more about the world than most people three times her age. Her confidence gave her a regal air that added to her beauty. No wonder the King had fallen in love with her, royal blood or not.

The trio, flanked by a force of a dozen or so men, stepped through a side gate and worked their way around to a section between the walls that opened into an outer courtyard garden. She saw her father waiting with a group of his own men, his numbers nearly doubling their own. Mahryn's heart, hammering beneath the bodice of her dress, plummeted at the odds. She questioned whether anyone really knew what they were doing. Surely they were stepping into a slaughter.

Movement on the wall above and in the bushes beyond caught her eye, causing her brows and her spirit to rise. Maybe she'd misjudged.

"School your features, my lady," Tahruk whispered. "They must surely know we have an advantage, though they are not yet sure exactly what." A silence followed before he added, "Don't help them."

Mahryn barely bobbed her head to confirm and turned to look toward the man who may have conceived her, but certainly had never been a true father, and suddenly her mother's words from her dream rang in her head. *Are you forgetting, Mahryn isn't yours?* She felt herself sway and had to force the dizziness away.

Tahruk positioned himself in the center of a handful of his men. They moved forward after he motioned for Mahryn to stay back with Christiana and the King. Another group of warriors closed ranks behind him and Mahryn grimaced, feeling another surge of threatening bile.

"Lord Tahruk. I suppose I should be surprised to see you here, though somehow I am not."

Mahryn cringed at the tone of superiority her father used with Tahruk, hated the way he always saw himself as better or above those around him.

Tahruk snorted, answering with his own question. "The better question is why are *you* here, Tedran?"

The older man flinched at the obvious snub given by using only his name. Mahryn watched his lips thin before he drew in a deep, uneven breath and, giving Tahruk a scathing glare, pulled himself taller. He looked past the men to where she stood near the wall, and she sunk back deeper into its shadows when his mouth curled up into what was intended to be a smile. She saw him look past her. Had she imagined him rolling his eyes?

"Isn't. This. Touching. The brothers of Zanak, gathered on the doorstep of Corigan's whore to protect *my* daughter."

Mahryn recoiled, disgusted by her father's words. She frowned, unable to understand Christiana's response. The other woman just chuckled and put out her hand to keep King Garrick from moving forward. She winked at Mahryn and whispered that they should wait to see how things played out. Was it to their advantage for her father to believe the King was Redahn? Being Tedran's daughter, she would have thought herself better at these games, though what sport was there when the lives of others were at stake?

"I ask you again, Tedran. Why have you come? You've been remiss to leave *your* King's side for some time now and yet... here you are. And how quickly you must have departed after word of your daughter's abduction reached the castle walls, it's almost as if you knew beforehand... One would have thought you would have left such matters to Dorengar's fighting men. Surely you had faith that we would bring her home safely."

Tedran remained silent for a moment and then shrugged, his face masked in indifference. "The how and why don't really matter. The facts speak for themselves and you have something that belongs to me. I want her back."

Tahruk's laughter that rang in the courtyard garden was hollow and mocking. "Just like that? You expect us to hand her over so that you can do what? Return her to the very men who my brother risked his life to save her from?"

Mahryn felt lightheaded. She slowly let out the breath she'd been holding.

Looking from Tahruk, his eyes skimming over Mahryn to land on the man he believed to be Redahn and then back to Tahruk, her father shrugged again. "She's *my* daughter. I will do with her as I please."

"Really?"

Mahryn wished she could see Tahruk's face. His voice, his inflection even in a single word, denoted power.

"You're wrong, Tedran," he countered. "You resigned that right when you sent her into the den of the Dremis Maidens. Her life is no longer yours. The Courts alone have the ability to make choices for her. And currently, they have put her under *my* father's authority. Not yours."

Closing her eyes, Mahryn leaned back against the wall, a surge of thankfulness shooting through her.

Until Tedran threw back his head and laughed. "You must believe me a fool, boy," he practically snarled.

A ripple of tense disbelief ran through the men opposing her father at the insolence thrown at their leader. Mahryn saw several hands go to sword hilts, though no one acted beyond readiness. Her father laughed again, making her shiver.

A moment of silence followed without Mahryn hearing

it. The sound of her own blood rushing through her body filled her ears and she grabbed her head before sinking to the ground. Visions swirled behind her eyes—her and her sister stumbling upon the men camped in the forest across the meadow. "No. No," she repeated, pushing away from Christiana who had squatted down beside her to offer comfort.

A toe-curling scream from behind Tahruk's men had them unsheathing their swords, momentary confusion parting their ranks and allowing Mahryn to storm through them. Garrick's warning to his cousin allowed Tahruk to grab the distraught woman before she could break free and cross the distance to where her father's men, who also stood with swords at attention, surely would have cut her down.

"Murderer!" she screeched, her eyes never leaving her father's face. "You killed them. As surely as if your hand had guided a sword into their hearts, you killed my sister and my mother."

"Don't point the blame in my direction, Daughter. It wasn't my idea to go into the forest that day. Whose was it? Yours? Yes, I see," he sneered when she recoiled against Tahruk. "You knew better than to leave the safety of the boundary wall and yet you went, sneaking out through the secret garden entrance. Had you not, the men would have come in the night and taken Mahryn. She would have been alive, and you and your mother would have been safe."

Murmurs ran through the crowd. Mahryn shook her head. "You are a madman. Have you no eyes? *I* am Mahryn!"

"Foolish girl. Have you not yet figured it out? You have no sister." He paused, letting his words sink in. "I did send a maiden to the Dremis. A maiden by the name of Mahryn Farling. A maiden who no longer exists, not my daughter."

"How can that be?" she whispered. "I am Mahryn. *I am*. I remember…"

"You remember what? Lying on a forest floor, your very life pouring from a gape in your side? Mahryn. Mahryn. Mahryn. You screamed her name over and over. Even when they told me what had happened and I returned home, that's all you would say. That's when I buried your mother and sent your grieving aunt away. And you took her place. You became Mahryn."

"You lie. How do I become who I already am?" She asked through clenched teeth, her nails digging into Tahruk's arm where she held onto him for strength. With her other hand, she touched her forehead.

Tedran nodded. "You know, don't you? You've tried so hard, all these years to block it out, but you know." He shook his head and made a tsking sound. "Poor, poor Hahna. A knock to the head and selective memory can only hide the truth for so long."

When Mahryn turned into Tahruk, her face pressed into his chest, he comforted her for a moment before leaning down and whispering. "Do you have your answers, my lady? We need to put an end to this…" He let the rest of what he had to say go unspoken, and Mahryn nodded. She took a deep breath, then shook her head.

"Just one more thing," she said, her voice muffled. Tahruk nodded, though she felt his hand leave her arm and move to the hilt of his sword. "She loved you!" Mahryn turned her head and called across the distance, making sure her father heard her.

"I did what I did because I wanted her to love me. I did it all for her, Hahna. Can't you see? She deserved a better life." He sighed. "Did you know it wasn't me she loved? It was a memory... my brother. She'd been matched to him since she was a small child. Only, he was killed and she got me." Tedran's laugh was hollow, pained. "With him, she had the promise of a grand life filled with beautiful things, just as she'd always had growing up in the house of an Elite. She was royal, and as a younger son I didn't have nearly as much. I just wanted to show her I could provide her with all those things."

Mahryn shook her head, tears beginning to trickle down her cheeks. "You're so wrong. She never wanted grand things. She was happiest in our home, with the people she loved, including you. There's so much I can't remember, but I do know that. Why can't *you* see?" She bit back a sob. "Because of you and your drive to succeed, she's dead. You may as well have ridden the horse that ran her down. You should have to relive the torment and terror in her eyes. Do you know what it's like for a child to have to see that?"

Her father's answering laugh echoed through the garden and Mahryn went from slumped defeat against Tahruk's chest to dropping down to grab the dagger out of his boot. Pushing against him as she rose, she spun away to cross the distance between the warring parties before anyone could react to the unexpected happenings. Tahruk's men quickly overcame their shocked reactions and moved forward to engage the opposing men who moved toward them. It was obvious to the trained that orders had been given on both sides concerning Mahryn. One was to protect her, the other not to touch her, though Mahryn was oblivious to it all. Her face twisted with anguish, she ran at her father, the dagger foolishly raised above her head. Tedran caught her by the wrist, and grabbing her other arm, he shook her, his face contorted in anger as he glared down at her.

"You think my men will let you live if you kill me?" Blue gold eyes locked with blue gold eyes, his nostrils flared. "Release the weapon, Hahna."

Mahryn cried out when the pressure on her wrist increased, though she kept hold of the dagger. "Hahna is dead. You made sure she was gone. You killed everything I love, and now I will kill you. I don't care what becomes of me." She tried to turn so that she could unhinge his balance, knowing it was her only defense, though he anticipated her move. Had he taught it to her? He reached up while squeezing her wrist even more, and plucked the dagger from her. Pushing her back, he held it out, pointed toward her heart.

"Hahna," he whispered. "Shall I end this now?" He stared at her, almost as if seeing her for the first time. "You have so much of her in you." His eyes hardened. "But you are also me. I see it in your eyes."

Mahryn looked at him and shook her head. "The only thing you see in my eyes is pity." She sucked in when she felt the pressure of the blade tip against her chest. "You don't have to do this," she squeaked when he stepped closer, causing her to backpedal toward the far wall.

"Death is the only thing left for us now. It's the only thing that will set us both free. I will kill you, and then they will kill me," he told her, just as her back hit up against the wall.

"Wrong, Tedran." Mahryn's eyes rounded when Redahn pushed through a hidden doorway near her. Her father stood still, confusion further contorting his features and giving Redahn the upper hand. "There's always a way in if there's a way out," he echoed what Mahryn had said about the garden at the cottage, then grabbed Tedran with an arm around his neck and pulled him away while Tahruk tackled Mahryn, pushing her to the ground.

"Stay down," Tahruk growled at her before his weight lifted. With the wind knocked out of her, Mahryn could do little more than comply while she worked to suck air. Mere seconds later, King Garrick slid down beside her, one hand on her back, the other holding his sword at the ready.

"No," she whispered when her stomach threatened to heave. She rolled over to where she could see her father and Redahn skirmishing on the ground not far from her. Redahn's body contorting in ways she knew it should not, he lifted up and landed a punch to Tedran's right cheek with his left hand. She heard him cry out as her father rolled him and he landed on his broken right arm. Still, he fought on, fiercely, bravely. She screamed when someone tossed her father a dagger and she saw him raise it in the air, intent on taking from her the last person who meant anything to her. Hands to face, she couldn't bear to watch.

Tedran's scream filled the air moments before all sound stopped. No more clashing of swords, no sounds of grunting or movement... Mahryn splayed her fingers, disbelief forcing its way out of her in the sound of a wail. She jerked away from Garrick and pushed herself into a sitting position, her wide eyes never leaving the scene before her.

Tahruk turned to look at her, his sword falling from his hand to clatter to the ground. He walked toward her and held out his hand. Mahryn shook her head, pushing away from him and using the wall at her back to support her as she stood.

His own chest heaving from the exertion still, Tahruk took a step back. "I'm... sorry, my lady. So sorry."

Mahryn looked from the ground to Tahruk, her face

void of emotion. She stared off into the distance for a moment before pushing away from the wall and stumbling toward the men on the ground. She dropped to her knees beside Redahn, then looked over at her father, thinking how he had taken so much from her, and claimed to have done it in the name of love. Now, he was dead, the blood from the wound on his back still coloring Tahruk's abandoned sword.

"He would have killed my brother, my lady. I couldn't let that happen." Tahruk's words pinged around in her head for a moment before Mahryn looked back from her father to Redahn's bloodied and bruised form.

Would have? She placed her hand on his chest and he sucked in a loud, hard breath that had her pulling back. Tears immediately pooled in her eyes, making it difficult to see the barely opened lids that lifted to reveal dark orbs shining with adoration. She touched a trickle of blood that ran from the corner of his mouth and he winced.

"For an old man, he still packs quite a punch," he groaned.

Mahryn's half-hearted laugh turned into a full-out sob and Redahn reached up with his left arm to pull her to him. She collapsed against his chest, both of them oblivious to the goings on around them.

When Tahruk finally lifted his brother to return him to his sickbed, he scolded him with harsh words, though the look of genuine concern as he cradled the broken body to him did not match his growled words. "What were you thinking? I had this handled, you big oaf!"

Redahn laughed and then groaned. "Ah, Brother. You know it's not in my nature to stand by doing nothing."

"I know you must learn to trust me. Besides, you're

always stealing my thunder where our ladies are concerned. I owed you one for saving Elenya." Tahruk looked over to where the King and Christiana were guiding Mahryn along the same path. "Be warned, cousin. Your lady Christiana is probably next."

They all laughed. Redahn groaned again. "I do owe her one since she has already saved me."

"Two, if you'll be paying off my debt to her from the time we were all held up in the abandoned settlement some years ago."

"What? Now I have to pay off your debts too?" Redahn teased. "I don't owe you for saving me. You're my brother. It's a given."

The two brothers continued their banter even after Redahn had been reinstalled in the bedroom inside the summer home. He held tight to Mahryn's hand as she sat beside him while they redressed his old wounds and patched up the new.

All in all, two of the Dorengar warriors were wounded, three of the men from Voringlok who fought on her father's side were dead. The rest, those who had not made their escape when her father had fallen, had been rounded up by men who would take them to Corigan's dungeons

As she lay beside Redahn after everyone had left them, words from her mother's study again drifted through her mind. *"I already told you, Saryn. I made a promise that I no longer wish to keep. Continuing to work my way into the Dorengar's inner circle, that's the better choice, only I'm afraid my momentary lapse in judgment that had me clamoring to accept a position within the kingdom of Voringlok has come with huge cost. Venderlay has demanded restitution for my backing out of his offer. I... I have no choice."*

King Garrick had told them one of the men had talked in exchange for a life of servitude instead of death or the dungeon. Tedran had promised his daughter to Venderlay's younger son as part of his agreement with them, though no one knew exactly what that agreement had been. What they did know was that when he'd reneged, Voringlok's King had demanded his daughter still, in exchange for letting him live. Apparently his son was quite taken with the idea of the young girl being his. And for some reason, Tedran had arranged for his daughter's kidnapping to fulfill the obligation. After he left, on his way to Dorengar, a group of men from Voringlok were to sneak in, take his daughter, and deliver her to the King. Only he'd told them wrong. It was the older girl, his niece—the real Mahryn, whose window he'd fixed for them to crawl through.

The other flaw in his plan was when his daughter and her cousin had snuck to the woods across the clearing from their home. That's when the two girls had stumbled into the camp of the men sent to retrieve Mahryn. Tedran had used the incident, telling Venderlay that his daughter had been killed. That had all been good and well, until recently, when Venderlay's son had learned Tedran had another daughter. He'd implored his father to let him have her instead, claiming that Tedran should have offered her after the older daughter's death anyway. Tedran had refused, sending her into the midst of the Dremis maidens instead. It was speculated that he expected Venderlay's son to decline once he knew her innocence had been taken. He'd been wrong and Voringlok's king had given him one option... the original one—allow him to take the girl, or die.

Mahryn had closed her eyes as the King recounted the man's tale. Even with all he had told them, so many questions remained unanswered. Her mind tried to sort everything out. Her father had said she was Hahna, that Mahryn was her cousin. Why couldn't she remember that? He'd said her mind had wanted to forget, making it easy to convince her that Hahna had been the one who died, that she was his younger daughter. Why? How? And other than bits and pieces, why couldn't she remember her life before that horrid incident? One thing she could have told them was why her father didn't give his daughter anyway—her mother's refusal drifting from the study window filling her thoughts. Deep down, he really had loved her mother, hadn't he? Somewhere, in his twisted mind, she believed he had. Was that why he'd sent her into the midst of the Dremis maidens? Because somehow, in some way, he loved her too? Those thoughts and more ran through her head as she drifted into a fitful sleep.

Throughout the night, the memories came in the form of dreams. Dark nights and gloomy days. Her grandmother dying, her mother crying, Senya's beautiful eyes clouded with terror as the little girl dangling from the man's side watched him wheel his horse and plow into her. And then the lifeless body of her cousin. Or was it her sister?

She'd cried real tears in her sleep. How could she live knowing she was responsible for that girl's death? Yes, she remembered that—convincing the older girl to take her to the woods to pick the yellow wildflowers that had just begun to bloom. Another reality… the one her father said was the real Mahryn, the girl she remembered as her sister, Hahna, would have been taken either way. But she wouldn't have had to die, especially the way she did. The thought of either of them being forced to live within the walls of men like those they had encountered in the woods, or those who had taken her near the home of Zanak's gardener, made her shudder. She hated the thought. Still, they would be alive.

All of them.

All the thoughts, all the doubts... it made her mind reel. Was there anything she could have done? Was there anything she should be doing now? She woke feeling dizzy with the weight of it all, feeling the certainty of madness setting in. Her father was right. Death was the only thing that would set her completely free.

In the dim light of a sun that had not yet completely risen, Mahryn could just make out Redahn's features. She pushed up on one elbow to study him, to remember. He looked awful, yet still he was so handsome that it made her breath hitch. An all too familiar longing surged through her, bringing with it tears for all she would never have.

She touched her fingertips to her lips, then pressed them to Redahn's. His only response was to pull in another loud, labored breath. A sad smile lifted the corners of her mouth. It was too bad he'd wasted his efforts on her. He should have let them take her. Or better yet, he should have let her die.

Choking back a sob, she rolled away from him and climbed from the bed. With one last look, she went to the door and walked out into the hall where she requested to be taken back to her own room.

Chapter 31

Mahryn was surprised to find her room occupied.

"I rather thought you might return, my lady," Christiana told her, looking up from where she lay atop the coverlet, the sleep quickly leaving her eyes.

Her eyes draped in wariness, Mahryn said nothing.

Christiana smiled and pushed herself into a sitting position. "I've taken the liberty of having the room cleared of anything I believed could be used to harm oneself." She chuckled when Mahryn sucked in a loud breath, then sobered at Mahryn's scathing look. "I've been where you are, my lady. Not the exact situation, no. But all our lives… we're not always provided an easy path." Her look softened at the new round of tears that began to roll down Mahryn's cheeks.

"I don't think I can do this," Mahryn croaked, her lips quivering.

"It's hard. Life can be cruel and underhanded. Ultimately, you'll do what you have to do, and I respect your choices." Christiana rose from the bed and walked to the middle of the room where Mahryn stood. She wiped at one of the tears on Mahryn's cheeks, then folded her in a hug. "You're stronger than you think, my lady. I sense that in you," she whispered. "I just want to make sure you think it through and don't do anything you can't take back. At least until you've given yourself more time."

Mahryn's answer was a loud sob, and the two women

sank to the ground where they remained until she had cried herself out. Her back becoming rigid, Mahryn sat upright and looked down, refusing to make eye contact with the mistress of the King's summer house. "I'm sorry." Her words were quiet.

Christiana shushed her, smoothing a hand over Mahryn's tangled hair. She smiled, tipping Mahryn's chin to where she had to look at her. "Your tears will simply add to all the others that have been cried within these walls."

A smile tried to form on Mahryn's quivering lips, though it faded quickly. "I'm sorry my father said what he did about you."

Already shaking her head, Christiana shrugged. "They were not your words to be sorry for. Besides, truth is truth." She began to rise, even before the last word was spoken.

Mahryn stared at her from her position on the floor. "The King... he loves you."

Christiana turned and looked down at her before offering her a hand. Eye to eye, she nodded. "Yes. I know." With a deep breath, she cleared her throat and was once again the near-regal mistress of the house. "Now, do you wish to have breakfast or would you like to rest?"

Mahryn frowned. Nothing had changed, and yet everything had. "I still don't know how I am to go on not knowing who I am anymore and not having all the answers."

"Honey, you're going to have to face the fact that you may never remember. Have you considered that maybe because you blame yourself for your cousin's death, you willed it to be you who died instead? That you so willingly allowed yourself to become Mahryn because that was your young mind's way of allowing her to continue to live?" Christiana paused for a moment to let her words sink in.

"And, if you never remember, if you continue to live as Mahryn, is that such a bad thing?"

Mahryn considered the wisdom of her words. What was done was done. She couldn't go back, couldn't change things. What she had was the here and now, people she loved, and people who loved her. She thought of Redahn lying in the room below, his body battered, broken because of her.

"What if Venderlay's men come back? The people I love have been hurt enough because of me and my father. I couldn't bear it if others I care for are hurt."

Christiana shook her head. "Your father's death absolved the original agreement. You are free from that threat. If Voringlok comes against one of Dorengar's subjects, especially one with ties as close to Andorak's family as you have, they will have your King and his elite forces to contend with. Had Venderlay's men not left as they did yesterday, that kingdom would have brought the wrath of both Dorengar and Corigan down on their heads. If they're smart, and we believe them to have at least some modicum of intelligence, they will not attack in attempt to get their men back or avenge those who were killed for the same reason."

"You seem to know a lot about kingdom politics." Mahryn raised a brow.

Christiana snorted. "You have to in my position, my lady. I see all and share little." She smiled and Mahryn nodded.

"Thank you," Mahryn told her after a moment of silence. "I think I'll take that rest now."

Patting Mahryn's shoulder, Christiana turned toward the door. "I meant what I said. Think before you act. Determine what is truly important. Look deep in your heart and know sometimes it's okay to live for the here and now. We don't always know what will happen tomorrow. It's best to take it one day at a time."

Mahryn watched the door close behind Christiana. Standing in the same spot, she turned around in a slow circle, not really seeing the room. More, she was feeling the aloneness that surrounded her. *Her.* Mahryn - Hahna. Who was she? Did it matter? Everyone in her life now knew her as Mahryn. She'd been Mahryn for the past six years, almost seven. She couldn't even remember being Hahna beyond occasional bits and pieces of that other life that slipped in. There was no one who knew... except Dara. She'd called her Hahna when Redahn had taken her to the gardener's cottage. The woman had nearly collapsed when she's said her name was Mahryn.

Mahryn thought of the dream she'd had, the one that had her scurrying to see Dara to find out if she had answers. Dara's eyes in that dream, the ones that had looked down on her in the forest, they'd been so nearly the same as her own, as her father's.

"Christiana!" she called out, even before she had fully opened the door, halting steps taking her to the lady who had stopped at the sound of her name. Midway down the staircase, Christiana waited, a slight smile lifting the corners of her mouth as Mahryn made her way to stand beside her. "When are the men to return to Zanak? There's someone close by who I need to speak to."

"Dara?" she asked, then laughed at Mahryn's gaping mouth. "I told you, it's my job to know." Smiling, Christiana nodded and motioned with her head for Mahryn to come with her. "Let's go find out. It probably depends on when Redahn is fit enough to ride. After we ask though, we must have breakfast. I'm famished, and surely you must be too."

Mahryn nodded, then shook her head. She was hungry, but the thought of food sent her stomach into sudden turmoil and she put her hand on her middle.

Christiana scrunched her brows, looking at Mahryn's midriff. "How soon after you met Lord Redahn did this aversion to food begin, my lady?"

Mahryn shrugged, looking away before her own brows drew down. "How did you know it was aft... Oh." She covered her mouth with her hands. "Oh no," came her muffled response. "You don't think..."

Christiana laughed. "I've heard that's how it happens." A hearty chuckle followed when a deep red crept with sudden speed into Mahryn's cheeks. "Perhaps we'll both know for sure in another seven or eight months," she leaned closer to Mahryn and whispered.

Eyes rounded, Mahryn smiled. "You?" For the first time in days, she laughed with sincerity when Christiana nodded. "Your first?"

Christiana nodded again. "And the King's first as well. This line is not known for their ability to sire children. You would do well to believe yourself to be as fortuned as I."

Mahryn nodded, though her mind had begun to whirl with thoughts and questions, all centered around a tiny life that may or may not be growing inside of her. She looked at Christiana, noting the woman's contentment and wondering if she'd ever feel that. Their situations weren't all that different, and yet they were worlds apart. Christiana knew her position in King Garrick's heart. He had ensconced her in one of his castles, had been willing to defend her honor even though technically she was what Tedran had called her. And he loved her. There was no way one could miss that just by the way he looked at her. If he didn't already know, he would be ecstatic that she was carrying his child, and somehow that child would grow up to inherit his kingdom. How would Redahn feel when he found out Mahryn had conceived? If she had. Would his reaction be as favorable as his cousin's? She sucked in a breath and looked at Christiana. "Our children would be related."

"Yes. Bonded by blood," Christiana confirmed before both women lapsed back into silence, each thinking of their unusual relationships with the men they loved.

Chapter 32

By the time they reached the dining hall and pushed through the doors into a room fit for a king, Mahryn was quite sure she was going to lose whatever questionable substance might be in her stomach, especially when Corigan's King and Tahruk stood from their seated positions at the far end of the table. From the corner of her eye she watched Garrick approach Christiana, him bowing slightly before holding out his hand, which was accepted with a smile. Theirs was a love that was never meant to be... a forest dweller and a king. Yet there they were, and her carrying his baby.

Tahruk had approached Mahryn more slowly. She tried to read the look in his eyes. Caution? Wariness? Had Redahn taken a turn for the worse after she left? She crossed her arms over her stomach, hastening his last few steps.

"You look like hell, my lady. Please, come and sit," he said quietly before taking her by the elbow and leading her toward the table.

Mahryn tried to swallow the dry lump in her throat so that she could speak, though the words refused to come until after she had taken a drink from the cup that was quickly placed before her. "Your brother," she managed to croak out. "Is he..."

Tahruk shook his head. "He's fine. Or he will be with a bit more time." Shifting restlessly in his seat, he looked down the long table at the small groups scattered here and there, enjoying their breakfasts, then looked back and studied her before continuing. "I wish to apologize again for..."

"No!" Mahryn's forceful interruption had the eyes of most of the room's occupants turning toward them. She looked down, waiting for the sounds of eating to resume. Christiana's hand covered hers beneath the table and with a deep breath, she looked up at Tahruk, her eyes glistening with unshed tears. "I cannot say when a man should die, nor do I believe now that I could have been the one to do it, but I am not sorry to know I will never wake again with his shadow hanging over me or those I care for." She closed her eyes, grateful that the table hid the hand she splayed across her stomach.

Tahruk began to say something, but she held up her hand. "He ceased being my father a very, very long time ago, my lord, and I will not pretend to mourn a relationship void of both respect and love."

There was silence for a moment before Tahruk finally nodded. "You deserve both," he said quietly, and they locked eyes. Was he wondering, as she was, whether she would find either of those with his brother?

As if conjured by her thoughts, the dining hall doors opened and a very bandaged and battered looking Redahn hobbled in. Heavily supported by a crutch-type apparatus on one side, and a rather large man to his other side and behind, he inched toward the group at the head of the table. Mahryn held her breath, unable to stand when the others had. She looked away only when she heard Tahruk's sharp intake of breath, and noticed the King's hand around the other man's arm, the tenseness indicating a warning to stay put. She knew Garrick was right—a brother's love should not override a man's sense of pride. And Redahn was one of the proudest men she'd ever known. She looked back, then down, her heart gripped with pain as he labored toward them.

"This is as far as I wish to go," she heard him say, her head snapping up to where her eyes locked with his.

His gaze never wavered until after one of the men pulled out the chair beside hers and they helped Redahn lower himself into the seat. He shifted with a groan and turned to thank the men before fixing her with one of his heart-melting smiles.

"You're a fool," she whispered, trying to control the quiver in her voice even while she could not contain the tears that caused her eyes to glisten.

"A damned fool!" Tahruk growled as he followed the King and Christiana's lead and sat back down.

Redahn's answering shrug was accompanied by a wince. "My bed and my stomach were both empty. I wasn't enjoying either." He winked at Mahryn. "Besides, the doctor said the faster I become mobile, the sooner I could go home. No offense, Cousin. Christiana. Your home is quite lovely, but I am looking forward to my own bed and Nema's doting hands."

They all laughed, except Mahryn. She smiled, then looked down, wondering where she fit in. Her hands beneath the table seemed to go of their own accord to cover her abdomen and she felt that increasingly ever-present gnawing on the inside of her stomach. *Deep breaths*, she told herself.

She felt a hand on her back, knew it was Redahn's. Even if her body hadn't responded with a flicker of desire, she'd still have known his touch anywhere.

"Are you not well?" he asked on a groan as he leaned

in and whispered next to her ear.

"Oh," she breathed softly, moved by the feel of his breath on her neck, the heat of his nearness. "I... I am... I am just... tired," she finally managed to answer.

He nodded, then grinned. "You should have stayed, though I'm not sure how much rest you would have gotten." He finished with a chuckle and Mahryn tried to laugh as well, only to burst into tears. Forgetting the pain she might cause him, she pushed her chair back and bolted from the room, leaving the occupants to stare after her.

"What did you say to her?" Tahruk growled.

Redahn shrugged again. "Nothing I haven't said before." He looked at Christiana who had recovered from her surprise and begun to rise. "I don't believe she is well."

Christiana threw her napkin on the table beside her half eaten food and shook her head. "It'll pass in a few months." She started to walk away, then paused to look back at the three men. "You'll all do well to remember her whole life has been changed by what happened yesterday. To you, it was simply a day doing what you do." She shook her head. "She has no idea what the future holds for her, where she'll go, or even who she is." Turning away, she mumbled as she left the room, "And to add a baby into that mix..."

Redahn turned back to his brother and cousin to find their eyes fixed on him. All three of their mouths gaping.

"Did... did she say... baby?" The battle-hardened warrior looked from man to man as if they had the answers to a decidedly difficult puzzle. He looked like a silly, love-sick maid with his eyes going dreamy and the corner of his mouth curving up on one side. "Mine?"

"Don't jump to conclusions, Brother. She was mumbling when she said it. We may have misunderstood."

Garrick was nodding in agreement, though the two older men exchanged a knowing look.

"I need to talk to her..." Ignoring Tahruk's warning, Redahn was already trying to push back his chair, prompting his brother to round the table at an unlikely pace.

"Sit." He urged his brother with hands on his shoulders. "Whether it be true or not, she doesn't need you right now. Christiana has gone to her. Besides, you need to let her tell you in her own time."

Garrick leaned back in his chair and looked at the two brothers now sitting beside one another. He chuckled. "Our children will all be very nearly the same age, though she has yet to confirm my suspicions either. But to me, it seems quite obvious."

"Ah! That's great news, Cousin. You'll have to congratulate your queen for us..."

The King interrupted his cousin with a hearty shake of his head.

"Christiana?" Tahruk asked with a grin.

Garrick responded with a nod and a bite to his lower lip, and the three fell into thoughtful silence.

With Mahryn still moving slowly, it didn't take long for Christiana to catch up to her. Side by side, they walked back to the room Mahryn was using, neither woman speaking a word until they were inside.

"Don't ask me what happened, because I honestly don't know," Mahryn said, forgetting herself as a lady and dropping across the coverlet. Propping her chin in her hands, she looked at Christiana who had lowered herself into a chair on the other side of the bed.

Christiana shook her head, though her smile was one of amusement. "You're going to have to talk to him."

Mahryn answered with a groan. "I know. It's just... I can't think straight when I'm around him. He looks at me or touches me and..." She shrugged as best as she could from her prone position.

"And you feel all aflutter inside and you want him to tell you he hung the stars next to the moon just for you." Christiana finished with her hands clasped in front of her and batted her long lashes before rolling her eyes. The two women laughed though both sobered rather quickly. "Give yourself time, my lady. You've been through so much."

Mahryn dropped her forehead to the coverlet, hiding her face in its softness. She knew Christiana was right, but she also knew she needed to get on, to figure out what the next step was that life had in store for her. With a fake cry, she raised her head.

"I failed to ask when there would be a party returning to Dorengar."

Christiana was already rising from her chair. "I'll find out for you, but I still think you need to talk to Lord Redahn, and the sooner the better. I think it will do your heart good, butterflies and all."

"I will," Mahryn spoke to Christiana's back. "I'll just rest for a while first."

Christiana chuckled and called back as she slipped through the door, "Just don't think about it too hard or too long."

Mahryn rolled to her back and threw her hands above her head with a loud sigh. She knew Christiana was right, but everything she knew to do seemed so much easier said than actually doing it.

Chapter 33

Mahryn bolted upright, looking around the sun-washed room with wild eyes. Her heart hammered in her chest as she tried to figure out where she was. A knock on the door had her placing a hand on her chest. She exhaled loudly and laughed. She must have dozed off and forgotten she was safe within the walls of Christiana's home.

Safe. The events of the day before had her shoulders slumping only to rise again. She'd been thinking about her father when she dozed off, was grateful he had not filled her dreams.

Something sparked within her. Was it hope? She laughed at herself. She still had no idea where she would go when she left Corigan. She wasn't sure whether she was carrying Redahn's child or not, or even if that would make any difference to him. She also knew that, as a woman, her life would never be completely her own, at least not until a time when society might change. She couldn't fathom that happening, but there was one certainty in her life, one truth that filled her with a spark of hope—she had moved beyond the shadow cast by her father.

Another more forceful knock on the door made her jump again, though this time she called out for its bearer to enter. The same young woman who had been outside her room the day before, the one who had showed her the way to Redahn's room stepped in. A wave of jealousy hit her as it had when she'd seen the girl slipping into his room when the party was going out to meet her father. She fought it down. She didn't want to not like this girl, especially when her feelings were unfounded. Redahn had left the girl's company to come and protect her. That thought made her heart soar. Twice now, he had been willing to give up his life for hers. That had to mean something. Didn't it?

The girl laughed when Mahryn practically sprang from the bed. It made Mahryn laugh too. "Will you take me to Lord Redahn's room, please?"

"Of course," she responded. "I was actually told to come to see if you'd be willing to go to him. He's been asking for you. Quite forcibly too."

Mahryn chuckled and shook her head. Another certainty to add to her list—Redahn seemed to remain the same, regardless of what was going on around or within him. The man was a rock and didn't even know it.

Outside Redahn's bedroom, Mahryn stood with her hand on the doorknob. Her head down, she breathed in and out slowly before biting at her lower lip. The girl had also brought her another piece of information. There was a group of Dorengar warriors leaving the next day and Christiana had arranged for two of her ladies and several of her own men to escort Mahryn should she decide to go with them. With a deep breath she pushed open the door.

Tahruk dozed in an oversized chair near his brother's bedside. She looked at Redahn, keeping her eyes on his chest as she crossed the floor. The slow, steady rise and fall filled her with a sense of comfort and she wondered how long it would be before he could easily move about and leave for home. If his visit to the dining hall that morning was any indication, he was in almost as big of a hurry as she was.

Stopping on the far side of the bed, Mahryn smoothed her hand over the silken coverlet before climbing up to sit beside Redahn. His eyes fluttered when her slight weight caused the mattress to dip down.

"Hey." His voice was creaky from his sleep. He smiled before slipping his good arm around her to draw her down to him. Mahryn settled her head on his shoulder, her hand lying softly over his heart. "They told me you were resting."

She nodded. "I was," she whispered.

"That's probably good for you," he mumbled and she wondered whether he was fighting sleep or the effects of some pain-relieving drug.

Neither of them spoke for a moment, his steady breathing leading her to believe he'd fallen asleep until he rubbed her shoulder with the arm he had curled around her. "Christiana says you may leave tomorrow."

She waited, hoping he'd say more. He didn't, leaving her no way to know how he might feel about her doing so. She nodded again and the silence stretched on.

"I wanted to see you before you left," he finally added, his voice more clear. "You could stay…" He let his words trail off then quickly added, "But I understand." She pushed herself up to where she could see his face—a futile effort since his expression was neutral. She frowned and he rubbed rough fingers across the lines on her forehead with a chuckle. "I know you need to speak to Dara and Christiana has already told me to give you time. I'll try, but you already know I'm not a patient man."

"You are an amazing man, my lord," she told him, her voice a bit raspy.

"So I've been told a time or two." He chuckled again,

then laughed louder when her cheeks flamed at his insinuation.

A groan from the chair at his bedside had them both turning to look at his brother who was rising. "I believe I'll take my leave before I see or hear something that will mar my brain forever," he grumbled.

Mahryn tucked her face into Redahn's shoulder and he laughed again before calling to his brother. "Let Christiana know Mahryn will be leaving in the morning."

Tahruk waited a moment, looking at Mahryn for her response. When he got none, he nodded and took his leave.

"I didn't say I was going," she said, lifting her face from his shoulder after the silence became too much. She looked down at him, her eyes questioning. Was he pushing her away? Did he want her to go? She stiffened and he shook his head.

"You have to go, Mahryn. If not tomorrow, then the day after, or the one after that… The questions you still have… they'll continue to eat at you. I know. I've been there. I'm still there, waiting to see what life has in store." He shook his head. "Besides, with you gone, I'll work that much harder to get home."

"And what if I still don't have all the answers?" she asked him.

Their eyes locked and, for a moment, Mahryn thought he was going to profess his feelings for her. That was just wishful thinking on her part. She thought of Christiana's jest in her room earlier when she spoke of men hanging the stars and the moon. Redahn could hang them for her. As far as Mahryn was concerned, he could do anything. He was her mythical god.

With a sad shake of her head, she tried to push herself away from him, only to have his arm tighten about her. "I should rest for the trip," she whispered.

He nodded, but didn't release his hold. "Stay here with me, Mahryn. Even if it's just for tonight."

His voice was thick, filled with a longing that gripped her heart and shot tendrils of desire through her. Her leaving would give him time to think, to realize his life was better off without her. He'd never promised her anything, but he was willing to give her this one last night.

Mahryn ran her fingers into his hair with a gentle pressure against his scalp that made him shiver. He watched her mouth intently as she moistened her lips then pushed herself up to rub them lightly against his full mouth.

"Be warned, Mahryn," he growled when she began to undo the buttons at the back of her dress. "I may just try to keep you here forever."

With effort, Mahryn quickly masked the sadness that tried to creep into the depths of her gold flecked blue eyes. She smiled instead. "Be forewarned, my lord, forever's a very long time."

Redahn didn't try to stop her when she climbed from his bed the next morning. In fact, he'd said little, just holding her close throughout the night, as best he could with his one arm. With his body so broken, she'd had to take the lead in their union. She'd seized the opportunity, using it to explore him, memorizing every minute detail of his body, storing it away inside her heart in the hope that it would fill the void she knew would come with being away from him.

After she'd dressed, she helped him into a more upright position, his hand resting on her waist while she propped the pillows around him. She could barely look into his eyes for fear of begging him to beg her to stay. And when the woman came to fetch her to leave, she could not bring herself to kiss him goodbye. She mumbled something about Godspeed in his recovery and for him to let her know when he returned home. She'd already told him she wished to see if Dara would let her stay at the gardener's cottage, and that he could find her there. Redahn nodded and looked away, his face still turned toward the far window when she glanced back quickly then softly closed the door.

Mahryn could see Dara pacing back and forth on the front porch, the cottage ablaze with welcoming light and color. She was glad Christiana had suggested sending a messenger beforehand so that her arrival would not come as a complete surprise. The journey back had given her much too much time to think since taking a carriage had taken longer. Nerves had kept her stomach in an uproar. Nerves and the child she was most likely carrying. She placed her hand on her abdomen, willing it to be so. Throughout the trip, the idea of a baby—her baby, Redahn's baby—had grown to be the most important thing she could ever imagine happening in her life. She may not know what else the future held, but a child to love and care for… especially the child of the man she loved…

Tears filled her eyes and she brushed them away, hopeful the speed at which she got emotional would diminish as her belly increased. She laughed at herself. It wasn't like the rest of her life wasn't in complete and utter turmoil.

"One step at a time, one day, one moment…" she whispered the words Christiana had told her just before she left Corigan. It was hard not to think toward the future when the future was all you had, but she would walk into it just as her new friend had said, one step at a time.

With a deep breath and a whispered prayer, she waited for the door to be opened and then took the hand of the corisan who would help her out. He smiled at her and she realized it was no corisan, but one of the warriors… the man she'd left standing in the Great Hall the night she'd left with Redahn instead of securing the match she was sure would have come.

"Welcome home, my lady," was all he said as he released her hand and bent slightly at the waist.

"Thank you." She frowned, watching him straighten and turn to rejoin a small group of warriors to the side of the porch. Guards?

"Lord Renaine thought it might be prudent to have you watched over."

Mahryn turned at Dara's voice as she came off the porch to join her when she didn't move from where her feet had first touched ground back in Dorengar. The older woman stopped just short of the spot.

"Are they to keep me safe or to make sure my whereabouts are known at all times?" Mahryn asked with an upward brow.

Dara laughed. "I'm glad to see your wit remains. It was always one of the things I loved about you. Even as a young child…"

Both women sobered, the questions and uncertainty radiating from Mahryn's eyes. Dara's face was awash with care and love which transferred to her embrace as she stepped forward and took Mahryn into her arms.

"Please," Mahryn whispered, "Tell me who you are. And why can I not remember…"

"You will, in time," Dara told her with a last squeeze. "Come." She stepped away and took Mahryn's hand. "Let's go outside where we can talk."

Settling themselves onto the same sofa where Mahryn had sat with Redahn in front of the fire, she was thankful for the refreshments Dara offered her, was surprised her stomach didn't balk.

They talked a bit about the events that led up to Mahryn's return, her suspicions that she was expecting, and eventually circled back to the question of Dara's identity.

"I'm your father's sister, his twin in fact. You might remember me as Darenda." Mahryn shook her head and Dara continued. "After Mahr... my daughter's father died, we came to stay with your family in Bander. It was to be for a short time only, though your mother asked us to stay on. I think she was lonely there without Tedran."

Mahryn thought for a moment then asked, "Why did you not stay... after?" She didn't need to finish. They both knew she was asking about the time after the incident in the woods.

"I did." Dara's answer surprised her. "It was you who left. That was when your father spirited you away. I assumed to live with him in the castle, though when I finally made my way here to look for you, I was turned away each time I tried to gain audience with my brother. Everyone I encountered that might know told me Hahna had died, and I began to believe it." She hung her head. "I'm sorry. I should have tried harder. I just never imagined he would have set you up to be someone other than who you were."

Mahryn shook her head and fought the urge to move closer, to wrap her arms around the woman. "How did you end up here?" she asked instead.

Dara took in a shaky breath. "Your father left me to care for his estate there in Bander. It was awful. Every day I roamed through those rooms, saw the shadows of lives that were no more. The only solace I found was working in the gardens. They became my escape, my world, and I turned them into a masterpiece." Her eyes grew dreamy and she smiled. "A man came to Bander... I had devised a way to keep the cold from nipping the life from my prized blossoms and the lady for whom he worked was interested."

Mahryn nodded. She remembered the contraption in Nema's garden.

"I honestly believed my heart as dead as those I loved, but when this man knocked on my door and I opened it..."

This time, Mahryn did not restrain herself. She leaned forward and wrapped her arms around Dara, welcoming the pressure of her aunt's returning hug. She may not remember much from before the incident, but her heart knew the feel of those arms. She started to cry.

"Shhh," Dara comforted, pushing her back just enough to where she could wipe away the tears from her niece's cheeks. "You can't change the past, love. Know your father can never again hurt you as long as you don't give him the power to do so. Let it go and be content with what you have."

Blinking to try to stop the tears, Mahryn nodded and wiped a hand across her face. Dara handed her a handkerchief and she thanked her aunt before looking down. She frowned. That cloth. She recognized it. On one corner was a shield with a lion in front and swords crossed over its middle. She pulled back, immediately taken to that place outside her mother's sitting room window. Running a finger over the image, she looked up at Dara. "What is this?" she whispered.

Linda Boulanger

Dara touched the embroidered piece, a sad smile lifting the corners of her mouth. "It's the crest of our grandfather, Roehrig Katsuran. It was said to bring peace and safety to all who carried its likeness." Dara looked from the cloth to Mahryn. "You would have liked him... your great grandfather, that is. He was a kind, gentle man. Much like you."

"And your father?" Mahryn covered her abdomen with her free hand.

Dara shook her head. "Our father was much like your own, I'm afraid. At least fate had the sense to have him send me to live with his parents when our mother died. My brothers, including Tedran were not so fortunate."

"Then I will pray those generations pass my son."

"And if your son turns out to be a daughter?" Dara asked with a raised brow. "I had expected a son as well."

A moment of pain passed through each woman before they hugged it away and Mahryn rose, asking that she be taken to her room, claiming she needed to rest.

"I am still sorry for the part I had in suggesting we go to the woods that day. I don't know if I can ever fully forgive myself for that. But..." She held up a hand to silence Dara's protest. "I know you're right. I can't change it and I must look to the future now." They smiled at each other and Dara rose as well, pulling her into another tight hug. Against her aunt's shoulder she mumbled, "Would... would you mind too much if I continued to go by Mahryn?" Dara tensed and Mahryn pulled back, only to see her aunt smiling through tears. She smiled as well. "I can't really remember being anyone else. Mahryn is who I am now."

Dara was nodding. "I wondered." She laughed. "I didn't want to ask for fear of upsetting you. I'd be honored, and I believe my daughter would have been too. She loved

- - 247 - -

you very much. You were the sister she'd always wished she'd had."

"Thank you," Mahryn whispered before they tightened the embrace again.

Dara kissed the top of Mahryn's head and gave her a squeeze. "I'm so glad to have you back in my life... Mahryn."

Chapter 34

Redahn paced around his room as best he could considering he still had a rather impeding limp and his arm remained in a sling. Against his will, and only at the physician's urging, had he stayed behind at Christiana's a week after Mahryn returned home. At least his leg had turned out not to be broken and as soon as he could sit up for a length of time, he'd taken his leave. Now, three weeks later, she still hadn't come to him and he felt he'd given her long enough.

With an impatient growl, he picked up her comb that he'd retrieved from the water's edge and put it in his waist pouch before turning to make his way into the garden outside his chamber. He looked around, surprised to see how much the colors were beginning to pop as his eyes roamed over the workers until he found the one he wanted. With a hobbling gate, he worked his way along the stone path to where Dara squatted beside a bunch of roses.

"Lord Redahn. You're just in time. Which color do you think? I can't decide between the peach or the coral." She smiled up at him only to frown at the downward curve of his lips.

"I need to see her, Dara. I can't keep waiting for her to come to me."

Dara laughed. "We've all been wondering how long it would take you to go and bring her home, my lord." He frowned as he looked down at her. "She's every bit as stubborn as you. Besides, she's fearful you no longer want her. I've tried to convince her otherwise, but she said something about asking you to come to her when she left Corigan."

"Foolish pride!" Redahn growled, making Dara chuckle and she almost lost her balance when she nodded in agreement. Lending a hand to help steady her, Redahn helped her to her feet. As she stood, she pulled a tiny ring from her pinkie and placed it on his palm that she'd turned upward. The ring was simple but beautiful, an intricate rose woven with sparkling jewels.

"This belonged to my grandmother. She gave it to me before I married." She paused and looked down. "I'm sure she expected me to give it to my daughter…"

"I'm sorry…"

"No. Don't. We can't change the past, my lord. Just… go and promise me you'll do your best to make her happy. Heaven knows her life needs a happy ending."

Redahn closed his fingers around the ring, then gathered Dara into a one armed hug that made them both laugh. Carefully slipping the ring in beside Mahryn's comb, he kissed Dara's cheek before turning to leave the garden, his garden. The bleakness of it had turned his nerves on end during his first week home. It felt exactly as his heart did without Mahryn, especially as he'd remembered her asking about his neglect of the space when he told her he had no use for it. She'd answered back that he surely would not always be alone and someday the woman he brought home would welcome the beauty.

The only beauty he wanted was Mahryn's.

He walked through his chambers trying to imagine her always being there. He smiled thinking how right the vision felt.

The sound of a horse's hooves had Mahryn's nerves instantly on end. Even the guards commissioned by the elder Sharanis to stand watch around the gardener's cottage couldn't fully allay her fears. The young warrior from the Dremis, the one she'd since learned was named Kadin, patted her arm in reassurance and rose from the chair where he'd been sitting while they talked quietly on the front porch. His hand rested on his sword hilt, though his orders called to the other warriors had them all waiting before taking action.

Mahryn stood too, her fight or flight reflexes stretched taut. She was about to move to the door when the rider broke through the clearing and her breath caught. From across the yard, she studied him, noting the dark hair that had grown even longer and more unmanageable since the last time she'd seen him. As he got closer, she could see that dark spots still covered parts of his face and chest—bruises that continued to heal. The sling around his sword arm reminded her of all he had lost and she knew she should have been surprised to see him riding so well. But this was Redahn. All he did was done well or he simply didn't do it.

A burden of blame for further robbing him of his future as a warrior shot through her. She'd heard the physician tell Tahruk that, because of the double break during his fall and the tear he'd received when he'd fought with Tedran, Redahn's right arm would most likely never work quite right again.

Redahn slipped from his horse, and even with his unsteady gate, a feeling of power still emanated from him. Only once did he glance away from Mahryn as he climbed the steps and that was to look at the warrior close by. He raised a brow and Kadin bowed slightly before taking his leave, though not before looking at Mahryn to wait for her nod. He returned the gesture and tapped his ear letting her know he'd be in earshot if she needed anything.

Another raised brow and a sardonic chuckle accompanied Kadin's exit and Mahryn knew she should be irritated by Redahn's demeanor. But she wasn't. As soon as he lessened the distance between them and their eyes met, she could see no one but him. She studied his face, saw the uncertainty and the longing in him—all the things she felt inside, and she closed the gap between them before her next breath could be drawn.

"I waited as long as I could." His voice was rough, gravely against her ear as he pulled her closer to him with his good arm. "I did my best to give you time." He pulled back just enough to look down into her tear-filled eyes. "I wouldn't blame you if you told me to go. I don't have a lot left to offer. I'll never again have the chance to be a great warrior… But I have reached my end, my lady. I can't stay away from you, and I want to be a good father to my child."

Mahryn's mouth opened slightly, her brows going up for a moment before she recovered enough to whisper, "You're wrong, my lord."

Redahn frowned. "You mean you're not…"

She was already shaking her head. "No, I'm pretty sure I'm carrying your child. What I meant was that you're wrong that you will never be every bit as great as any man who wields his swords on a field of battle. Can you not see all that you've already done, that the only difference is you offer salvation one subject at a time? Are we not every bit as important?"

He thought about what she was saying. There'd been

her and Elenya… even Corissa. What about the help he'd offered Dahru, his father, and the King? Did they not all say brains were every bit as important to the military as brawn? He may never again be the man he'd once been, but did that make him any less of a man?

Elenya was right. It was all a matter of how you looked at it. Only it took him nearly dying… again, and the recollection of words from the women he loved to make him understand. Elenya had always told him the shadows he lived beneath were of his own making. So had Mahryn, Dara, and Nema… just in different words. If that was true, it was time he moved beyond them. Had he not come to Mahryn as a first step to taking charge of his life again? He looked down at her and smiled. He'd start with the biggest and most important decision of his life… the one that would seal the hole in his heart forever.

"If you'll have me, Mahryn, I'd like to ask for your hand... I'll make my request to the King's Courts as soon as you say yes."

She looked at him through instantly misty eyes. "You don't need my permission," she barely managed to get out.

"No, I don't. But I'd like it. In case you haven't figured it out yet, I respect you and I'm thinking I'm maybe just a little bit in love with you."

She couldn't hold back the floodgate. "I have loved you since the first time I saw you, long before that night at the Dremis Ball. I just... I never dreamed you might return it."

Redahn leaned down and kissed her moistened cheek. He slipped his hand down to cover her belly and frowned. "I can't feel a thing through all these skirts."

Mahryn laughed, even as the tears continued to flow. "It's too soon."

His brow hitched up, taking with it the corner of his mouth. "You may have to show me," he whispered, his lowered voice sending a shiver through her.

"I wouldn't be opposed, my lord."

Swiping her hand across her cheek, she wiped it on her skirt and then took his hand. Without looking around, she led him to the room she'd been using—the room they'd shared when they first became one. It seemed fitting they should consummate the promise of forever there—a forever she hoped would take a very, very long time.

Epilogue

Mahryn rolled over, snuggling her backside against Redahn and adjusting his arm over her swollen stomach. The baby moved and kicked against his hand, making her chuckle. He growled behind her and nuzzled her neck.

"I'd bet my horse you're carrying a girl this time," he whispered against her ear.

Mahryn shivered. Only her curiosity won out against her desire to forego asking him why in hopes that he'd continue touching her the way he was. But she knew he loved that horse almost as much as he loved her and his son. She had to have an answer.

"You see the way she treats me. Always kicking when I touch you..." He hitched a brow as he rolled Mahryn to her back and kissed her belly. "Roehrig would never have done such a thing to his father," he spoke to the moving bundle before beginning to work his way back up to look down at the woman smiling up at him. "Besides, you're carrying her differently. Much as Elenya carried Emylene and the one she's carrying now. I'm beginning to think Rennie and Roehrie are to be the only boys to carry on the Sharanis name."

Mahryn studied him, first surprised that he would notice the difference in the way a woman carried and then wondering if it would matter greatly to him if there were no more boys in this second generation of Zanak men.

"There were only two of us," he told her, reaching

down to rub his nose against hers.

She smiled, marveling at the way he so often seemed to be able to read her mind.

"You could be wrong, my lord."

He shook his head. "I'm not."

Mahryn laughed and the baby kicked harder against Redahn's belly that pressed against her. "My proud, arrogant man. You will never change, will you?"

"You have changed me plenty, my love. When I could no longer fight, I thought there was nothing to live for, but you showed me I was wrong." He kissed her, his lips playing over hers as he caressed her cheek, then moved his hand lower, his fingers dancing over her awaking a desire that seemed only to grow stronger with the years. She still remembered little of her past though it didn't seem to matter so much because she knew her future, *their* future was right there, together, walking through life side-by-side. When she pressed herself against him, he growled. "When this vixen is gone from your body, I shall ravage you like the starved man I am." He then proceeded to make love to her more gently than even the most gentle of men.

"If you are right and this baby is a girl," she told him after as they lay close together, "I'd like to name her Hahna."

He kissed the corner of her quivering mouth then wiped away a tear that she couldn't blink back in time before it spilled onto her temple. Running his fingers through the strands of her blondish brown hair, he smiled. "I can't imagine a name that would suit her more." He nodded and wrapped his arms more tightly around her. "I think that would be perfect. *You* make things perfect, Mahryn."

"I love you, my lord," she whispered, not trusting her

voice to say more. Snuggling closer, she laid her head against his chest, finding comfort in the sound of his beating heart.

The End

Author Note

Thank you for spending time with me in the *Land of Riandus*. Would you be surprised if I told you I originally intended to kill off Redahn in *Dance With the Enemy*? I did, but he wouldn't hear of it. I'm so glad his voice was big inside my head, because he turned out to be a favorite.

If you're just jumping into this fantasy land, be sure to grab a copy of *Dance with the Enemy*, Tahruk and Elenya's story. It's currently available only on Amazon, and while each book is a complete story in itself, you can never go wrong with getting to know the characters from the beginning of their creation in my mind.

Joining my Facebook Group is a great way to stay informed and enjoy the one on one that comes from being a part of an interactive group. Just look up Linda's Dragon Guardians. We'd love to see you there!

Until the next story...
Thank you for being a part of my dream,
~Linda

Acknowledgments

I've said it before and I'll say it every time, I'm sure. The birth of a book is not a solitary venture. I certainly can't imagine taking this journey alone, and there are so many people I want/need to thank... but that would take a book in itself, so I'll just highlight a few. The rest of you know how much I love and appreciate you!

To my wonderful friend who assisted me through this book, Kristina Haecker... you seriously saved my sanity.

To my street team... you guys (mostly girls) are the absolute best! When I need something read, shared, or just conferred upon, you are on the spot. Your excitement about my characters is the first step to me breathing life into them on the written page and I thank you from the bottom of my heart.

Krissy Smith Proofreading (who did not proofread the acknowledgments) ... I so appreciate your services and your excitement over enjoying a story that is seriously out of your genre of choice. I'm glad you liked it.

As a book cover designer, I've made a lot of author friends over the years. I want each one of you to know how much I have appreciated your support of my writing ventures. I won't name drop all of you, but you know who you are. When I say "author friends" I meant that. You're not just clients, you've become true friends.

I do have to mention one author friend by name, and very few will be surprised that it is Andrew E. Kaufman. At the time of writing this, we were "celebrating" one of his books hitting #2 on the Top 100 with him sick in bed after radiation treatments. #stillfighting ... you've got this, my friend.

Pat Sipperly ... you'll be named in every one of my books, because without you, I'd probably still be wishing I could figure out how to live this dream. "Let's make it happen ..." – words that opened doors. Thank you.

And to those of you who picked up *Beyond the Shadows* and read to the end. YOU are true granters of dreams. Thank you for being a part of mine.

About Linda Boulanger

Linda Boulanger is a happily-ever-after author, wife, and mother of four human children and two fur babies. She has an eclectic mix of published books, numerous story singles and short stories in a few group anthologies, plus a slew of always evolving works in progress.

Along with being an author, she designs book covers for herself and others through *Tell~Tale Book Covers* and *TreasureLine Designs*, all from her desk just north of Tulsa, Oklahoma.

Other place to find Linda:

Website
LindaBoulangerBooks.com

Blog
writersshelflife.blogspot.com

Facebook
www.facebook.com/TheShelfLifeOfLindaBoulanger

Facebook Group
www.facebook.com/groups/664151640414859

Email
lindaboulangerbooks@gmail.com

Amazon Author Page
www.amazon.com/Linda-Boulanger/e/B002NPYDC6

Linda's Writing

Novels/Novellas
On Wings of Time
On Wings of Fire
A Leap of Faith
Stirring Up Some Love
Dance With the Enemy
Beyond the Shadows
Arms of an Angel

Mini-Novella
Makinna's Secret
A Warrior's Christmas Gift

Anthologies
Echoed Heartbeats
Time Out on a Roller Coaster
Becoming…
Whispered Beginnings

Color Illustrated Children's Book
When Sadie Learned to S.M.I.L.E.

Short Story Trios and Singles
Up To Bat / Center Stage / Best Friend Rules
Face of an Angel / Life Changes / Talk With Me
Secret Shame

www.ingramcontent.com/pod-product-compliance
Lightning Source LLC
Chambersburg PA
CBHW051423170626
46809CB00006B/2290